UP IN ARMS

KINDLE ALEXANDER

Up In Arms
Copyright © Kindle Alexander, 2012, 2022
ALL RIGHTS RESERVED

Edited by Jae Ashley
www.jaeashley.com
Cover art by Reese Dante
https:// reesedante.com
Cover content is for illustrative purposes only. Any person depicted in the content is a model.

ISBN ebook: 978-1-941450-40-6
ISBN printbook: 978-1-941450-43-7

This is a work of fiction. Names, characters, places and incidents are either the product of the author's imagination or are used fictitiously, and any resemblance to any actual persons, living or dead, events, or locales is entirely coincidental.

TRADEMARK ACKNOWLEDGEMENTS

The author acknowledges the trademarked status and trademark owners of the trademarks mentioned in this work of fiction.

SPECIAL THANKS

To our friends in
Kindle's Krew
How would we ever do this without you?
So much love to you guys.

(Confused by the *us* and *we*? Check out our About Me at: https://www.kindlealexander.com/our-story/.)

AUTHOR NOTE

We all have a first, and *Up In Arms* is ours.

Up In Arms is a story of a love that grabs you and holds you still until you've done whatever it takes to make it last forever. A deep, soul touching love, inspired by our Facebook role-play days. Those were great days, but a story for another time. <3

We never intended to publish Up In Arms, but as the role-play experience ended, we needed to commit our characters' journey to paper. At the time, those were lofty goals for two people who knew absolutely nothing about writing a book or thriving in the publishing world.

We enlisted the help of authors, editor-friends, role-players and critique groups. Advice flowed freely. We received a crash course in writing style, pacing, point-of-view, and dialogue. Serious effort was made to incorporate everything we learned back into *Up In Arms*. Eventually, all the well-meaning advice began to contradict itself and the learning curve left us confused and frustrated…and with a story that wasn't ours.

But it was from that confusion and frustration that we learned to write with our hearts, to let our characters lead the way. If you look closely at *Up In Arms*, you might even see where we began to find our own voice. Since then, we've followed our hearts and have loved the evolution of developing our characters into who they are today.

We've always viewed this Kindle Alexander world as a team effort and given credit to every professional, friend, and reader who's ever opened one of our books. There's no way you'll know the depth of gratitude we hold for each and every one of you. Thank you for reading our books, loving the characters, and staying with us through the years.

On a side note. A thank-you to Reese Dante for designing all our self-published covers to date. They're beautiful, sexy, and captivating. Reese also introduced us to our editor, Jae Ashley. Jae's tough, thorough, and in our opinion, the best editor in the business.

We also can't talk about our beginning without including Denise Milano Sprung. The blogger who took our books and insisted they be read by everyone she knew. Without these people and many more, we would not be where we are today.

Please enjoy *Up In Arms*. Be patient with the story's evolution. Remember, it was our first. :)

XOXO,

Kindle Alexander

CHAPTER 1

"Damn! Calm yourself down." Reed Kensington fumbled over the last button on his silver Gucci button-front shirt. He lectured himself to take it easy as he nervously smoothed his palm down the length of the sleeve.

Slow down. He could be a few minutes late... Except Reed really wanted to arrive at the ballroom before his brother and future sister-in-law made their grand entrance.

He couldn't believe his younger brother, Rylie, was getting married. The big rehearsal dinner tonight kicked off the multi-day wedding festivities. A few days from now, his brother would be a married man. How could Rylie be old enough to be married? Where had the time gone?

Reed and his brother were six years apart in age. The last time he'd spent any real time with Rylie, the kid had been a lanky teenager who did little more than play video games for most of the day.

Today, Rylie stood close to Reed's six-three stature. What used to be an almost too thin frame had become muscular and solid, with not an ounce of fat anywhere to be seen. They both shared the same chiseled facial features, naturally blond hair, and deep emerald-green eyes. But after five years in the military, and a chunk of it in the Marine Corps Special Operations Command, Rylie's eyes held something more—the weight of a seasoned warrior and a battle-weary fighter.

Forcing his mind away from the lingering thoughts of his brother, Reed hurried back into his bedroom, glancing at the small alarm clock on his nightstand. He headed for the two printed silk ties lying on the hand-carved antique dresser he'd discovered in a little antique shop in Europe. He chose the pink and purple silk tie by Saint Valentine by Hermes. The small imprinted pink and white hearts were perfect for this special occasion. With a flip of the collar on his neatly pressed dress shirt, Reed stood in front of the dresser's mirror and absently tied a Windsor knot. He'd tied this same knot almost every day of his adult life and didn't need the mirror to execute it perfectly.

He thought back to the day his brother had announced his engagement. Reed truly couldn't have been happier for the two of them. The love Rylie held for his beautiful bride, Elise, shone brightly in his eyes every time he spoke of his childhood sweetheart. The love and romance of the situation made Reed wonder about his own life. If maybe someday his brother might stand next to him and be his best man at his own wedding.

In that moment, Reed recognized the long history of the Kensington men falling hard and fast, with no instances of divorce or separation appearing anywhere in their long and twisting family tree. And that was as far as that thought went.

He chuckled at the absurdity of such a fairy tale. Who was he trying to fool? Too many lovers had passed through his front door, and he had never considered sharing his life with any of them. Hell, if truth be told, those guys weren't even his lovers. They were merely tension relievers, distractions to help pass the time.

Many of his friends and colleagues considered Reed a

playboy. He had rightfully earned his reputation as a hard-edged lawyer who would fuck you in and out of the courtroom, but very few knew it was all a game to him. Europe didn't have the same deep prejudices as many here in the United States did, or at least he hadn't experienced it. And boy, had he experienced plenty while in that part of the world.

But the game had grown tiresome. Reed secretly craved relief from some unidentified missing element in his life. His deepest, secret desires were the love and romance of finding his one true connection like all the Kensington men had. He wanted the one person he might wake up to and go to sleep with every single day for the rest of his life. And if the fairy tale ever presented itself, he would readily hang up his playboy ways and give himself as freely as Rylie had to Elise.

Maybe moving back to his hometown truly was the best possible choice. He had spent the last few years abroad, learning from the largest international law firms from around the world. Rylie had chosen the military route, working for years at a time overseas. Their schedules rarely matched up. Time passed too quickly.

While Reed kept up with Rylie through text, email, or the occasional phone call, he still regretted not being there to play big brother to him. When Baker & Pruitt offered him a full partnership with an obscenely large salary, Reed seized the opportunity and happily moved back to DC, the area where he'd grown up.

Lost in his trip down memory lane, Reed absently selected a pair of onyx and diamond cufflinks and secured them through his cuffs. After a spritz of his favorite cologne, he picked up the black bespoke suit jacket laying across his bed. He slid it over his shoulders before making his way back to the mirror. With one last glance, Reed ran his fingers through his thick blond hair and grinned at his reflection. Everything in place.

He grabbed his phone, the keys to his new Porsche Carrera GT—Reed's gift to himself for the promotion—and headed out the door.

The valet stood ready and waiting as Reed pulled into the circle drive of Hotel Zaza. He quickly leaped from the car, tossing the keys to the valet.

"Take care and park her close by," Reed said, pulling cash from his wallet and handing it to the young man.

"Yes, sir. I will. Thank you!" the valet called out after Reed as he made his way inside.

He walked through the bronze-plated front doors of the elaborate hotel. Reed spotted a young man guiding the guests to the Grand Ballroom across the atrium.

This wasn't a traditional rehearsal dinner. With the wedding only a few days away and most of the guests already in from out of town, it had become more of a wedding event in the lavish style befitting his mother's party planning skills. This dinner could be considered more of a kick-off to the next few days than an actual rehearsal where only the wedding party would be in attendance. His mother had planned luncheons for the women, golfing for the men, and ongoing celebrations until they finally reached the true reason they were gathered: Rylie's wedding.

Strolling into the ballroom, Reed looked around, a grin tugging at the corners of his lips. As usual, his mother had outdone herself in her venue selection. The marble flooring, gold fixtures, and thick crown molding added an air of sophistication to the room. In the middle of the spacious ballroom hung a large, ornate crystal chandelier that transformed the room into a palace. Fresh flower arrangements and pictures of the engaged couple had been placed with care across tables and pedestals. Each centerpiece held a snapshot marking a special moment in Rylie's and Elise's lives. He swept his gaze past all those thoughtful touches until he spotted his parents chatting with friends and headed their way.

"Mother, it's stunning as usual. Rylie will be proud," Reed said, leaning in to kiss her on the cheek.

"Thank you. I wanted it to be nice for them." His mother, Olivia, beamed at the compliment. "And you look dashing as ever."

A waiter walked past, carrying a tray of champagne flutes. Reed carefully took one while turning his attention to his father.

"Son, I want you to meet the Hendersons. Darlene, Jacob, this is my son Reed. He's just accepted a partnership with Baker & Pruitt." Carson, Reed's father and a United Nations ambassador, never stopped working, and of course, Reed knew the drill well. He shook both the Hendersons' hands and began the small-talk thing he'd done for most of his life.

Behind Reed, the large ballroom doors whooshed open followed by a sudden burst of cheers. He refocused his attention toward the doors and placed his now empty glass on a side table to clap along with the other guests as his brother and future sister-in-law entered the crowded room.

The couple came in holding hands. They smiled and blushed, but one of Rylie's friends flanking Elise's side drew all of Reed's attention. His heart picked up a beat, pounding until it threatened to leap from his chest. He glanced down at his mother, wondering if she'd noticed his sudden breathlessness.

Evidently not. Her gaze remained fixed on Rylie, and she lifted her hand to wave at him.

"Oh, Rylie looks so handsome, and Elise is like an angel next to him," Olivia said, smiling up at Reed. She stepped closer, intertwining her arm with his. "I want this for you someday. And look there at Trevor and Brody. My three soldiers, all in their dress blues. I'm so glad they went that direction and not the suits I tried to buy for them. They all look so distinguished."

"Yes, they do. You did well in not forcing suits on them," Reed agreed, keeping an eye on one of the two soldiers with his brother. Leaning in toward his mother, he asked the name of the one with auburn hair, who stood just to the right of Elise. At his question, his mother turned to Reed with a knowing smile.

"That's our Trevor, dear. He's a good man. Very stable, quiet, and extremely reserved. He's the one that your father and I welcomed into the family. Poor thing lost his parents. He was an only child. He has no one but us. You have to remember me telling you about him."

Reed watched Trevor closely. A vague memory surfaced of meeting Trevor a few years ago at a family gathering, or it could have been at Rylie's graduation from boot camp. But, damn, the guy had changed and filled out rather nicely. Trevor held his broad shoulders back and his head high, a vision of pure confidence. But the deeply furrowed brow let Reed know that, while Trevor might appear confident, he was having trouble dealing with the crowd circled around them.

Reed thought over some of his past conversations with Rylie. He'd now be able to place faces to the names. The soldier to the left of Rylie had to be Brody. All three of them were part of MARSOC, the Marine Special Forces division. Rylie didn't say much about that side of his life, but Reed knew the three of them were tight. Best friends.

Brody's short-cropped, black as coal hair added to his handsome yet rugged good looks. The young man carried himself with an arrogant strut. He looked a little edgy, as if he might be itching for a fight. He was indeed impressive, but it was Trevor who fascinated Reed. Actually, he did much more than intrigue him.

Reed had always been attracted to a man in uniform, but Trevor made his body quicken.

For the briefest moment, his and Trevor's eyes met, drowning Reed in a sea of cerulean blue. The look in Trevor's eyes seemed to reach out and speak directly to his soul. Reed tried to hold the gaze for as long as he could, but a hint of bewilderment crossed Trevor's features and he turned away. Perhaps the man truly was shy. He looked nervous, maybe even embarrassed.

Then the oddest thing happened. A need to comfort Trevor

emerged from some hidden, hollow place within Reed.

An abrupt small laugh burst from his lips at the idea of lending comfort to another person, and he couldn't help but be baffled by this sudden nurturing side. Usually, his first thought would be about all the things he could do to such a hard body. Strangely enough, sex hadn't crossed his mind. Well, until that moment, as he envisioned what awaited him under that perfectly starched uniform. Reed grinned to himself and shook his head to clear the now very explicit images of all the ways he could comfort the redhead.

Olivia stayed on Reed's arm as they worked their way through the crowd. After his little outburst of a laugh, all he could do was shrug when she looked up at him questioningly. It took some time for them to wend their way through the room and past scores of well-wishers to get to the couple. Once there, they congratulated his beaming brother and fiancée.

Reed spoke briefly to Rylie, giving him a quick, hard hug. His brother didn't let go, and he could feel the emotion pouring off him.

"Have a good night, brother. Let the stress go. Worry again tomorrow. Tonight's for you and your lovely bride-to-be," Reed whispered, giving him another good hard pat on the back before moving aside.

Rylie kept eye contact with Reed, the moment still storming in his gaze as he nodded. Reed allowed himself to be pushed away, and when his brother was absorbed into the next group of people, Reed turned, searching for Rylie's friends. He wanted to introduce himself, but his brother's entourage had vanished into the sea of people still converging on the happy couple.

Reed found he also had to suffer through too many hugs and congratulations on his brother's behalf. His relatives drove him crazy. Their questions never stopped coming and were always the same.

"When are you going to settle down, Reed?"

"Are you seeing anyone, Reed?"

"Can you believe your little brother's going to beat you to the altar, Reed?"

Needing a few minutes' reprieve, he spotted a bar in the very back of the room, away from all the festivities. Reed dodged a few more nosy relatives, finally making his getaway.

CHAPTER 2

Perched on a barstool, Trevor intentionally ignored the stares directed toward his best friend Brody. Everyone always watched the man, no matter where they were. Trevor got it. He didn't begrudge Brody the attention. The guy was by far the best-looking man he knew. Blessed with devilish good looks, a hot, hard body, and a cocky grin that made Trevor's body burn…

Yeah. He let go of a deep sigh. Trevor's heart was locked in a constant state of hidden pain as his best friend flirted shamelessly, hitting on everyone in sight. Well, everyone except him.

Brody charmed both men and women alike. When Brody found his mark, they could usually be seen slipping off to one of the restrooms or a dark corner. It didn't take much for Trevor to imagine exactly what they were doing. It was all nothing more than a big game.

The entire time Brody played, Trevor sat back and watched. Watched and hurt, but the hurt changed nothing. Trevor kept his emotions under wraps, never able to man up enough to share his desires.

Brody was Trevor's exact opposite in every way, and he'd been infatuated with his best friend for some time now. At some point, that feeling intensified. He'd tipped the scale into falling for the guy. But being a gay man in the military left him with challenging choices. And the strain of secrecy had started to catch up to him. Loneliness was a constant companion. He wanted a relationship, and apparently, he wanted it with his whore of a best friend.

Trevor forced a mental shift in his attention, looking around the room. This ballroom felt alive tonight. The joyful murmur of guests mingling and lively music from the band filled the air. A sense of happiness, excitement, and love poured out to Rylie and Elise from both sides of their huge families. Everyone in attendance seemed genuinely thrilled about the impending marriage.

Trevor took the last swig of his beer. He lifted his heels to the bottom rung of the stool, getting more comfortable in his stay at this bar.

With a glance over his shoulder, he lifted and shook his empty longneck bottle, signaling to the bartender for another. As he turned back to the crowd, his gaze collided with Rylie's older brother, who took a seat at the opposite side of the small L-shaped bar.

Butterflies flitted in his stomach, his heart did a quick nosedive, and all he could manage was a slight nod in Reed Kensington's direction. For the second time that evening and the first in years, Trevor realized there may be someone on the planet better-looking than Brody. Outside of the pictures inside Rylie's apartment, where he and Brody were staying this weekend, Trevor had only seen Reed once before, years ago, at their graduation from basic training.

Reed stood slightly taller than Rylie. His blond hair, emerald-green eyes, suntanned skin, and broad shoulders were impressive all on their own, even before throwing in all those movie-star good looks. While Rylie looked a lot like his brother, he had a more serious, harder edge to him, where Reed was just smooth and captivating.

Now, seeing the guy in person, Trevor realized he'd missed Reed's best feature: the most perfectly formed lips he'd ever seen. Reed's lips were the sexiest part about him, which seemed an odd thing to think since the guy was so very good-looking. But those lips were full and thick, spreading easily into a wide, sexy crooked grin. Trevor forced his eyes away and turned fully back in his seat toward the crowd.

"Trevor West, right?" Reed said, extending a hand across the bar toward him, drawing his attention back to the man.

"That's right. And you're Reed, Rylie's brother. I've seen your pictures. Nice to meet you." Trevor gave a firm, quick handshake, surprised that Reed would remember him.

He did make eye contact, but under the intensity of Reed's green stare, he quickly averted his gaze. Rylie talked about how smooth his brother could be, how shrewdly he handled himself, winning his cases and moving quickly up the ladder. Face-to-face with that devilish smile and those mesmerizing eyes, Trevor could see how easily Reed was able to disarm those around him.

"I've got your beer coming," the bartender said in Trevor's general direction before turning to Reed. "What can I get you, sir?"

Reed's eyes stayed trained on Trevor as he replied, "I think I would like a bottle of your finest champagne and two glasses, please. You know," he said to Trevor, "I've met you before. At your graduation with Rylie. It's hard to believe that the lanky kid I met all those years ago grew up to be such a handsome man."

The compliment startled Trevor, his stupid nerves making his hand shake until he sloshed a drop of beer from his bottle as he rested it on the bar top. He quickly glanced around, wondering if Brody had approached. It made better sense that Reed's compliment had been directed toward his buddy. The bartender chuckled. And still, that intense stare of Reed's was focused just on him.

"Will you join me? It's difficult to toast alone," Reed asked, though he didn't wait for Trevor's answer. He took the bottle, quickly popping the cork, and poured a glass of champagne. Reed handed the glass to Trevor. If for nothing more than something to occupy his hands, Trevor took the flute, setting it next to his cold beer on the bar. He was so out of his element in this conversation with this man that he felt three steps behind everything Reed suggested. It didn't seem to stop Reed; he filled his glass, turned his gaze back to Trevor, and lifted his flute in the air.

"To Rylie and Elise. Two souls with but a single thought. Two hearts that beat as one. May they have a loving marriage and a happy home filled with the sounds of children's laughter." Reed reached across the bar and clinked their glasses together before taking a long drink. Trevor was slower to lift his glass to his lips. "I have to say, Rylie's a very lucky man. He fell in love with his childhood best friend. Elise in return is a lucky woman, because we all know a good man is hard to find." Reed inclined his head as he lifted one of his perfectly arched brows. A mischievous grin parted his full lips. "But as I've always said…a hard man is a much better find."

The innuendo caused Trevor to choke on his sip of the cold, fizzy champagne. Reed chuckled, taking a drink from his own glass while reaching over with his other hand to slide Trevor a cocktail napkin.

"Here, you might need this, handsome."

While trying to regain his composure, Trevor took the napkin, wiping the champagne from his chin. He looked down to see if any spilled on his uniform. Everything about Reed threw him into a tailspin. Trevor's normal, quiet acceptance had turned into a bumbling mess of nerves. His heart beat harder, and the heat from a scalding blush crept up his cheeks.

"I'm sorry... I must've misunderstood something about what you said. I wish the best for both of them too. They're a good couple," Trevor said, sitting back on his stool, still coughing just a bit. He picked up the glass but turned in his chair, focusing on the surrounding crowd. He desperately needed to put some distance between himself and Reed before he completely embarrassed himself.

With his fair skin, the heat suffusing his cheeks was no doubt a strong visual indicator of how uncomfortable he already was in this conversation. To embarrass himself more just wouldn't do, since he would be relocating to this area very soon. After his mother's death, Reed's family had become his family, and Trevor didn't need it to be awkward every time he saw Reed from here on out.

Then the most terrible thought occurred to him, and he nearly gasped out loud: Rylie must have sent his brother back here to talk to him. His heart sank and he gave an inward groan. This wasn't the first time something like this had happened, but usually his friends sent over a woman. And never before had Trevor sat so completely spellbound by anyone obligated to speak to him.

Trevor cringed inside and just felt incredibly pathetic to be gushing over someone burdened with spending time with him.

"So, Trevor, are you hooked up with some nice woman? Is there someone special in your life?" Reed asked.

Though the blush still burned on his cheeks, Trevor glanced over. Reed kept those penetrating eyes fixed on him, and just as Trevor opened his mouth to answer, Brody appeared out of nowhere. He positioned himself between Reed and Trevor, giving him a quick fist bump in greeting. Brody lifted his foot, perching it against the bottom bar rail, and leaned in to rest his elbows on the bar ledge.

The move effectively blocked Trevor from Reed. For the first time ever, Trevor had completely forgotten about Brody being in the same room with him. No one ever took his mind off Brody. With that thought came another, causing Trevor's heart to skip. Trevor prayed Brody wouldn't turn his attention to the handsome Reed. Could there be any chance Brody wouldn't go there because Reed was Rylie's brother?

"I'm Reed Kensington. Rylie's older brother. I believe you're the other friend, am I right?" Reed asked.

"Yep, I'm Brody Daniels. Nice to meet ya." A cocky grin spread across Brody's lips. A quick waggle of his eyebrows indicated Trevor needed to watch his next move, but Trevor didn't want to be a party to Brody's games. Not this time. His heart gave a small ache as he watched Brody swivel back toward Reed.

With effort, Trevor spun away, forcing his mind elsewhere. He took small sips of his champagne and focused on anything that might draw his attention from the scene unfolding next to him. The pain in his heart kicked back up, his breath hitched, and the heat of his blush consumed his cheeks, but he pushed the two men out of his mind. With any luck, he wouldn't be aware when they left to find some hidden spot where Brody's charm would seal the deal. Trevor absolutely hated feeling like such a baby about it all.

"Excuse me, Brody."

Lost in thought, Trevor felt a light touch on his arm. He looked over his shoulder, thinking the bartender may be asking if he wanted another beer, but Trevor found no one there. He lifted his eyes, scanning them in the general direction of Reed and Brody, preparing himself for what he might see. The touch could have been a simple goodbye, letting him know they were taking off together. Instead, Trevor saw Reed leaning around Brody.

"You sure are quiet over there. Are you okay? I'm still waiting for the answer to my question."

Both men were staring at him. Brody looked confused, his brow furrowed, and disbelief flashed in his eyes. Reed's lips pulled into a sexy smile, showing his perfect white teeth.

After a minute of all three just staring at one another, Trevor finally asked, "I'm sorry. Were you talking to me?"

"I was asking if you have someone special in your life?" Reed repeated in his rich, deep cultured voice, his brow arched in question.

"No, not at all." Trevor shook his head, a grin spreading across his own lips at the brutal honesty of his answer. He didn't sugarcoat it. Brody chose then to step back, once again blocking Trevor's view of Reed. Brody motioned for the bartender, requesting another beer, and stayed right there between them.

Trevor looked around his friend as Reed stood, picking up his glass and the bottle of champagne. Reed circled Brody and took a seat on the empty barstool on Trevor's other side. Reed took Trevor's glass from his hand, topped it off with more champagne, and handed it back with a wink.

"This is much better. It's easier to chat when I can see your handsome face."

Just then, before Trevor could recover from his shock, an announcement introducing the engaged couple sounded overhead. Both Reed and Trevor stood, placing their champagne flutes on the bar to clap.

Rylie and Elise moved to the front of the room. Rylie took the microphone to say a few simple but heartfelt words of gratitude. After a moment, Rylie called his family to the front with him.

Reed turned to Trevor, looking disappointed. His sexy grin spread across his lips, and Trevor watched the movement, his heart reacting with a strong lurch, wanting to bind itself to the allure.

"Looks like I'm needed. Too bad. I would have liked to get to know you better." Reed held out his hand.

Trevor hesitated before taking it. His pulse hammered wildly, and the contact of Reed's warm skin sent electrically charged impulses racing up his arm. He was afraid his hand might be trembling in Reed's grasp. Without question, Brody had never stunned Trevor like Reed just did. The handshake lasted a moment or two longer than appropriate.

"It's been a pleasure speaking with you, Trevor," Reed said. Trevor pulled his hand away to find Reed had discreetly slipped him a business card. "I'm looking forward to finishing our conversation soon. Perhaps over a nice dinner." Finally, after an extended minute, Reed turned away and crossed the room to join his family.

"What a jerk," Brody muttered. "I can't believe he's the beloved brother Rylie talks about all the fucking time. What an ass."

Trevor almost laughed. He'd completely forgotten Brody was standing next to him. His best friend wasn't used to getting shut down this quickly into the game. He eyed Brody for a split second but turned back to watch Reed leave.

"I didn't see that at all," Trevor said in an octave above a whisper, giving a slight smile, keeping his gaze on the sway of Reed's perfect ass as he sauntered away.

"Whatever. You want a pompous dick like that, go for it. I'll stick with the regular people." Brody grabbed his beer before stalking off. Trevor just stood, stunned, looking down at the business card in his hand.

Reed Kensington, Attorney at Law.

He lifted the card to his nose, inhaling deeply. The card smelled of Reed's cologne. Biting his lip, Trevor thought of Reed's sexy smile one last time. He dropped the card inside his wallet for safekeeping. Hopefully, he'd run into Reed Kensington at Rylie's bachelor party the following night.

CHAPTER 3

"Hey, man, I'll get you another beer," Trevor slurred and staggered the step or two to the bar. The bartender was on his game tonight and pushed three Corona bottles in his direction without him even having to ask. Trevor handed one to Rylie and one to Brody.

"Nah, I've had enough. Give it to Brody," Rylie yelled over the blaring music.

Brody didn't hesitate. He grabbed both beer bottles, holding one in each hand, giving Trevor a sloppy, teasing grin.

"Thanks. This is a damn fine rockin' party you planned, buddy. You havin' a good time?" Brody leaned in far enough to shout in Trevor's ear.

The hot shot of breath caused goose bumps to spring up over Trevor's arms. Trevor turned his head to bring his mouth close to

17

Brody's, only to lose his balance. He stumbled back a few steps and slammed into the wall near their table. Brody watched him with a laugh before lifting the bottle to his lips then turning back to the party and heading into the crowd.

Everything about Brody called out to him. The way the guy moved, dressed, spoke, smelled... The sway of that tight ass as he sauntered away. Trevor wanted to run his hands across the denim so badly. Even in his drunken state, his cock sprang to life. It struck Trevor—there was only one other ass that could draw his focus and make him completely forget about his best friend, and it belonged to Reed Kensington. His plump cock grew stiffer thinking about the gorgeous blond.

Trevor had thought about Reed several times since their meeting last night, easily chasing Brody from his mind. The card Reed had given him was now rubbed well worn. Trevor had traced his fingers across Reed's name over and over while thinking of his smile and dreaming of his touch.

Why hadn't Reed come tonight?

As Rylie's best man, Reed should be here, even if it wasn't his normal scene.

The rumors circulating about Reed were plentiful.

A ruthless attorney.

A self-made man.

A notorious international playboy who enjoyed a variety of men.

Trevor had nothing to offer Reed. He wasn't wealthy or handsome. Trevor couldn't even offer to be another notch on Reed's bedpost, as he didn't sleep around. He would never be that kind of guy. Even years ago, when he'd slept with women before he'd given in and faced the truth of his own sexuality, sex had still meant something.

Plus, if it meant something to him and nothing to Reed, he wouldn't be able to handle that, which would make everything very awkward around Reed's family. He just couldn't risk his relationship with them. They were the closest thing to family he had.

A burst of laughter tore across Trevor's drunken mind, then out of his mouth. He had as much of a chance with Reed Kensington as he did with Brody. Actually, Trevor would have a better chance with Brody than ever drawing the attention of Reed. Hell, the gorgeous blond probably wouldn't even remember him from last night. And clearly, if Reed had wanted to see him, then he'd have been at the bachelor party. Looking out across the crowded bar, his thoughts jumbled in his head.

Trevor took another long swig of his beer, thinking how he wished Reed were here anyway, and how nicely the night had turned out.

Elise had asked Trevor to personally plan this party, happy to leave all the arrangements to him so long as he followed one strict rule. She'd made it perfectly clear—no strippers dancing naked or grinding on her future husband. Trevor honored her wishes. And from where he stood, it seemed a reasonable request. He didn't know how the other guys felt about it, but since Brody rarely went after the men they worked with, the party was turning out pretty cool for Trevor. He wouldn't have to watch Brody hanging over anyone tonight. They stuck to things like darts, pool, foosball, cigars, and beer. Lots and lots of beer.

Cheers suddenly erupted, and the music in the bar swiftly changed. Trevor stood up from where he still leaned against the back wall, pushing himself forward to see the cause of this commotion. His eyes went wide as they fell upon four scantily dressed women. All high heels, long hair, and longer legs. They strutted through the crowd, asking for Rylie by name.

Confusion clouded his drunken mind. Moving forward, Trevor went to tell Rylie the strippers were not his doing. Brody must have invited them. He only made it so far before watching one of the women try to sit on Rylie's lap. His buddy denied her, standing quickly, only to draw all the women to him. Rylie tried hard to avoid their roving hands.

He struggled to move away from the pack until Brody jumped in to save the day, taking Rylie's place. That was all it took. The women danced around Brody. Cheers erupted again while their clothing was teased away.

"I'm sorry," Trevor said as Rylie stepped out of the circle of coalescing bodies. "I didn't know they were coming. Brody must have—"

"It's not a thing." Rylie lifted a hand to stop Trevor's apology. "I just promised Elise I wouldn't get involved."

Now, the two of them stood completely on the outside of the circle surrounding the women. Brody sat in Rylie's chair, patting his lap to encourage any of the women to sit on his muscular thighs. Every bold move Brody made caused the cheers to grow louder. Unable to force his eyes away, Trevor watched Brody run his hands all over the writhing body on his lap. After a little coaxing, Brody captured her lips and ground his hips forward, making his intentions more than clear.

Just like that, with Trevor's thoughts on Brody's little sex show and Reed a no show, his cool, easy on the heart night plummeted into the abyss.

***

Traffic was a bitch. Parts of the highway were shut down for construction. Reed took what he thought might be a shortcut, but it turned out everyone else had the same idea. It took him and his father, Carson, well over two hours to get across town to Rylie's bachelor party, and they'd been late to begin with.

For most of the day, Reed couldn't escape the thoughts of the stunning soldier he'd met briefly the night before. Trevor wasn't his usual type. Reed tended to lean more toward flamboyant men, both bold in voice and in action, but Reed couldn't seem to keep his mind off the unassuming military man.

Trevor's strong, chiseled jawline, deep cerulean blue eyes

framed by a thick fringe of dark lashes, and full, pouty lips just begged to be kissed. They kept his fantasies playing over and over again for the entire day. Reed felt an instant animal attraction for Trevor that he could find no explanation for.

When they'd stood together at the small bar last night, clapping for his brother, Reed had glanced over at Trevor. The moment Trevor had met his gaze, an instant blush had stained his cheeks, and Reed's heart melted. He thought Trevor experienced the moment too. At least he hoped so, but a twinge of disappointment filled him when Trevor hadn't called today. Reed didn't want to be wrong and have this deep attraction be one-sided.

"Place looks packed," Reed said to his father, finding a parking spot in the back of the lot. "I hope we haven't missed too much." He'd made record time, parking, shutting off his engine and leaving his car, tapping his foot as he waited at the hood for his father.

"These were great parties back in the day. I'm surprised Trevor invited me tonight. This is a young man's tradition," his father said as they headed for the front door.

"Dad, get your foot out of the grave. You aren't that old. You belong here with your son tonight." He opened the front door of the bar for his father and held out his arm in a sweeping motion. "After you, old man," Reed added with a grin.

The potent combination of booze, sweat, and sex hit him as he entered. The music blared, and he scanned the room, watching the strippers work the men. A redhead straddled Brody's lap, gyrating her hips back and forth. From the look on Brody's face, Reed assumed she hit all the right spots.

A cheer arose from the crowd when Brody removed her sequined top and buried his face between her large silicone-enhanced breasts. Brody waved her skimpy top over his head like a lasso and then tossed it to the roaring horde. Reed guessed the 'no touching' rule didn't apply tonight, and Brody looked to be enjoying the evening's festivities a little too much.

"Dad, over here. Rylie's over here." The loud music made it hard to hear. Reed pointed his finger in the direction of the back of the bar where his brother stood. And next to him...Trevor.

Reed's heart clenched. He stood there for a brief second, just staring. He took a deep breath, letting his heart have this moment. Never had the organ pounded so wildly at the sight of another man. His eyes took in the tight-fitting, royal blue knit polo stretched across Trevor's broad shoulders and muscular chest. All that hard-muscled goodness tapered into a small waist.

Although tempted, Reed thought it best not to look much lower. Instead, he shifted his gaze up to Trevor's face. Trevor seemed to be concentrating hard on Brody. Reed knew Trevor's eyes were a deep ocean blue—he'd fantasized about them for most of the day—and the color of Trevor's shirt would complement that unique hue. Pieces of his short auburn hair fell across his forehead, giving a youthful charm to his classically handsome features. Watching Trevor now, he realized he'd missed his slightly crooked nose and wondered when exactly he might have broken it.

Guiding his father back to the two men, Reed considered Trevor's fair complexion. Did he have freckles? Reed didn't remember seeing any the night before, and the question had plagued his mind for most of the day.

"Sorry we're late. I see we arrived just in time for the show though," Reed shouted after finally reaching his brother's side. Rylie looked incredibly uncomfortable, and his father jumped to Rylie's aid right away.

"Come have a seat with me. This music's too loud for me to hear my own thoughts." In his father's usual way, he took control of the situation, ushering Rylie off to a table on the far side of the bar. Reed watched them for a moment before turning to acknowledge the handsome man beside him.

"Good evening, Trevor," he said loudly. He could tell the guy must have drunk quite a bit by the way he swayed, but Trevor also looked visibly upset. Waving his hand in front of Trevor's face, Reed shot him a flirtatious grin, trying again to gain his attention. "Trevor…hello…?"

Reed followed Trevor's line of sight to where Brody rose from the chair with the redhead stripper's legs locked around his hips. Her clothing was now gone except for the spiky high heels digging into Brody's ass. They made their way to the side of the bar with the nearest restroom.

Trevor spun away, a look of shock crossing his face when he finally noticed Reed. He gave a smile, and the worry lines creasing his forehead simply vanished. His eyes lit as his drunken gaze focused intently on Reed's face for several long moments. Reed hoped this look meant Trevor was genuinely happy to see him. His gaze softened and a deep need showed plainly on his face.

"You have beautiful lips," Trevor murmured, grabbing Reed's shirt. "I'm tired of waiting. I thought about you all day." Trevor pulled Reed forward, crushing their lips together.

The moment Trevor made contact, Reed circled an arm around his waist as the soldier leaned back, taking Reed with him as his ass hit a back wall. Reed caught up quickly. It took less than a second before he met Trevor's velvety tongue until what had seemed like a wall became a door and gave way behind Trevor.

They both tumbled out a side door, into the night. Reed pitched forward, stumbling hard, but not letting go of Trevor as he struggled to keep them both on their feet. They performed the silliest uncoordinated dance, trying to stay upright. The music from the bar faded to a muted bass beat as the door closed behind them, leaving him alone with Trevor.

"I thought for a moment the earth was moving beneath my feet," Reed teased once he steadied them, curling his lips into a dark grin.

Trevor didn't say a word, but a drunken smile slowly slid across his face. His hands snaked out, reaching for Reed again.

Everything seemed to happen in slow motion. The intensity in Trevor's gaze caught Reed completely off guard. The sexual tension wafting off the man took Reed's breath.

This time, when Trevor tugged him forward, he carefully brushed his lips against Reed's ever so lightly.

Oh, hell yeah.

Reed seized the moment, unwilling to let the opportunity pass. He leaned in, pressing his lips to Trevor's. He gently let his tongue trace across the seam. Oh Lord, he wanted inside Trevor's mouth. Hell, Reed just wanted to be inside Trevor; something he'd fantasized about for most of the last twenty-four hours.

Tugging Trevor closer, Reed stayed within a breath of Trevor's mouth. He softly cupped Trevor's face, running his thumb across that plump bottom lip. "Since first laying eyes on you, I've thought of little else."

He slanted his mouth above Trevor's, kissing him hard again. His breath hitched as Trevor parted his lips, allowing immediate entrance. Their tongues mingled and swirled. Reed opened wider, and Trevor pushed his tongue deeper inside. His first instinct was to suck Trevor's tongue even farther into his mouth. Reed wanted to completely fill himself with this man.

As he smoothed his hand over Trevor's neck and chest, he let his fingertips glide down Trevor's sides and around his waist. He devoured Trevor in a slow dance of teeth, lips, and tongues. The feel of Trevor's mouth working beneath his, the urgency of the kiss, sent Reed's head spinning. God, Reed longed to be deep inside this man.

Need nearly overwhelmed him. He had never felt such an intense connection in his life. Reed's breath hitched again when Trevor's strong hands gripped his rock-hard cock, rubbing him with urgency. He let his own hand slide down Trevor's firm ass, then around his hips to grind against Trevor's thick dick, delighted to find Trevor as aroused as he was. The contact caused Trevor's kiss to become harder, more demanding.

Reed deepened the kiss, matching the hungry touches with his own. Trevor shoved Reed backward. And a small sound escaped his lips when his back hit the hard brick wall.

Oh dear God, this was going to be good.

"You're beautiful… I've waited too long and I'm tired of being without," Trevor said sloppily, taking the step to Reed, laying a hand on the wall to steady himself. With his other hand, Trevor tried to unbutton his own pants. Frustration crossed his brow. "Damn these pants are fuckin' hard to undo."

Reed spent much of the day thinking of how he wanted Trevor. He'd envisioned hours of exploring every inch of Trevor's muscular body with his fingers, mouth, and tongue. Reed wanted Trevor to tremble beneath his touch. He wanted to torturously draw out the time to pleasure Trevor properly.

But hell, he could play this way too. Reed liked it rough, hard, and fast. If Trevor wanted it like this, who was he to deny the guy? Opening his eyes, Reed moved to help Trevor unbutton his slacks, hoping to move things along.

"How does it work from here? I haven't done this before, and I need you to be gentle. Am I supposed to ask that? If not, ignore it. Any way's good," Trevor said.

Reed smiled as Trevor's eyes rolled to the back of his head when Trevor slid his own hand inside his pants. Reed would have gladly helped Trevor out, but Trevor's mumblings stopped him from going any further. He could easily take advantage of this situation, and lord knew that was what he wanted to do, but his heart told him Trevor would be worth the wait. Besides, Trevor was too drunk to make a conscious decision. Reed should have realized it when they'd tumbled out the door.

Fuck! Where the hell did this bout of conscience come from?

Groaning, Reed placed his hands on Trevor's waist. But Trevor stayed focused on pulling himself free of his clothing. Reed needed to make sure he'd heard right, praying desperately he hadn't.

"Trevor, hold up and look at me." Reed waited while Trevor's sexy gaze slowly focused on him before he quietly asked, "Have you ever been with a man before?"

"No. But he doesn't want me, and I want to have sex. It's cool. It's dumb to be saving myself. That's just fuckin' dumb." Frustration laced Trevor's words.

Trevor pushed away from the wall, stumbled back several steps, but stayed on his feet as he shoved his pants down.

"Oh yeah, look, I'm really ready! I want this. I want you," Trevor said as he reached down to grip himself, stroking tip to base. Giving a little moan of pleasure as his fist slid along his shaft.

With his pants jumbled around his ankles, Trevor took small steps back to where Reed still leaned against the wall.

"I really want you. I want to kiss you again. It was a good first kiss, right? I've never kissed another man before." Trevor's brow furrowed. "Damn, I can't understand why I'm saying all this shit to you. I need to shut the fuck up. I sound pathetic as hell. I never talk and can't seem to shut the fuck up now…" Trevor shook his head and stumbled a small step forward. "Whatever, just fuck me." He grabbed Reed's hand and shoved it down to his swollen cock. Trevor stumbled again, bumping hard into Reed's chest with his arm and shoulder.

A deep resigned sigh tore from Reed as his head fell back against the bricks. Reed struggled to push all his salacious thoughts from his mind, but man, he wanted to stroke Trevor.

Get a grip, Reed.

Hell yeah, he wanted to get a grip. He desperately wanted to wrap his fingers around Trevor with both his hands... No. Fuck his hands. He wanted to take Trevor with his mouth and tongue. Just the thought made Reed harden even more.

Yes, his mouth would be a much better choice, allowing Reed to feel and explore every beautiful inch of that glorious cock. All the time Reed battled with himself over right and wrong, Trevor continued to stroke himself as if nothing else mattered. Reed's hand finally snaked up Trevor's back, cupping the nape of his neck, drawing Trevor back to him.

"Trevor, listen to me. You're pushing every boundary I have." Reed groaned breathlessly as he lightly slid his mouth across Trevor's. "I can think of no better pleasure at this moment than to shove you against the wall and grant your wish."

Reed tightened his grip on the swollen cock, allowing his thumb to circle the thick, broad head. His tongue slowly slid across Trevor's trembling lips.

"Listen to me. You're not pathetic and it's not dumb to save yourself. The man who pushed you away is a fool. I don't know how he could do it because I'm having a hard time controlling myself right now. I want you badly." Reed smiled softly, watching Trevor. "And if that was your first kiss with a man, then I am honored you chose to share it with me. If I have my way, I can assure you it won't be our last."

Leaning in, Reed again pressed his lips to Trevor's. He wouldn't let it go any farther than this, but Trevor needed to be reassured he was wanted. Trevor stroked himself, moving Reed's hand faster as the demanding kiss continued. Reed struggled with his inner self, his hand riding with Trevor's.

Do I stop him? Do I let him finish?

Reed wanted to push Trevor's hand out of the way, drop to his knees, and take him into his mouth to help him find his release. But Reed knew where that would lead, so instead, he broke from the kiss long enough to grab his handkerchief from his pocket. He spun Trevor so his back rested against the wall.

"Oh yeah…that feels so fucking good. I need it harder. Shit, the fuckin' spinning won't stop," Trevor said, opening his eyes wide, gazing up into the night sky. "This feels so good." Trevor's hips bucked back and forth, pushing into Reed's fist.

Forcefully, Reed slammed their lips together again, sucking Trevor's tongue deep into his mouth. Reed strengthened his strokes.

"This is all I can do for you right now, Trevor. I want you so fucking bad, but not like this, not with you this drunk." Again, Reed questioned this newfound conscience. He ran his lips and mouth across Trevor's jaw and neck, whispering sweet words of encouragement against his warm skin. Trevor was intoxicating. Reed's own arousal throbbed, straining against the confines of his slacks. He ached to be touched. Instead, he kept to his word. His pants stayed zipped. His hand remained on Trevor as his breaths deepened, becoming erratic.

Trevor's head rolled back against the wall. He parted his lips as his body tightened. He was close. Pulling back, Reed looked down to make sure the handkerchief was open before he lowered it.

"Trevor, look at me. I want it to be me you see when you come," Reed whispered urgently. Trevor's half-lidded gaze met his, his body bucked, hips arching forward, and he pushed his arousal hard into Reed's hand. Trevor shuddered, but his blue gaze stayed focused on him as the release came. After the last spasm shook Trevor's body, Reed wrung the last drop from him before disposing of the cloth. Reed kept Trevor in his arms, slanting his mouth over his still parted lips. He couldn't help but push his tongue into Trevor's mouth, their eyes locked as they kissed.

After a minute, Trevor pulled away, leaning his head back against the brick but keeping his eyes on Reed. A sultry smile spread across his lips. "I finally had sex the right way—with a man. Damn, it was so good. I knew it would be." Trevor suddenly pitched forward, grabbing for his stomach, pushing hard from the wall. He muttered, "Oh hell!" Stumbling over his pants still trapped around his ankles, Trevor threw up.

"It's okay, Trev. I'll get you home. Although I must say I've never brought on this reaction from anyone ever before," Reed said, lightly patting Trevor's back, chuckling at his own remark. "Here let me help you with your pants," he added once Trevor appeared to be finished.

Reed squatted and angled his head, looking up the long line of Trevor's body. The guy was built like a Greek god, and even with his cock half erect, Trevor was still impressive. Sighing, Reed rose, pulling Trevor's pants up his muscular thighs. He laughed at the helpless, drunken flailing of arms which meant Reed had to do all the work. Reed quickly tucked Trevor in his pants, zipping and buttoning him up, and then placed an arm around his shoulders to hold him upright.

"Come on, handsome. Let's get you home."

They made their way across the parking lot to his car. Trevor shuffled awkwardly and stayed quiet except for the occasional moan. Reed propped him up against the side of the car, making sure he wouldn't fall over. With his free hand, Reed took his key fob from his pocket and unlocked the doors.

"Here we go. Why don't you sit right here? Let me help you." Reed lowered Trevor into the passenger seat and reached across Trevor with the seatbelt. "Let me just find the buckle, babe."

Trevor's hand cupped Reed's cheek. A velvety moist tongue licked up his neck. A shiver ran up Reed's spine when Trevor gently bit the soft skin of his earlobe before sucking the tender flesh into his mouth. But then a moan that was decidedly unsexy escaped Trevor's lips as he dropped his head back to the head rest and once again held his stomach.

"Shit, I shouldn't have done that. Crap, I feel like hell."

Stunned completely, Reed blinked at Trevor. The feel of Trevor's tongue and teeth on his skin had shot straight to his already aching cock. Thank goodness the fresh bout of nausea halted Trevor's pursuit, because Reed couldn't have held back much longer. He placed the tip of his finger on Trevor's chin, pulling his head back down, looking him directly in the eye.

"You seriously keep pushing at my boundaries. You afford me too much credit as a gentleman, much more than what I truly deserve," Reed said in a strained whisper. Trevor's face paled and Reed quickly added, "Hold on. I'll get you home."

Leaning over, Reed placed his keys in the ignition and started the car. He turned the air conditioner on full blast and rolled down the windows. He stood outside the car and pulled out his cell phone to send a text to his brother.

"I've got Trevor. He's drunk and sick, ready to go home. I'll make sure he gets there. Please get Dad home safe. If you can't, tell him to text me and I'll come pick him up. Love you, brother."

Reed hurried to his trunk, hoping he had anything to use as a trash can just in case Trevor didn't make it out the window.

Finding a grocery sack, he snagged it then slid into the driver's seat. Trevor sat very still with hands across his stomach. He placed the sack in Trevor's lap, beseeching Trevor to use it if anything more happened, "If you feel sick, please throw up in there. Got it?"

Trevor let out another groan, which Reed took as a yes. Satisfied his interior was as safe as possible. He pulled out of the parking lot and onto the street.

"Did I please you?" Trevor mumbled softly. "You know, did you... Was it good for you too?"

Reed took his eyes from the road to look at the gorgeous drunk man peeking at him with only one eye open and his head awkwardly pressed against the passenger seat. Reed grinned; the sweet question took him off guard. Thinking for a moment on how to respond, Reed turned back to watch the road in front of him. By the time he glanced back over at Trevor to answer, the man had passed out.

As Reed pulled onto the highway, he reviewed the night and how the shy, sexy man utterly fascinated him. With an almost silent chuckle, Reed amended his thought—oh, how Trevor intrigued him. The vision of Trevor with his head against the brick wall, the look of pure ecstasy crossing his face, the sounds escaping through his full lips when his body released, all caused Reed to shift uncomfortably in his seat.

Reed never turned down sex. It didn't matter where or with

whom, he never said no. And he certainly never required anyone to look at him when they came. But every instinct told him Trevor was special. Reed needed to do everything he could to hold on to this man.

Driving past the front gates of Rylie's apartments, Reed snaked through the complex, pulling into the parking spot closest to his brother's door. He sat there a minute and hoped Trevor didn't try anything else because his resolve weakened with each touch or shyly spoken word. Slowly, he let out his pent-up breath and killed the purr of the engine with a flip of his key.

"Trevor. Hey, handsome. Wake up," Reed said, opening his car door. It might be better if he tried not to jostle Trevor too much. He circled around to the passenger side and opened the door. He leaned in and unfastened Trevor's seat belt. Reed lifted Trevor's arm to slide it around his neck, pulling him from the car with a groan.

"Damn, you're heavy. Just hold on to me." With a gentle kick to close the door, Reed added, "Come on. Let's get you inside. It's chilly out here." He kept a tight hold on Trevor as they stumbled across the dark parking lot; the chilly late April air danced across his skin, encouraging him to hurry Trevor to the front door of the apartment.

"Here we are. Home at last. Shit!" Reed reached for the front door. Locked. Propping Trevor against the bricks, one steadying hand on Trevor's chest, Reed searched the man's pockets for the house key. "Trevor, did Rylie give you a key? I need your keys. Help me out here. Keys, please."

Trevor looked at Reed, his eyes just barely small slits, and a grin spread across his lips. "My name is Trevor, not Key. The Keys are in Florida." He snapped his mouth shut and glanced off to the side, an adorably confused furrow marring his brow, before he continued, "I think. I can't really remember for sure right now though. You have the most striking eyes. Did you know that?" Trevor looked around the porch, then down to where Reed's hands were moving over him in search of the keys, and his grin widened. "I don't think it's a good idea to go at it on the porch with the lights on, but move your hand over just a little and yeah…" As Trevor adjusted his position, moving his cock closer to the graze of Reed's hand, he let out a moan before dropping his head back with a thump on the brick wall.

"No, don't stop," Trevor said, jerking his head forward when Reed finally found the keys. Reed reached over to unlock the front door then pushed it open. He pulled the drunken man forward, trying to get him through the door. Trevor cooperated but stumbled, then fell hard against Reed's chest. Reed let out an oof as he balanced their weight.

"Are you all right?" Reed asked, trying to help keep Trevor on his feet.

"I don't normally drink this much. Hang on. I got this. Come on," Trevor replied, lurching through the living room. Reed stayed directly behind him, keeping the pictures on the wall and the furniture upright.

"Stay here. I'll be back," Trevor said as he reached the door of the guest bedroom. He wobbled off to the en suite bathroom, and Reed smiled as he looked around Trevor's room. Even though Trevor had been there for a few days, the room was spotless, not a thing out of place. No suitcase or travel bag anywhere in sight. Reed ran his finger across the various bottles of expensive colognes set out on the dresser. He palmed the closest bottle, lifting it to his nose, inhaling deeply. Trevor had worn that scent tonight, and it suited him completely. A small collection of cufflinks lay neatly together beside the bottles. Expensive cologne and cufflinks. Reed needed to remember those for any future gifts.

He picked up a few snapshots on the dresser. Rylie, Trevor, and Brody...all in combat gear. Reed looked closer; the three men smiled in the pictures, but they looked more like warriors than soldiers. Rylie carried a sense of weariness in his gaze, and Reed noticed the other two men wore similar expressions. Perhaps weariness wasn't the right word. Maybe it could be categorized more as a sadness of things they'd witnessed over the years. They were too young to bear that kind of knowledge, those kinds of memories, without it changing them on some intrinsic level.

A loud crash startled Reed from his musings. He hurried to the bathroom door, knocking lightly. "Everything okay? Do you need any help?"

"Nah, I'm good. Hang on. Don't leave."

Another loud bang carried through the door, and then several minutes passed before the door opened. Reed's lips slid into a slow, wicked grin as he gazed at the suddenly naked man. Trevor's hair was wet, standing up in every direction, but Reed paid it no attention. His full concentration remained fixed on Trevor's body. Just as he'd guessed, there wasn't an ounce of fat anywhere on the sculpted man standing before him. Pure muscle from head to toe. Trevor's thick cock jutted straight out, begging to be touched.

"You're still here?" Trevor asked, walking forward, pushing Reed backward while at the same time reaching to kiss him. The bed hit the back of Reed's legs, and Trevor fell with him onto the mattress. A constant barrage of kisses stroked over Reed's neck and jaw. Slick tendrils of wet hair brushed against Reed's chin. Trevor's soft lips nipped and sucked all along his neck, driving Reed to the brink of insanity. Reed ran his hands down the length of Trevor's firm naked body, and he struggled with himself for the third time that night. He didn't know if he could maintain himself this time around.

Trevor gazed down at Reed. A sexy smile spread across his lips. "I want you to want me." The confession stunned Reed, stopping the play of his hands edging down to Trevor's tight ass as his heart took in some of the sweetest words he'd ever heard.

"I do want you. Can't you feel how badly?" Reed asked, running his lips across Trevor's jaw. His mouth slowly found Trevor's. Reed moaned as he pushed his tongue forward. The hint of cool mint toothpaste invaded his mouth, and he grinned into the kiss, deepening it. He never stopped stroking the rigid muscles running up Trevor's back.

Not allowing himself to think, Reed opened his legs more, cradling the naked body between his thighs. He slid his hand up, allowing his fingers to tangle in Trevor's hair, and then ground his arousal against Trevor's. Reed groaned, knowing he must do something fast because he was quickly losing the battle with his will.

"Trevor, go out with me tomorrow night."

In one quick movement, Reed flipped Trevor on his back, brushing the wet hair from his brow. He stared down into hypnotically beautiful blue eyes; eyes he found himself wanting to look into many times over.

For the first time, he understood the rumors about the men in his family, how they'd just known the first time they laid eyes on their mates. Not only did he comprehend, he could confirm the truth of the tales. Reed's pull to this sexy drunk man lying underneath him nearly undid him. And the revelation made his heart slam against his ribcage.

"Will you let me take you to dinner tomorrow evening? I want to get to know you. Please say yes."

"How can you talk with all this spinning?" Trevor asked, reaching up to grip Reed's shirt. "We have to stop the spinning." He shook his head as if forcing himself to stay awake. After a moment, deep-etched concern filled his eyes. "Shit, I must've been drugged. They must've drugged me. I should've watched for that tonight. I thought I was safe there. Damn it. Yes, I'll say it, yes, but don't let them drug you." A soft snore ripped from the back of Trevor's throat as his eyes fluttered shut.

Reed would take that yes, although he couldn't be sure Trevor truly understood what he'd agreed to. He smiled as he rolled off the bed. Trevor looked exquisite in sleep. Reed reached down to pull the duvet up, tucking Trevor in before he bent to place a tender kiss on his forehead.

Trevor would need aspirin in the morning and perhaps a glass of water during the night. Reed went to the bathroom only to pause at the door. The bathroom was in complete shambles as if a tornado had tumbled through. The towel rack lay on the floor, wrenched right off the wall. Clothes were scattered about, along with various bottles of gel, toothpaste, aftershave, and an electric razor. Reed shook his head. What a mess. He gathered the items off the floor then placed them on the counter. He picked up the clothes, folding them neatly as he went. The small medicine cabinet door fell off in his hands as he opened it. Setting it to the side, Reed found the aspirin and glanced around for a glass, finally finding a small disposable one in the cabinet.

Reed tiptoed back into the room with the essential supplies, which he placed on the bedside table. Luckily, he found a pen and pad of paper inside and scribbled a quick note.

> *Trevor,*
>
> *You've agreed to see me tomorrow night. Thank you. I will be here to pick you up at seven. Dress casual.*
>
> *You have my number so do not hesitate to call. I'm looking forward to seeing you again.*
>
> *Reed*
>
> *PS: I thought you might need the aspirin. You had a little too much fun at the bachelor party.*

> *He propped the note next to the water glass and bottle of painkillers. With one last look at Trevor, Reed whispered, "See you tomorrow, Trevor West. Sleep well."*

CHAPTER 4

Late in the morning, Reed wiped the steam from the mirror to better see his reflection. He raked his fingers through his thick blond waves to achieve the latest hair style. It only took a minute. Satisfied with the result, he smiled as his mind returned to the intriguing man who hadn't strayed too far from his thoughts. Those mental images of Trevor caused his body to harden for the third time that day. The last episode of pleasuring himself in the shower, only thirty minutes ago, still hadn't squelched his need for Trevor, no more than it had that morning when he'd woken. Trevor had him all wound up.

Reed stood there, staring at himself, letting his mind wander again to last night. He pictured Trevor outside the bar. Trevor's pants hitting the ground while the soft breeze blew his short auburn hair. Need filled those ocean blue eyes when Trevor stroked himself. The image captivated him, forever etched into his mind.

Reed closed his eyes and remembered every little detail as he slid his own hand down his ripped stomach, vividly recalling Trevor's rich dark scent, and how Trevor's sweet mouth and wicked tongue moved in perfect rhythm with his own. Reed's breath hitched as his fingers wrapped around his aching cock. He stroked from base to tip, needing to again release more of the built-up tension raging through his body. Reed groaned as he remembered the sensation of Trevor's thick, hard cock sliding against his bare palm.

With each stroke, Reed's thoughts centered on what it might feel like to drop to his knees and take Trevor's beautiful cock fully into his mouth. The thought caused his hips to buck forward, thrusting his swollen dick harder into his tightened fist. Trevor's body had responded to his as if they were made for one another. His cock throbbed as he wondered what it would feel like to make love to Trevor for the first time, how it would feel to have his big body quiver with need as Reed pushed into him, inch by delicious inch. Reed moaned aloud, picturing Trevor's body gripping and milking his cock as he pounded into him.

His breathing deepened. The searing thoughts of Trevor continued to play in his mind. The hot, delicious friction of his hand caused his hips to buck. His body involuntarily arched forward, forcing his cock deeper into his palm. He continued to stroke. The release took him by force. His body quivered uncontrollably. The erratic pounding of his heart had him gasping. The memory of Trevor's full, slightly parted lips, lost in his own pleasure, coaxed an even stronger shudder to overtake him. His body spasmed as the last of his hot seed shot out, splattering against the marble sink.

After several long moments, Reed gathered himself and turned on the faucet to wash away the remnants of his excitement. His cell phone rang, drawing his attention. He inhaled deeply, and draped a towel around his waist, making his way to his phone on the dresser. With a sigh, he declined the incoming call with a swipe of his finger. The only person other than Trevor he wanted to speak with was Rylie. He needed to text his brother to find out a few things about Trevor before he finalized their evening plans, so he sent a quick text to Rylie.

"How's my favorite brother on this very fine day?"

Reed brought the phone to the closet with him to dress. It took a few minutes before his phone beeped. Reed read the reply.

"Hahaha! Your favorite brother, huh? If I remember correctly, I'm your only brother! This brotherly love can only mean one thing—you need something... What do you want now?"

Reed chuckled. Rylie knew him too well.

"I have a few questions about your boy, Trevor. Is he seeing anyone? What does he like to do? I want to know everything you know about him."

A tap on the screen sent the message. Reed stood naked in his closet, waiting on pins and needles for Rylie's response.

When the text didn't come right away, he forced himself to focus on getting dressed. He selected a dark red Armani button-down, and a new pair of D&G jeans. He dressed quickly, watching his phone all the while. Finally, as he was sliding his shoes on, the phone beeped. Reed scrambled to open the message.

"Trevor's one hell of a soldier. He's shy, hasn't dated since his last girlfriend back when we were like 19 or 20 years old. He's not a casual relationship kind of guy. Honestly, I think he has a thing for Brody; not sure though. He's never actually come out and admitted he's gay. Trevor's smart. Spends his free time reading, going to art showings or museums by himself. Mom loves all his manners. Why? What happened last night?"

Reed grinned at Rylie's questions as he stepped from his closet, quick with his own reply.

"Thank you for the info. Now you really are number one on my list of favorite brothers, lol! You know very well I won't discuss what I did with your boy, but I can tell you, Trevor piqued my interest. I want to get to know him and you have been quite helpful. Thank you but I've got to run...talk to you later."

With Rylie confirming his mother's opinion on Trevor's shyness, Reed didn't want Trevor to be uncomfortable tonight. He would change his plans and move slowly, like his gut had already warned him to do. Reed grabbed his car keys while forming a mental shopping list. There were hours to kill before their date, and he needed to have everything just right.

***

"Oh fuck," Trevor groaned, turning over only to stop in mid roll. The movement along with the sound of his own voice pounded through his head. It took a full minute for Trevor to realize something woke him other than the nonstop pain shooting through his brain. It took another full minute to decide whether he cared what it might be until he heard Brody letting out a string of obscenities.

"Damn, man, what the fuck did you do to your bathroom? You tore that shit apart." Opening one eye, Trevor slowly raised his head to see Brody exiting his bathroom to stand over the bed. Brody was up and dressed, looking ready to take on the world. Partying hard on the regular had its benefits the next day if Brody were any indication.

"What time is it?" Trevor croaked. His one opened eye went back to its preferred position: closed.

"Late. Two in the afternoon. I gotta get these women out of the house before Elise shows. I was just checking on you. You disappeared last night." Brody picked up the glass of water, handing it and several aspirin to Trevor. "Looks like someone hooked you up, bro."

Trevor propped himself up on his elbow to swallow the water and aspirin, staying as still as humanly possible, waiting to see if his stomach would cooperate in keeping everything down.

Satisfied, he gently laid his head back on the pillow, hoping the intense throbbing might magically come to an end. Out of the corner of his eye, he watched Brody pick up a piece of paper.

"What's this shit about?"

Brody's voice pierced his brain. A whole new round of pain shot through Trevor, and he flopped back, shielding his eyes with his arm. Brief images of girls and lap dances filled his mind, making him sicker over that than what he appeared to have done the night before. His memories were just too hazy. "You didn't bring me home?"

"Nah, man, but it looks like someone did." A none too subtle sneer caused Trevor to lower his arm to watch Brody flip a piece of paper onto the bed. Then Brody reached down and yanked the bedspread away from Trevor's body.

"You're naked. You never sleep naked. What the hell happened last night?" Brody demanded.

For the first time in his life, Trevor didn't care if anyone saw him in the buff. He needed the throbbing to stop, and that meant Brody needed to shut the fuck up. Rolling to the side of the bed, Trevor rose, sitting there for a second while assessing his body's current situation. A loud beep jarred him.

"Take your girls home. Check me later. I have no clue how I got here, but my stomach...just go." Trevor shoved to his feet, dropping his hands down to cover himself but leaving his bare ass exposed. He walked to the dresser, picked up his phone, and stopped the offending noise. Trevor watched from the dresser's mirror as Brody kept quiet with his eyes pinned on Trevor, looking as if Trevor had suddenly grown two heads overnight. Thankfully, with nothing more than a scoff, Brody finally left the room.

Trevor took the phone and inched his way back to bed. He crawled under the covers before opening the text message from the unknown number.

"Good afternoon, Trevor. I hope you're feeling better. I

wanted to make sure we're still on. I'm looking forward to tonight. Reed."

Scanning the words with little interest, Trevor closed his eyes only to have them pop back open. Trevor sprang forward, jerking to a sitting position. He ignored the pain the sudden movement caused as he racked his brain over what may have happened the night before.

Strippers, lap dances, and Reed Kensington just didn't fit together no matter how hard Trevor tried to reorganize that puzzle. He couldn't even remember seeing Reed last night. Panic gripped his heart, and he sent Rylie a quick text asking how he had gotten home from the bachelor party.

The throbbing bass drum in his head became second to the fear of what he may have done. Trevor wobbled to the bathroom, frowning when he got to the door. The bathroom looked like a disaster zone. Pushing towel rods and a toilet seat cover aside with his foot, Trevor made his way to the sink then splashed cold water on his face. After brushing the fuzz from his teeth, he again doused his face, as if the water would give him insight into his missing chunk of time. Nothing came to him as he toweled himself off.

He wrapped the towel around his waist and headed back into the bedroom where he saw the piece of paper Brody had flicked onto his bed. His eyes focused on Reed's signature.

Hesitantly, he picked up the note, studying it. Nothing made sense. Trevor plopped on the end of the bed when the phone beeped again. Rylie's reply didn't help in giving him any clues.

"Reed texted he was taking you home. Talked to him this morning. What did you do last night? He wouldn't say."

Trevor racked his brain as he dropped back on his bed. He lay there several minutes, looking at the rotating ceiling fan, willing himself to come up with something. When that failed, he decided not to respond to Rylie's text because, really, what could he say? He returned to the bathroom to examine its torn up state. Some of the repair would require a trip to the hardware store. He found his clothes folded on the sink which absolutely didn't make any sense, given how everything else was trashed. He dug through them for clues but came up empty-handed.

Taking these clothes, he packed them, and then dressed, trying hard to manipulate his mind into believing he felt better than he really did. He stayed just as lost, with no memories resurfacing. Trevor reread the text from Reed, as well as the note. Both were short and sweet, providing him with zero recollection of what he may have agreed to last night.

On so many levels, this was a horrible turn of events. Trevor never let anyone know his feelings about his own personal relationships. He figured Rylie and Brody knew the truth even though he'd never said the words aloud. Heck, they were his best friends. But if Reed had been there last night, after Trevor had obsessed about the guy all day yesterday… And then he'd been in such a state of drunkenness… Who knew what he'd let slip.

At this point, all he could do was hope he hadn't looked like too big an ass in front of Rylie's family. But that wasn't the worst of it. Sudden fear gripped him, making it hard to breathe. What had he done in front of his team?

Damn, had he come out to everyone last night? Surely not. Rylie didn't know what happened. If he left publicly with Reed, Rylie would have known. Right?

Trevor glanced at his phone. He typed a text to Reed, then retyped it, finally settling on, "I need help remembering what happened last night. I'm sorry. And what exactly did we decide to do tonight?" Trevor fell back on the bed while he waited for a response.

Thankfully Reed replied quickly. "Hahaha! I'll tell you tonight. We're just going to hang at my place and cook some steaks on the grill. Or if you'd rather go out, we can go to dinner somewhere. It's up to you."

Relief flooded him. So he had been freaking out for nothing.

Just because he crushed on Reed all day yesterday didn't mean he'd acted like an ass the previous night. He was now picturing a much better scenario than anything his overactive imagination had conjured up. Tonight just sounded like a couple of guys buddying around.

Reed was a seriously hot guy who could have his pick of men. Trevor certainly didn't fall anywhere in that category. At very best, and in a dark room, Trevor might be considered average. So it couldn't be an interested "let's date" thing. Reed had just moved back to town. He needed a friend or two. Yeah, Trevor could see that so much easier than thinking Reed wanted a date. Feeling better, back on stable ground, Trevor went downstairs to find something to eat.

Nothing more than sheer willpower kept the turkey sandwich down. Trevor chugged a large glass of soda and sat at the small kitchen table in Rylie's apartment, finally finding the courage to text Reed back.

"Your answer makes me nervous. I hope I didn't embarrass myself or Rylie too badly. I'm not a big drinker. I'm good with just hanging. Whatever you want to do is fine by me. I could meet you wherever. You don't have to drive all the way here. I can borrow Rylie's truck."

It wasn't a moment later before Reed replied. "I don't want you to be nervous. We'll discuss what happened later. You didn't embarrass yourself at all. I enjoyed our time together. I gathered you weren't a big drinker; I'm not either, but I am looking forward to tonight. I have to go to the store anyway, so I'll pick you up."

After scanning the message a couple of times, Trevor decided it all seemed reasonably clear-cut in his mind. He washed his dishes while keeping a steady stream of hydration pumping into his body to counteract his choices from the previous night. Grabbing two water bottles, he went up to his room to get ready. A long hot shower helped his head, and the food seemed to settle his stomach after the initial rebellion. Wiping a towel over the bathroom mirror, Trevor ran through his manscaping routine:

shaving, clipping his fingernails, removing all unwanted hair.

Hair gel came next. Trevor always used hair gel when going out. Lifting the plastic tube, he stopped mid-motion. This wasn't a formal going out deal; they were just planning to hang out at Reed's house. No gel needed. Trevor looked at the tube and shrugged, picking it up again. It always helped to look your best. Once more, he put the bottle back down. Standing in front of the mirror, Trevor stared hard at himself for several long moments.

"Looking your best for what? Reed's freakin' hot and you're not. It doesn't matter how you look tonight. It's just two guys hanging out," Trevor said directly to his reflection, and then reached his hand out to pick up the gel, cocking an eyebrow at his reflection.

"But what if he has friends over? Maybe there'll be someone better suited for you to meet. Ever think about that?"

Trevor put the gel down, still talking directly to himself as if saying it out loud made it an easier debate.

"If Reed has friends, he wouldn't need to hang with you, dumbass."

Finally, Trevor swiped the bottle off the countertop and squeezed a small amount onto his fingers. He ran it through the wayward pieces of hair, trying to tame those few odd strands which seemed to fall straight onto his forehead. Then he padded to the closet. Time ticked by while Trevor contemplated all the clothing he'd brought. He tried on jeans, slacks, then back to jeans, only to finally decide on slacks. He went from a short sleeve button-down to a long sleeve, to a pullover, to a polo, then back to the short sleeve button-down.

A critique of different belts led to a crisis over shoes. He tried on every pair he'd managed to stuff in his duffel bag: dress shoes, loafers, even tennis shoes. While stuck in the middle of his quandary, the doorbell rang. Completely caught off guard, he glanced down at his watch, surprised at how much time he'd taken to dress.

CHAPTER 5

Trevor's ultimate strategy to get through the night boiled down to two words: stay quiet. He'd formulated this plan in the first few seconds after his doorbell chimed and his nerves skyrocketed. No doubt his fair complexion had sunk into a deep crimson just knowing Reed had arrived. Trevor absolutely hated his blush. He could never hide his anxiety because his stupid face always gave him away. He chugged the last of his water bottle and walked through the apartment, fanning his own face with his hands. He tried to take deep breaths, centering himself in hopes the pink would leave his cheeks before Reed noticed.

"It was quite a party you had last night. Did Dad get home okay?" Reed asked Rylie as Trevor rounded the corner to enter the small living room.

"Yeah, he drove me home then took my truck. They brought

it back this morning. You ducked out early last night. You weren't there more than a minute," Rylie said.

Trevor dodged eye contact with them both and initiated his stay quiet plan while the brothers chatted. He took a seat in an armchair close to Rylie, taking care not to wrinkle his slacks.

"Are you ready?" Reed asked. Trevor looked up quickly, caught in the act of running his hands down his pants legs, smoothing the wrinkles free. Reed stood and Rylie followed his cue. Then both looked directly at him. Rylie wore a little smirk on his face, and Trevor immediately stood in a clumsy movement.

"Ah...sure. Yeah. Yes. I'm ready."

"We're out of here, little brother. Enjoy your night with Elise," Reed said as he made it to the front door and opened it wide, before stepping aside for Trevor to lead the way. It wasn't in Trevor's nature to go first; he always held the door for everyone. He stood back now, waiting for Reed to walk through first. Reed did the same, and their gazes collided before Trevor could look away. Reed's sexy grin sent goose bumps springing up across Trevor's arms.

"After you, handsome. I insist," Reed said with a soft chuckle at their stalemate.

Rylie took the matter into his own hands and gave Trevor a little shove from behind to get him through the open door. Unsure how to act, Trevor scolded himself for getting into this situation in the first place. He reaffirmed his oath of the day: he would never drink again.

At the end of the porch, Rylie gave him a second push. Trevor immediately saw a need to alter his strategy for the night and added ignoring his best friend to the overall plan. Between all the little shoves and all the questioning looks Rylie sent his way, Trevor had become even more unnerved. If that were remotely possible.

Somewhere between the last step off the porch and Reed's high-performance car, Trevor's awkwardness reached an all-time high. He kept stepping into Reed, brushing against him, or just flat bumping into him. Fortunately, Reed seemed to be doing his best to help him out, never acting as if it were much of a problem.

Trevor absorbed himself with the car to help excuse his actions. It was easy to focus on the sleek vehicle. He'd never ridden in anything so extravagant. Without thinking, he allowed Reed to open his car door and help him inside. Reed's car was impressive, and Trevor lost himself in scanning the instrument panel and all the fancy buttons across the console. He feathered his fingers along the gearshift and inhaled deeply, appreciating the new car smell as Reed lowered himself into the driver's seat.

"How long have you had this?" he asked as Reed started the car. The stereo came on, lighting up the well-designed dashboard, impressing Trevor all the more.

"I got her when I returned to town a few months ago," Reed said, gripping the stick, sliding it easily into reverse. He backed out of the space in one fluid motion. Trevor watched Reed's hand on the stick shift and looked up to meet Reed's gaze. His heart slammed hard in his chest. The compact interior of the car cocooned them in intimacy. The intensity of Reed's stare took his breath away and held him captive for several long seconds.

Trevor finally averted his gaze and tried to think of something to say, praying his voice didn't shake and betray his anxiety. "I've never ridden in anything so nice," he said lamely, focusing his gaze out the front windshield.

Reed pulled onto the street and casually replied, "I was thinking perhaps we could take her out for a ride before you leave town. There's a beautiful mountain range nearby. I think you may enjoy the scenery."

Heat crept back up his cheeks. He hoped it was dark enough for Reed not to notice the blush. He tried to relax and focused on straightening his slacks while he did a couple of breathing exercises. Somehow, his left hand landed right on top of Reed's. Utterly mortified, he jerked it away from the grasp it apparently tried to make all on its own accord.

"I'm sorry," Trevor croaked again, clearing his throat. There was no way Reed wouldn't notice that one. His eyes darted in Reed's direction to gauge his reaction but flitted away just as quickly as Reed looked over at him.

"You have nothing to be sorry about," Reed said, trying to watch both Trevor and the road at the same time. His cheeks had to be bright red. Why had he ever agreed to any of this in the first place? He was too attracted to Reed, and way outside his comfort zone. He didn't know how to act normal around the guy.

Luckily, Reed kept a steady stream of conversation, which didn't require Trevor to speak. Which was good since Trevor refused to say anything more for fear of embarrassing himself further.

"We're here. I don't know about you, but I'm starving," Reed said, pulling onto a treelined street in a gated community.

Within minutes, he slowed to turn into his driveway.

"Come on. Let's eat."

Again, there were more awkward moments as Trevor opened his door and ran into Reed who had jogged around, apparently to open it for him. Reed seemed frustrated by his reaction when he spoke again.

"Trevor, I've invited you to my home. It's my responsibility to get your doors."

Trevor didn't know how to respond, so he just stood there, shoving his hands into his slacks pockets and looking blankly at Reed. They stood just like that, staring at each other for several long moments until Reed's face changed, and he chuckled, lifting a well arched brow, and then extended his arm. "Please, after you."

Trevor gave in, just to get out from underneath the weight of Reed's smile. He stepped past Reed only to bump into him yet again as he walked by. Trevor jerked out of the way, giving a quick apology for being clumsy as he walked straight to the front door. His heart hammered in his chest while his mind ran double time as he mentally chastised himself. He needed to focus on staying as far away from Reed as he could. He reached to turn the front doorknob and used his body to push against the heavy wood door. It wouldn't budge.

"Here, let me get this for you."

Trevor registered the faint brush of Reed's palm on his back and arm as Reed stepped closer to the door. Trevor's cock pulsed and strained against the binding material of his dress slacks as Reed's other hand ran across his ass and around his waist. He was pressed between Reed's muscular body and the front door for several long seconds.

As Reed slowly maneuvered to unlock the door, his fingertips briefly caressed Trevor's hand at the same time Reed breathed across the skin of Trevor's neck, sending a shiver rolling down his spine.

Trevor's dick couldn't help but take notice before he could even think to get out of the way. Reed didn't step away or give Trevor any room as he worked the lock near Trevor's hand. Trevor shimmied out the side to get out of the way.

No way had Reed caressed him, right? It was an accidental touch, nothing more. Trevor stepped further down the wraparound porch, trying to move out from under the porch light, all the while hoping Reed couldn't see what was going on inside his pants.

Trevor grew more frustrated with himself by the second and demanded his body get a hold of itself. He dropped his hands in his pocket and tried in vain to adjust the hard-on tenting out for all to see. He spun around, feigning interest in the yard as he begged his body to calm down and cooperate.

"I could have borrowed Rylie's truck. You didn't have to come get me," Trevor finally said, after several long moments of desperate adjusting. When Reed stayed quiet, he looked over his shoulder. Reed stood in the open door, leaning against the frame, watching him with an amused grin.

"Welcome to my home, Trevor. I'm glad you're here." With a confident wink, Reed gestured for Trevor to step inside.

Trevor stayed out from under the porch light. Reed didn't move from the doorway, so Trevor had no choice but to turn sideways to ensure their bodies didn't touch as he entered the house. His new surroundings held little interest with all thoughts devoted to the difficult task of making sure he stayed at least three feet away from Reed.

Reed insisted he lead the way, inevitably ensuring Trevor took a wrong turn here or there. And when he did, Reed would extend his hand to guide him back on course. Those small touches caused Trevor's already strained body to harden to even more painful degrees. His hands remained crammed in his pockets to keep his traitorous dick from bulging out. For about the hundredth time, Trevor swore if he made it through this evening, he would never willingly put himself in a similar situation again.

"It must—" His voice breathless and strangled, he cleared his throat before continuing. "It must be hard to have all this and not have your friends around to share it with. Rylie's glad to have you back. After things get settled for him, I'm sure he'll be around more, and friends will happen. Do you keep in touch with any of your old buddies? Or is that just weird with all the time that's passed?"

Relief washed over him when Reed finally stepped around him as they entered the large kitchen. Trevor searched the room for anything to hide behind, grinning when he spotted the large center island. Perfect. He could move around in a full circle and keep his lower half hidden from Reed.

"I have plenty of friends in town." Reed went to the refrigerator as he spoke. "I grew up here. In fact, last weekend I had a big party for Rylie's return. I wish you had been here. You could have met everyone. You're being relocated here soon, right?" He pulled out vegetables and steaks, setting them on the closest counter.

Confusion clouded Trevor's mind. He furrowed his brow. Why in the world was he there if Reed had plenty of friends in the area?

"What would you like to drink?" Reed asked, poking his head around the refrigerator door.

"Whatever you're having's fine. What can I do to help?" Trevor continued to stumble over his thoughts as Reed handed him a bottle of wine.

"Here, you can open this," Reed said with a grin.

Possibilities charged through Trevor's mind. Maybe Rylie wanted to be alone with Elise tonight. Maybe Elise and Rylie set up a double date for Brody and needed to ditch him for the night. Maybe Rylie figured out Trevor was gay and asked Reed to spend some time with him to help him learn to feel okay with it. The possibilities were endless, but no matter how he tried to spin it, none showed Trevor in a positive light.

Trevor concentrated on the bottle opener, wrenching the cork from the top. The little pop sent the fruity aroma from the bottle into the air. Thankfully, his stomach didn't roil. Reed came in from behind Trevor with a couple of wineglasses, which he placed on the counter. Reed's chest brushed against his back, and Trevor quickly looked down to make sure his erection stayed hidden.

The few minutes of trying desperately to figure out why he was in this house had allowed his hard-on to soften just a bit, but all it took was one touch from Reed and his dick stood at attention, demanding to be noticed.

Trevor had to force himself to focus on pouring the two glasses of wine.

"I thought we might eat outside. The weather's been beautiful. All the flowers are in bloom. I think you'll like the view from the deck. It's rather charming in the spring." The entire time Reed spoke, he watched Trevor over the rim of his wineglass before taking a sip.

Reed set the glass down and slid the cutting board, with a pile of vegetables on top, toward him. "Are you handy with a knife?"

They worked on dinner together, and thankfully, as his hands became occupied, so, too, did his lustful thoughts. Reed prepared the steaks while Trevor diced the vegetables. For a moment, Trevor thought he could handle this evening after all.

"My mother's excited about Rylie being home. Excited you and Brody will be relocating soon. Do you have living arrangements yet?"

Popping a piece of zucchini in his mouth, Trevor's hard-on continued to slowly fade.

This time, he was able to answer Reed's question without sounding like a rambling fool. "I'll get a place somewhere close to base. I haven't thought that far ahead yet."

"Mmmm, well, I'm sure I can point you in a direction if you need help finding a place. Rylie told me your parents are no longer with us. You know, if there's anything you need, my parents and I are here for you. My mother considers you one of her own already."

"Your family's been exceptionally good to me. Your mom sends birthday and Christmas gifts every year. I try to do the same for her, and on Mother's Day. She's the best." Trevor could tell he'd switched himself into survival mode and almost laughed at the ridiculousness of this whole situation. "She met my mom one time briefly at graduation, right before she died. Your mom and dad even came to the funeral. They flew out since Rylie couldn't be there. My mom was sick for a long time. Breast cancer. She fought a hell of a battle, but she couldn't shake it. I'm happy she's not in all that pain anymore. Your mom helped me see that too."

"Yeah, my mom's incredible. I'm lucky to have her. I'm glad you have her too. What happened to your dad?"

"Dad died in the line of duty. He left the military and became a police officer. He was shot serving a warrant. I was a few months old."

"You don't have any brothers or sisters?" Reed asked, looking up at Trevor while seasoning the steaks.

"No, Mom never remarried. It was just me and her. She was a good woman, a great mom." Trevor continued dicing, his body finally settling down enough he could move around a little more freely and actually make brief eye contact as they spoke.

"Your mother has an amazing son. I'm sure she was proud. I'm going to get these started outside. Come out when you're finished," Reed said, balancing the steaks in one hand, and his wineglass in the other. Trevor waited, letting his body completely relax before manning up and following along.

"The night's perfect," Trevor said as he opened the door and stepped outside. Despite his more relaxed state, he still stayed many feet from Reed.

"It is. How do you like your steak?" Reed asked from the front of the grill. "Wait, let me guess. I bet you're a medium type of guy."

"That's right. How do you like yours?"

"I'm a medium type of guy myself. Have a seat or take a look around. I've been working on the spring garden over in the far corner of the yard. It won't be much longer before these are ready," Reed said, carefully turning the steaks over.

A small breeze blew across the backyard. Trevor took that tour around the yard as opposed to sitting and staring at Reed. He walked the length of the deck to relax himself. Trevor finally brought the glass of wine to his lips. With the smallest of sips, he carefully swallowed, relieved the wine stayed down after his overindulgence in alcohol the night before.

He walked alongside the swimming pool, then out into the yard. The night was dark. The moon peeked from behind a cloud, lighting the yard just enough for him to notice exactly how well-manicured Reed kept the landscape.

Trevor used this time to think back over the events of this evening up until now. He assessed his current demeanor as somewhere between awkward and bumbling idiot. He seriously needed to spend more time with people in the future, because after tonight, he saw himself clearly as a social imbecile.

Heading back toward the deck, Trevor spotted the smallest of blooms just starting to open in the flower bed along the deck. He loved flowers and the commitment and care it took to grow them.

Kneeling he looked over the new blooms, still contemplating the evening. After this first hour, surely Reed would see that a friendship with him didn't fit in his world. He figured Reed would probably return him to Rylie's apartment immediately following dinner. Reed was too nice of a guy to abandon the meal he'd already started cooking to take him back now. Besides, Trevor did have the pity card going in his favor after they'd talked about his mom and dad. Guilt, if nothing more, would force Reed to keep him here through the entire meal.

Rising, he started to move away from the flowers. Maybe this whole night was at Rylie's mom's request. It was the one idea that made the most sense, and it surprised him that he hadn't thought of it sooner.

What would Reed go back and tell his mother about their evening together? They were clearly as different as two people could be. Lost in thought, Trevor walked back up onto the deck, scanning over the backyard again, taking in the swimming pool and the large custom-built deck and huge flower garden. His gaze strayed up to the beautiful Victorian style home, which he stared at as if seeing it for the first time.

Trevor chuckled to himself. Reed was so far out of his league. He had nothing to worry about. No way would Reed want to spend any more time with him after tonight. Regardless of what embarrassing details Reed might relay to his parents, Trevor felt much better about things.

However, his heart gave an odd little ache at the thought this night would be the last he spent in this home.

CHAPTER 6

The steaks were close to done. Reed turned the grill's knob to lower the flame, then closed the lid to let the steaks sit for a few more minutes. He'd secretly hoped he and Trevor would have been in his bed by now, but instead, Trevor continued to act anxious, apologetic, and uninterested. Reed lifted his wineglass and took a long drink, watching Trevor explore the backyard.

Reed's hands itched to pull Trevor close. With each inadvertent touch, he prayed Trevor would take him in his arms and kiss him like he had the night before. He longed to rekindle some of the magic they'd shared, and despite how torturous this little game was, Trevor was worth the wait. Slow and steady were the best way to capture this gorgeous man.

If it weren't for the huge and very noticeable bulge in Trevor's pants, Reed would be convinced Trevor wasn't interested in him at all. Now, he just needed to figure out why Trevor's actions said one thing while his body showed another.

Taking another sip of wine, Reed gave Trevor space and stayed as far away from him as possible. He went back into the house to gather the rest of their food, and brought it all outside, setting the table. As he worked, he kept one eye on Trevor, who still completely avoided him.

On a whim, he scooted Trevor's seat closer to his at the large, round patio table. Trevor was extraordinarily handsome to Reed, and fit in his home perfectly, suiting its sophisticated beauty. None of Reed's strong feelings for Trevor had faded. They were only growing stronger with each passing minute.

While waiting for the steaks to finish, Reed casually went to stand behind Trevor at the edge of the deck, where he was once again focused on the backyard. Reed made sure to keep a considerate distance, but after a moment, Trevor's body tensed. He looked down and stepped to one side.

"I'm sorry. I'm in your way again," Trevor said, staying close to the railing, looking confused and trapped. All Reed could do was watch, keeping his hands tucked away inside his pants pockets. He had to will himself not to reach out and touch Trevor again.

"No, you're not—"

"Why am I here? I honestly don't remember last night. Is this a pity thing? Did your mom want you to be nice to me? I'm not trying to ruin the night. I just can't figure out why I'm here."

Reed watched the anguish cross Trevor's brow seconds before he schooled his features.

The question caught Reed momentarily off guard. He blinked, then blinked again. Then everything slipped into place and made a hell of a lot more sense. He smiled, letting it reach his eyes as he cautiously stepped in a little closer. "You're here because you agreed to go on a date with me. You honestly don't remember?"

"No, I don't. I can't figure any of this out," Trevor said, a quiet desperation filling his voice.

"That explains everything." Reed took another step closer, his chest almost touching Trevor's. "I assure you this has nothing to do with pity. In fact, I can't seem to get you out of my head. You're all I've thought about since I ran into you at the rehearsal dinner. And after last night"—Reed's gaze dropped to Trevor's plump lips—"I crave the taste of your lips against mine again."

Reed placed his hand on Trevor's arm and leaned in closer, inclining his head so his lips hovered slightly over Trevor's. "Will you let me kiss you again?"

Trevor said nothing as his breathing quickened, his chest heaving several breaths. His eyes went wide, and that sexy blush suffused his cheeks. All at once everything came together perfectly in Reed's world. Trevor inched closer. His hard arousal brushed against Reed's own aching cock, causing it to throb. Trevor lifted his lips in a silent invitation.

Oh dear God, yes…he wants me too!

The slight tilt of Trevor's head was all the agreement Reed needed. He took Trevor's face between his palms. Reed pressed closer, desperately needing to feel the hardness of this gorgeous man's body against his own. A slow slide of his tongue across Trevor's full bottom lip was rewarded when Trevor's eyes slid closed and his lips parted, opening for him.

Ah, that's right...kiss me.

Reed's tongue surged forward, meeting Trevor's. A groan vibrated deep inside his chest. His senses flooded with desire. Trevor's kiss tasted so much sweeter than Reed remembered.

He loved the way Trevor responded to him.

Reed feasted on Trevor's mouth, his tongue tasting, swirling, and eagerly probing. He wrapped Trevor in his arms, pressing head to toe against Trevor's hard body. He wanted this man so badly it hurt.

Oh, you're magnificent, Mr. West.

Reed burned to take Trevor to his bedroom, slowly undress him, and explore every part of that rock-hard body. He wanted to hear Trevor gasp his name in pleasure. Reed groaned. His cock twitched. Yes, he wanted to pleasure Trevor, over and over, hour after hour, and lose himself until he didn't know where Trevor ended and he began.

What the hell was wrong with him? After this one kiss, he wanted to pick out china patterns with this man. Lord, he already had it so bad, and all he could hope was Trevor shared his feelings.

With great restraint, he drew Trevor's tongue into his mouth one last time before easing from the kiss, keeping Trevor tucked in his arms. He didn't know if Trevor could sense his urgency or his desperation, but he didn't want to scare him off.

For Reed's own sanity, as well as Trevor's comfort, Trevor would have to set the pace of their relationship.

"Mmmm, I like kissing you," Reed whispered, the gravel of passion littering his words. It took a moment for Trevor to open his eyes. Confusion clouded his gaze, and Reed's heart skipped a beat. He prayed Trevor wouldn't bolt.

Then Trevor asked, "I'm sorry, what did you say?"

Reed grinned at the sweet response. The tip of Reed's thumb traced the outline of Trevor's full bottom lip one last time. "I said your kiss is intoxicating. Thank you for allowing me the pleasure."

Reed laughed as the smell of sizzling meat grabbed his attention. "See what you do to me? I almost forgot about the steaks." Reluctantly, Reed moved from Trevor's arms and raced to the grill, quickly yanking everything from over the hot coals. "Perhaps a little overdone, but let's eat."

They sat together at the patio dinner table well into the night. Their empty plates pushed out of the way, wineglasses filled for the third or fourth time that evening. Reed kept their fingers entwined, using his thumb to trace small circles into Trevor's palm.

Since the kiss, Trevor seemed more at ease. He opened up and became very comfortable to be with, not to mention amazing to look at. They never went more than a moment without something to say. Reed happily discovered they shared many things in common, from movies to books and almost all their music choices. They both loved art and museums. Reed realized, with more than a little fear, he was falling hard for this wonderful man.

But all too soon Trevor glanced at his watch, and Reed knew the magic of the evening had come to an end. It was late and Rylie's wedding was the following day.

"I should go," Trevor said while rising. He picked up the plates from the table. "Tomorrow's a big day for you. I can take a taxi home."

"I'll get these, you're my guest. Please sit and enjoy the evening. It'll only take a few seconds for me to clear the dishes."

Trevor started to protest, but Reed quickly appeased him.

"No, I insist. And I will be taking you home. It's only right. So, sit while I take these dishes to the sink. I'll be right back then I'll take you home."

Reed drew out the cleaning process just to keep Trevor at his home a little longer. It was time for the date to end, but he just couldn't bear to have him go yet.

Shutting the screen door, Reed strolled over to where Trevor stood, leaning against the railing. Dare he hope Trevor waited there for him. "Beautiful night, isn't it?"

"I think it's you that makes it truly beautiful," Trevor said, smiling shyly. "I'm happy to be here. Your house is perfect. You can tell you took the time to make it your home. My mom always wanted a backyard like this. She would have loved it."

Reed was touched at the way Trevor's eyes lit up as he spoke of his mother. He stepped closer. A smile gently tugged at the corners of his lips as he placed his arm around Trevor's waist. "She was lucky to have you as a son." Reed brushed his lips softly across Trevor's. "I'm sure you made her very proud."

Reed kissed Trevor tenderly, gently. He wanted to ask him to stay the night, but he needed to tread carefully. After all, this was only their first date. Rylie said Trevor was a classic gentleman. Did a gentleman have sex on the first date? Chuckling to himself, Reed admitted he always had sex on the first date, because there were no second dates. With Trevor, Reed wanted a second, a third, a fourth, a fifth…

"I should go," Trevor said as they parted to take in some air. "You have a big day tomorrow. Rylie will need you early. It sounds like the wedding will take all day and the reception all night. Are you sure you don't want me to call a cab?"

"No, I'll take you. Tomorrow's the big day, but I don't have to meet Rylie until after lunch, so I'm fine." Taking Trevor's hand in his, Reed entwined their fingers. He spoke softly as he gazed into Trevor's blue eyes. "Before we go, I need you to know I've enjoyed myself tonight. I hope you have too. I really like you." Insecurity stopped the flow of Reed's words. He glanced down at their joined fingers, and then back up again. He was nervous and rambling. His stomach fluttered. He felt like a silly schoolboy trying to be cool in order to impress his first crush. Taking a deep breath, Reed focused his eyes back on Trevor. "Would you think it too forward of me to ask you to be my date to Rylie's wedding? I know we're both going anyway, but I would really love for us to go together."

Trevor lifted his eyebrows, only to drop and narrow them as he answered, "Sure, I mean, would your family be okay with it all? I don't want to intrude on your family time. And... well...I don't know if I can...be with you...with my team being there. I should probably tell them before I just come out." Through his reply, Trevor tightened his hold on Reed's hand and his eyes focused on Reed's lips, his head lowering to them. "I didn't want this to be the last time I might see you," he whispered before capturing their lips together.

Reed melted into Trevor's kiss, his arms sliding around his waist. He pulled Trevor's hips into his and deepened the kiss; his tongue probed and teased Trevor's. Trevor gripped Reed's head, tangling his long fingers in his hair. Reed stepped forward, pushing Trevor against the rail. A needy groan escaped when Trevor's hips rolled and his arousal ground against Reed. Reed's wanton hands smoothed down the curve of Trevor's tight ass, gripping him, tugging him tightly against his hard-as-stone arousal. Trevor needed to feel how badly he was wanted. Slowly, Reed pulled himself from the kiss, trying to remember the importance of slow and steady.

"You're not intruding. You could never intrude. I want you with me. We can keep our dating quiet. No one has to know. It's enough for now that I know you want to be by my side." Reed traced the outline of Trevor's full lips with his tongue.

Trevor's lips parted and his tongue came forward to brush against Reed's. Reed responded voraciously. Trevor tightened his grip as the kiss heated. Delicious friction sent Reed's body soaring, more aroused than ever before in his life. His breathing faltered; his heart echoed in his ears. Everything about Trevor completely overwhelmed him.

Gasping, Reed broke from the heated kiss, his eyes locking with Trevor's. He'd never experienced anything this intensely before. Reed laid his forehead against Trevor's and closed his eyes. Small pants of breath escaped as Reed softly whispered, "Stay... Please stay with me tonight."

Trevor's hips rolled forward, but the deep lust Reed saw reflected in Trevor's eyes slowly morphed into some logic that didn't appear inclined to go in his favor. Trevor reached forward, lightly capturing Reed's lips for a small kiss before answering.

"I have a fierce battle going on between my heart, my legs, and my head. I've never been the guy for one-night stands. I want to stay, but I'm not that guy. I'm sorry. I'm deeply sorry." Frustration crossed Trevor's brow, and he lowered his head to Reed's shoulder, hiding his face. "I don't make a very good gay man, do I?"

Tenderly, Reed brought a hand to Trevor's neck, placing his

index finger underneath Trevor's chin to lift his face. "Let's just be very clear here. I want more from you, much more, than a one-night stand. I want to take it slow for you. I've never felt what I'm feeling right now. If I'm to be completely honest, the reason I want you to stay is…I'm afraid."

Reed inclined his head to focus on Trevor's face, pausing briefly to memorize every curve and line.

He smiled when he realized there were no freckles on that sexy face. "I'm afraid if you walk out that door, it'll be the last time I see you." Bringing their joined hands to his lips, Reed kissed Trevor's knuckles. "I want to give us a chance. You've promised to be my date tomorrow. We'll see what tomorrow night holds for us."

CHAPTER 7

Arriving early to Rylie's apartment, Reed found the front door unlocked and let himself in. He wound his way first to Rylie's bedroom to check in on the groom before making his way down the hall to find Trevor.

He tapped his knuckles lightly on the slightly ajar guest bedroom door. He pushed it a little further open with his foot and caught Trevor's reflection in the bathroom mirror.

Trevor wore no clothing, just a towel draped loosely around his hips as he fixed his hair. His sculpted, muscular chest and big broad shoulders all tapered into a narrow waist. Every one of Trevor's movements caused the muscles in his arms and back to ripple and flex as he worked his hair in place. Reed's own body responded to the sight, tensing with the need he couldn't quite sequester since meeting Trevor.

Reed cleared his throat and took a step back. "Can I come in?" he asked loudly.

"Sure, come on in. I'll be out in a minute," Trevor said, looking over his shoulder. A little crimson flush showed on his cheeks as he shut the bathroom door.

"Did you sleep well?" Reed called out, seeing the uniform placed neatly on the bed. A devious grin spread across his face as he wondered how Trevor planned to get the uniform into the bathroom to finish dressing.

"We didn't sleep much. Rylie was too wired. We ended up playing poker until about five thirty this morning. How did you sleep?" Trevor asked through the closed door.

After a moment, Reed decided to give Trevor a break. He picked up the hanger holding the uniform, walked to the bathroom door, and gave a quick knock. Trevor opened the door a crack. The relief on his face was evident when he saw the uniform.

"I thought you might need this." Reed pulled the uniform back just as Trevor reached for it and pushed the bathroom door a little further open with his foot. "How about a kiss first?"

The endearing flush on Trevor's cheeks darkened. Reed decided then and there that he loved to watch that slow tinting of color. He found it very sexy and somewhat fulfilling to know he had the power to provoke such a reaction. Reed leaned in and received a quick kiss, with just a tease of the tongue. It wasn't near enough.

Reluctantly, he handed over the uniform. "You're welcome... and I did sleep well once I finally fell asleep. I had very, very sweet dreams too."

"Hang on. I need to put this on." Trevor finished dressing but didn't quite shut the bathroom door all the way this time. Minutes later, when Trevor stepped out, Reed couldn't seem to take his eyes off the man.

"You're truly devastatingly handsome, Trevor." Reed narrowed his eyes as he swept his gaze down the length of

Trevor's body. "I'm going to have to keep my eyes on you tonight. I wouldn't want anyone trying to steal you away from me."

"I'm sure you have nothing to worry about," Trevor added dryly, dismissing Reed's utterly serious remarks as nothing more than inconsequential ramblings.

"I'm not so sure. You're a striking man, Trevor West." Reed gave Trevor a wink and moved to the door, trying to keep his hands to himself. Trevor looked deliciously handsome and incredibly shy about it all. It was a tempting combination. "We'll be late if we don't hurry. Let me check on Rylie's progress."

***

Though Brody tried his best to get into Reed's sports car, Rylie kept a firm hold on their friend, shoving Brody into the passenger seat of Rylie's truck, giving Trevor enough time to slide in beside Reed.

Once Reed pulled from his parking space at the apartment, he reached over to link their hands together. Then he chatted steadily throughout the ride to the church, thankfully not requiring Trevor to say much. He liked how Reed did that for him, just filled the silence, keeping everything comfortable. Trevor had sat through too many awkward silences in his life to not appreciate Reed's efforts in keeping the dialog fluid.

They weren't in the car for more than ten minutes before pulling into the chapel's parking lot. The way Olivia spoke of the place, it sounded tiny and quaint, but this was a large, sprawling mega church. It made sense considering the number of guests attending today. Reed shifted the car into first gear and turned the ignition off before turning to Trevor.

"I wanted to kiss you before I get out of this car, but I don't want to embarrass you in front of Rylie or Brody. I'll be thinking about my unfortunate luck in having missed out on your kiss. I tried to lose them, but Rylie ran that last light, ruining my chances.

I'll have to be sure to thank him for that later." Looking into his rearview mirror, Reed kept his eyes locked on something. "My brother's always so serious. I worry about him. I'm going now. I'll see you as much as I can."

Reed quickly exited the car and hurried past Brody, only giving a quick nod before wrapping his arm around his brother, hugging him tight and patting him hard on the back.

"Okay, little brother, today's your big day. Are you holding up okay?"

Trevor watched the exchange from the hood of Reed's sports car, giving the brothers a small degree of privacy. After a moment, Brody came to stand beside Trevor.

"Shit, I don't think I remember the vows. Did I forget my copy?" Rylie asked, worry crossing his brow while he patted his pockets.

"You'll be fine. It's only pre-wedding jitters. Everyone gets anxious, little brother. Come on. Let's get this show on the road." Reed turned his brother toward the church, heading in the direction of the front doors where an elderly man waited.

Pastor Hamilton, as Rylie introduced him, seemed like a kind old man. He stood, holding the heavy oak door open, welcoming them to the church.

As he and Brody lingered behind in an effort to give Rylie and Reed a moment alone. Brody said, "Yeah, I'm lookin' sharp. You don't have to say it." Brody playfully elbowed Trevor in the side, giving him the grin which always drew people to Brody.

"You don't look too bad. Of course, technically, we all look the same in this uniform. How's Rylie?"

"Nervous as hell. By the way, how was your night last night? Did you finally get a little ass?" Brody asked while walking backward, lifting his fist in the air for a quick knuckle bump. Trevor looked over at the pastor. Clearly, he, as well as Rylie and Reed, had heard the crude comment. Brody seemed immune to the astonished stares, but Trevor couldn't ignore them and left

Brody hanging with his fist in the air.

"Dude, really? We're at church. That's wrong even for you," Trevor hissed and walked past Brody.

"Well, I'll take that as a big ass no. It might help if you would pull out the fucking corn cob that's stuck up your tight ass, man," Brody called out even louder than before. Trevor ignored him completely. When Brody got on a roll, nothing stopped him.

Reed stood in the door, holding it open. The pastor stood just inside with Rylie. Trevor couldn't quite make eye contact with Reed when he walked inside. Reed looked angry and all that anger was centered on his loud-mouthed friend following behind.

In unison, Trevor, Brody, and Rylie's cell phones alerted them that an official message had been sent. When a notification came from the federal government, everyone took notice of the loud tone echoing through the room, it didn't matter if the phones were silenced or not. Rylie turned quickly, his eyes going wide, before Trevor could get his phone from his pocket.

"Don't worry. They aren't calling us in. We're on standby." Trevor read from his phone, then looked up to check the groom. Momentary relief shone on Rylie's face. Reed stood beside his brother, staring at Trevor for a long moment as the weight of the situation settled in on all of them.

"They do this all the time, Rylie, and never call us in," Trevor reminded him, trying to keep the concern from his voice.

"Right... You're right," Rylie said, giving a solid nod as if to confirm his words.

"Then let's go get you married, brother," Reed said, concern still marring his features, but he clamped Rylie reassuringly on the shoulder. No more words were necessary as the brothers turned and followed the pastor into his office.

CHAPTER 8

The wedding ceremony went perfectly, which made Trevor happy for his friend. Reed stood between Rylie and Trevor. All throughout the ceremony, Reed found reasons to turn Trevor's way, always with a brief smile or slight wink. When the wedding ended and it was time for Trevor to walk back up the center aisle, Reed casually placed a hand in the small of his lower back. The touch turned into a caress, dipping low until deft fingertips ran across the bridge of his ass. His body hardened under the touch and his face heated as he met his assigned bridesmaid and walked her up the aisle.

A formal dinner reception followed at the hotel where he'd first met Reed. The guests seemed happy, relaxed, and ready for the reception celebration. Reed had stayed close to Rylie's side for the entire afternoon and most of the evening.

The security around Reed's parents was incredibly tight. If the United States had gone to such lengths to protect the Kensingtons, something must be going on in the world, but Trevor had not been privy to the information. One thing was for sure, nothing going on in the outside world dampened the atmosphere of this evening.

Elise had tried several times over the years to fix Trevor up with the petite woman who turned out to be the bridesmaid and dinner companion at his assigned table. Trevor remembered her name to be something like Karen…or Karri…or maybe Karol. Whatever her name, she turned out to be the perfect company for Trevor. She spoke easily, talking and filling in the gaps in conversation when he stayed quiet.

Despite the pleasant company, Trevor's thoughts strayed regularly to Reed. His gaze constantly searched out the family table for just small glimpses of him. Every time he looked up to find Reed, their eyes collided. This time, Reed tipped his glass in Trevor's direction, giving him a wink. He couldn't help but grin, and the heat of a blush rushed back over his cheeks.

Once dinner ended, they were all ushered to the reception hall for the party. Karen-Karri-Karol stayed close by Trevor's side. She was a beautiful woman, and it wasn't a hardship to have her nearby. Trevor noticed Mrs. Kensington's excitement while watching them.

Reed didn't seem able to shake free of his best man responsibilities. He was always needed for something. Rylie and Elise went through the traditional wedding festivities: cutting the cake, taking pictures, and having the maid of honor and the best man speak. Trevor and Karol were standing in line for cake when Reed came to the microphone to give his best man's speech. Every eye turned his way. Reed drew people to him like no one Trevor had ever seen before.

"If everyone will grab a glass, please, I have something I would like to say. For those of you who don't know me, my name is Reed, and for those of you that do, well, consider yourself extremely blessed. My full name is actually Reed Would You

Like A Drink for those of you who I meet in the bar later tonight. Please don't forget what I look like, and I'd appreciate it if you could use my full name." The room burst into laughter. Trevor watched Reed look over at his brother, giving a wink, letting the joke settle.

"I'm actually Rylie's older brother, and isn't it good to see that I'm finally receiving the recognition I deserve by being named best man for the nuptials of Rylie and Elise? It's a well-known fact that I can talk, and I couldn't help but notice that there's a betting pool on the length of my speech. Well, just to let you know, having timed my speech at two hours thirty-seven minutes and the pool payout is currently standing at somewhere around nine hundred ninety-three dollars, I must apologize in advance. So please make yourself comfortable and enjoy the ride."

Reed laughed, this time with the guests while turning to his brother and Elise. "All kidding aside, I'm honored to stand here this evening and celebrate the love and life you have chosen to share with one another. When you realize you want to spend the rest of your life with someone, you want the rest of your life to start as soon as possible. I understand that feeling, so I will be brief." Reed looked back over the guests until his eyes locked on Trevor's. Breath froze in his lungs at the power in that gaze. In that moment, Reed spoke directly to him. All others in the room just simply faded away. "A wise person once told me that magic happens at the most unexpected times. I would have to disagree to an extent."

Breaking the stare, Reed turned back to his brother and new sister-in-law. "Today has been planned for months and months, and it was still filled with unexpected magic. I've known Rylie all his life and I've never seen him happier than when he's with Elise. Also, I have never seen Elise without a smile on her face when she and Rylie are together. This magic that makes them glow today is love. Love, however, isn't always simple. You will fight and disagree, but as long as you love each other, the magic you feel at this moment will never die. May the rest of your lives be filled with magical moments. I love you both."

Reed raised his glass. "Finally, it gives me great pleasure to invite you all to raise your glasses to Rylie and Elise Kensington. I'm sure everyone here today would like to wish the newest Mr. and Mrs. Kensington love, life, laughter, and a happily ever after."

Trevor stood fixated on Reed, watching everything about him as he spoke. The guy was so polished, so sophisticated, and he held this audience in the palm of his hand. The admiration this room held for Reed transcended his sexuality and focused on respect. Trevor was in awe, wondering what someone so magnificent could possibly see in him. Reed needed someone who complemented him, who was equal to him on every level.

Out of nowhere, Brody came barreling toward Trevor. With both fists, he grabbed Trevor's uniform jacket and pushed him back several feet from Karol, who stood clapping with everyone else for Rylie and Elise.

"Dude, seriously, why do you keep staring at him? He's a player. You were played. Get the fucking stars out of your eyes. You look lovesick. It's pathetic, even for you." Brody got up in Trevor's face, standing nose to nose with him. Seeing where this conversation was headed, Trevor herded Brody through a side door to the kitchen, separating him from anyone who might overhear.

"Man, what's your problem tonight? You're being a bigger ass than normal," Trevor responded, glaring.

Brody didn't stand down, nor did he step back, but his lips curled in a mocking smirk. "Do you think he's into you? Is that it? Like it's more than a fuck?" He paused for a second, tilted his head, before continuing. "You do! You actually think you're more than a fuck." Brody gave a snide, harsh laugh, and Trevor could do nothing more than stare at the man he thought was his best friend. Brody was so angry, so insistent, and up in his face. It took time for Trevor to process it all, still confused over what could have bothered Brody so badly.

"It's not like that."

Brody cut Trevor off to continue his hateful tirade. "You think he's into you. Oh, that's sweet. Okay, watch this. I know his kind. I'm his fucking kind. He's not into you. He's into himself and the next fuck, and he'll say whatever it takes to get it. Watch, better you should see it now." Brody left as quickly as he came, barreling through the door, letting it swing wide. Trevor stared at the door's back-and-forth motion until it came to a stop.

He didn't want to watch the impending scene. Somewhere deep inside his heart, he wanted to believe Reed desired only him. Unable to stop himself, Trevor pushed open the door and stepped aside, watching Brody stalk across the large room toward Reed. Trevor's heart ached as he tracked each one of Brody's steps. He desperately wanted to stop Brody but saw no way possible without causing a scene.

Trevor realized the years he spent pining for Brody were nothing more than his safety net. He never experienced the depth of emotion or the sheer utter romance with Brody that he had with Reed. The slow creep of pain made its way to his heart. Brody was going to ruin it all. If Reed had played him, then so be it. For now, Trevor was happy. If at the end of the weekend, or hell, even the end of the night, Reed never contacted him again, he would have at least the memory of tonight to look back on.

As Brody rounded the corner to the front tables, Trevor's heart broke a little more. Brody moved forward with a single-minded purpose. He only looked back over his shoulder once, as if to make sure Trevor was watching. Brody approached Reed from behind, where he sat listening to the next speaker.

Every moment slowed for Trevor. Brody placed a hand on the small of Reed's back. Reed turned to Brody, and Brody leaned in, whispering into Reed's ear. Trevor's heart sank to new lows at the smile spreading across Reed's face.

What was wrong with him? Trevor had only known Reed for a matter of days.

Closing his eyes, he took a deep breath. Brody was completely right, and he felt totally pathetic on every level.

"Trevor, I need my drink refilled. Do you mind? I'm being called to the front for the bridesmaid toasts." Trevor turned away when Karol touched his arm. Self-reprimands and ridicule slowly poured through his mind. Mechanically, Trevor smiled down at her, trying to hide the pain crushing his heart.

"Sure," Trevor said, praying he could save some of his dignity if Brody or Reed happened to look his direction as they left together. Trevor blindly walked to the bar, chastising his delusional romantic dumb thoughts.

CHAPTER 9

Involuntarily bouncing his leg, Reed looked down at his watch, wishing he could escape. Elise's chatty little maid of honor, who sat to his right, wouldn't stop prattling on about the wedding and how she didn't like being single. All Reed wanted to do was get his hands and lips back on the shy man standing across the room. Trevor stood in the back of the reception hall, looking sexy as hell, and Reed literally ached to get back there with him. He honestly didn't know how much more of all this he could take.

Completely lost in the deep thoughts of Trevor's lips and how they moved against his own when they kissed, Reed was surprised to feel a warm hand on his back. A smile tore across his face at the caress. He turned, hoping Trevor might be standing behind him. Instead, he was momentarily caught off guard when he looked up to see Brody.

Brody leaned in, not waiting for an invitation, and whispered in Reed's ear, "I've watched you all night. I want you. I'm versatile, whatever way you want, I'm there." Brody's hand never stopped the annoying caress on Reed's lower back.

"Is that right? All night?" Reed asked. He almost laughed out loud at the audacity. Not a chance in hell, pretty boy. Brody was a player, no doubt about it.

"Yeah, I want to suck you off. I want to feel your cock jerk as you shoot your load down my throat," Brody added, his voice so quiet Reed almost couldn't hear him. Brody's hands increased their pressure as they slid deliberately up and down his back, making Reed want to cringe.

Any other time, Reed would have taken the guy up on his offer. You didn't have to like the person to have sex. Sex was sex, and Reed always enjoyed a good fuck. But listening to Brody talk, Reed realized without question, the only man he wanted was the auburn-haired one who haunted his thoughts. How could Brody be so stupid as to throw away someone like Trevor? Reed turned his head, so his lips were only inches from Brody's and looked him firmly in the eyes before flashing his trademark grin.

"Why don't you go ahead; I'll meet you in the bathroom. Give me five minutes." Motioning for Brody to lean closer, he whispered in his ear, "You can go ahead and start without me. I like to watch. It turns me on."

Brody didn't respond, but straightened to his full height, stuck his chest out, and strutted off alone to the bathroom. What a stupid fool. Reed chuckled to himself as he rose from his chair and headed across the room.

He spotted Trevor at the bar. Reed wound his way through the throng of guests, not allowing anyone to sidetrack him as he went. When he finally reached Trevor, just the look on his soldier's face made him furrow his brow in question.

"You look surprised to see me. Are you?" When Trevor didn't readily reply, only his Adam's apple bobbed as he swallowed his confusion, Reed continued, "I should apologize for my dating skills, or rather lack thereof, that is. I would ask you to dance, but your girlfriend might not like it." Reed chuckled at his own words, knowing there were some jealous overtones in what he said. He had wanted to be the one by Trevor's side tonight.

They stepped forward as the bartender asked for their drink order. Reed placed his order after Trevor's, recognizing Trevor still had not responded.

Reed turned to the handsome soldier, his tone apologetic and sincere when he spoke. "I'm sorry for all of this. I really need some alone time with you. I hear the view from the balcony is quite lovely. Care to meet me there?"

Silence held Trevor for a couple of long moments before he spoke. "Let me get this to Karol and excuse myself. I'll meet you out there in a couple of minutes." Trevor would barely look Reed's way.

Some hint of sadness lurked in those blue eyes, but all he could do right now was watch Trevor walk away with both drinks in his hands. Something wasn't right. What happened? Had he missed something?

Reed excused himself from his family obligations, telling his brother and parents he would be back a little later. Through the exchange, he kept an eye on Trevor as he slid out a side door. He watched as Trevor removed his uniform jacket and placed it carefully on the back of a chair. The thin material of his shirt stretched over that wide, expansive chest, causing Reed to lose all ability to think straight. He stood there staring until Trevor walked to a far corner of the balcony, out of sight and breaking the spell.

He became a man on a mission. He stopped by the band, requesting a song, instructing them to wait fifteen minutes before playing it. Reed purposefully ignored everyone and everything between him and those balcony doors.

Walking out, Reed vowed he wouldn't let too many more

nights like this happen. He must do whatever it took to win Trevor over. Trevor needed to be by his side; that was all there was to it. And Reed would be proud to have Trevor there. He didn't want to have to sneak away for a simple touch or a quick kiss. Hell, with the possessive turmoil coursing through him this entire evening, Reed wanted those touches and kisses to show everyone around that Trevor was his.

Reed inhaled the fresh scents of spring as he walked out into the night. The unusually warm late April evening gave a perfect feel for any guest who cared to venture outside.

Giving his eyes the second or two they needed to adjust, Reed scanned the two dark corners Trevor could have retreated to. The balcony was longer than it looked, with a large area completely hidden from the ballroom's windows. His heart kicked up when he spotted Trevor next to the railing, facing away from him, staring out into the night.

What has you so deep in thought?

"I love spring evenings, don't you?" Reed asked, striding over to stand beside Trevor. Reed rested back against the balcony rail.

Trevor slowly turned to face him but didn't speak. He hoped Trevor was as overwhelmed by him as he was Trevor. Finally, Reed's gaze shifted and moved around the balcony, taking in the view.

"It's beautiful out here, isn't it?"

The balcony was draped with thousands of twinkle lights. Beautiful fragrant flowers and greenery filled the space. Several small tables sat to the side, decorated with linens matching the bride's colors inside. Delicate flower arrangements adorned the center of each table. Large candles filled the empty spaces, giving off a soft romantic glow. It was beautifully decorated and charming but had nothing compared to the soldier standing next to Reed.

"You're the beautiful one, Reed," Trevor finally said, shifting to mimic Reed's position.

Trevor leaned back against the rail, spreading his legs apart. Reed took it as a silent invitation. "Ah, finally…I get what I've wanted all night," Reed purred, his hands slipping around Trevor's waist as he slid between his thighs, pulling him close.

Holding Trevor in his arms, Reed didn't move. He didn't say anything more, just held Trevor tightly.

The welling emotion had Reed resting his head on Trevor's shoulder, breathing in his wonderful scent, watching the candle flames dance in the evening breeze. Everything slowed when Trevor wrapped his arms around Reed, returning his embrace. And in that moment, everything righted itself in his world. He'd met his one.

Reed felt a connection to Trevor's soul. It didn't matter if it was three days, three hours, three years, thirty years—Trevor belonged with him. If soul mates were real, Reed had met his match.

Holding Trevor this way, tight in his arms, comforted Reed. Never had his soul felt comforted by the closeness of another. A lump formed in his throat as emotion rolled through his heart. Please need me like I need you.

Reed looked up at Trevor who quickly averted his gaze. Did Trevor feel this same pull and just couldn't look him in the eyes from the sheer emotion of it all? He lifted a hand to Trevor's chin, turning him to look Reed in the eyes. Trevor seemed relieved yet resigned. A sadness lingered in his gaze. Not quite the look Reed hoped for but one which caused him to pull Trevor closer against his body. No words were said as Reed wondered if this look had anything to do with Brody.

It may be best if everything were laid bare between them before his runaway heart took him too far. Reed needed to know what he had to do to keep Trevor all to himself. Rylie said Trevor might have feelings for Brody. He needed to know for sure. Reed pulled back a little, watching Trevor for a moment before he spoke.

"I know I've only known you for a short time, but I feel differently about you. I really would like to try a relationship with you," Reed said quietly. He looked down, searching for the right words. After a moment, he lifted his gaze, looking directly in Trevor's haunting eyes. "What happened between you and Brody in the reception hall? If it's none of my business, just tell me." Reed's throat went dry. He swallowed hard but forced himself to continue. "I don't want to intrude or come between you and him. If this was just sex between us, I would have no problem. But I want something different with you, and I want to make sure we're straight from the start. I couldn't help but see Brody pulling you aside; I watched you for most of the evening. I can assure you I'm not dating anyone…but I want you to be honest with me. Are you and Brody together?"

"No," Trevor said, his chest swelling with an almost silent mirth. "Not at all. I'm not seeing anyone. That has to be painfully obvious." Trevor couldn't quite hold Reed's stare as he averted his gaze, searching for his words. "Brody is, well, I guess he's family to me. I thought more at one point, hoped for more even longer than that, but he would never be right for me. I wasted a lot of time waiting and watching Brody. I guess I needed that time to come to terms with who I am. I didn't accept this about myself for many years." Trevor paused for several long seconds, staring hard at Reed, looking as if he wanted to say more. "Reed, I don't want a relationship filled with sharing partners. I want one of honesty and faithfulness."

Trevor said more in those few moments than ever before. Reed could see Trevor's heart on his sleeve, but Trevor also never said he wanted to continue this with Reed.

"I want honesty and faithfulness too," Reed said, hoping to draw Trevor into the part of the conversation that mattered most. "I'm not sure I could share you easily either. I found myself jealous over the bridesmaid by your side tonight. I've never been jealous one day of my life."

"I'm glad you aren't in a restroom with him right now. It would've been hard on my heart. Once I got out here, I thought it may have been a ploy to get me away from the scene," Trevor replied. His voice grew softer as he spoke.

Trevor reached up and ran his fingers over a stray piece of hair dropping down on Reed's forehead. The action seemed bolder to Reed, more open. Trevor drew him closer while he spoke, his hands roaming over Reed's back, waist, and pushing under the hem of Reed's jacket. Trevor was touching Reed without being prodded. He loved those honest caresses, and the possessive grip Trevor made when he spoke of restrooms and Brody.

There were still no words from Trevor about commitment, but he had said enough for Reed to see how Brody had used them both tonight. He didn't like being a part of anything that might leave Trevor hurt in the end. After a minute, Trevor ran the pad of his thumb across Reed's lower lip, caressing as it went.

"I like the idea of dating you," Trevor whispered, reaching to lightly kiss Reed's parted lips.

"I want a relationship with you, Trevor. Something so much more than just dating," Reed said lightly against Trevor's mouth. "I can't believe I just said that. That's a first for me. I know you've never been with a man. I want to be your first, if you will allow me. I want to be the only person you need. I want to make love to you, and just to you." Reed massaged Trevor's back, feeling the cool cotton shirt give beneath his palms.

"If you come home with me tonight, I promise you won't ever regret it," Reed whispered in Trevor's ear. He let his tongue slide across the vein in Trevor's neck and smiled when Trevor shuddered under his touch. Reed licked a path up Trevor's neck, then again spoke quietly again in his ear. "We'll only go as far as you're comfortable with. I'll be satisfied to just hold you if that's what you wish." Reed lifted his head to look Trevor in his eyes, a sly grin formed on his lips. "Well, that's a lie, but I promise to follow your lead."

Trevor remained quiet, just watching Reed, holding him close. As he spent more time with him, Reed could see Trevor wasn't shy, just quiet, and perhaps reserved.

Reed pressed into Trevor. "I want you."

He ran his tongue lightly across the seam of Trevor's lips. "Mmmm, I've waited all night for this." Reed growled, fully taking that sexy mouth with his own. Trevor's lips parted as Reed's tongue slid deep into his mouth. He cupped Trevor's face tenderly, deepening the kiss.

The song he'd requested, "Save the Last Dance for Me," started to play. Somewhere in the back of his mind, Reed heard it and broke from the kiss, smiling at the beautiful man standing before him. Trevor looked dazed; his heart pounded against Reed's chest.

"There's something else I've wanted to do all night," Reed said, stepping back, smiling as he slid his jacket down his arms. He laid it on the nearest chair, turned back to Trevor, and held out his hand. "Can I have this dance, handsome?"

Trevor watched Reed curiously while several bars of the song played. Just when Reed thought he was going to be denied, Trevor smiled at the outstretched hand and looked around the balcony. They stood completely alone. Trevor allowed Reed to bring him forward. Reed's breath caught in his throat when Trevor tugged him against his body. They held each other close as they swayed to the music. Trevor bent in, running his nose along Reed's neck, into his ear and through his hair. His hot breath tickled the little pieces of hair on the nape of Reed's neck, sending chills racing down his spine. Trevor lifted his hand, seductively fingering the collar of Reed's dress shirt before dragging his fingers into his hair.

They moved together, fluidly. Reed led, and they found their rhythm easily. "I love your scent," Trevor whispered against Reed's hair.

Reed closed his eyes, allowing his body to melt into this man.

The cool night air blew across his skin, and he pulled Trevor closer to him. Their bodies moved together as one, twirling around the edge of the balcony. Reed spun Trevor then dipped him, laughing. He could tell the sudden bit of playfulness caught Trevor off guard, but he went with it, chuckling when he was pulled back up. When their hips fused back together, Reed smiled wickedly, feeling Trevor's hard arousal brush against his with every movement. Oh yes, baby...I want you too.

Everything about this moment was perfect. As the song ended, Reed softly brushed his lips across Trevor's. "Thank you…"

Trevor stayed wrapped around Reed well after the song ended and a new one began. Not sure why exactly, but Trevor seemed more confident. Maybe it had to do with Reed's declaration of a relationship between them. Trevor still hadn't committed, but he hoped he would soon. Trevor continued to hold Reed tightly to his body, breathing in his scent. He ran his fingertips gently against the back of Reed's neck, and into the small hairs brushing against his shirt collar. Trevor's sweet lips turned in, licking Reed's earlobe before whispering ever so softly.

"I'm not sure what's driving me to say all this. Maybe it's what's lying so heavy between my thighs." A breathless sigh came from Trevor's lips as he spoke. His warm breath slid across Reed's ear, causing him to harden to painful degrees. Reed closed his eyes, listening. "I want to know what it's like to have you buried deep inside me," Trevor whispered just enough to be heard, while running his nose the length of Reed's ear.

"I want to lick you and taste you here." Trevor's hand pushed between their bodies to grip Reed's hard cock to emphasize his words. "I want to kiss you when you finally come deep inside me. I crave the taste of you. I want something I've never known, but I know it's you I crave."

Reed's cock jerked, and he fought the urge to come at the delicious feel of Trevor's palm rubbing against him. The feeling stopped Reed's heart, and a sudden exhale burst from his lips.

"I want to know what it's like to be inside you too, Trevor. I want to hear my name cross your lips when you're lost in the pleasure I'm giving you. I want us to make love. I want to feel you in me and me in you, until we're both spent and sated. I want to fall asleep in your arms and wake to your sweet kisses."

A smile spread across Trevor's lips. He held Reed in place, looking him directly in the eyes. "And when you're done with me, you tell me. I don't want to be that guy sitting by the phone, waiting for the call that isn't coming." Trevor didn't wait for an answer but captured Reed's lips with his own. He drove his tongue into the far reaches of Reed's mouth. The urgency of Trevor's kiss floored him.

Reed shuddered while the kiss continued, but those words confused him, causing Reed to pull away for the briefest of moments. "I have no desire to leave you by the phone. I want you too," Reed said, pushing Trevor into the far reaches of the darkened corner, against the railing. "I need to touch you...let me touch you," he growled against Trevor's lips. Reed slid his hand around to the front of Trevor's trousers, his fingers working quickly to undo his pants, sliding the zipper down. His own breath deepened as he eased his hand in between Trevor's skin and the material of his slacks, moaning when the warmth of Trevor's thick cock pressed against his palm.

"You're not wearing any underwear...all the better for me." Reed grinned into the kiss, groaning when Trevor's hips surged forward for his touch. He wrapped his fingers around Trevor and stroked.

"Let me make love to you," Reed pleaded, his smooth rich voice now raspy with need. His lips trailed across Trevor's jaw and down the column of his neck while he worked Trevor's arousal with his hand.

Lowering his head, Reed ran his mouth across Trevor's chest, biting and nibbling his tightly budded nipple through the smooth cotton shirt. Reed lifted back to a standing position, taking Trevor's mouth with his once more. He kissed him completely, sucking his tongue in time to the rhythm of his stroking hand. Reed was lost in Trevor.

Just when he began to lower himself to his knees and take Trevor's beautiful cock with his mouth, Reed heard the annoying sound of someone clearing their throat. An all too familiar voice called his name. Groaning, Reed pulled his mouth from Trevor's, but he never let go of Trevor's rigid cock. He simply turned his head to glare at his brother.

"What's so important that it couldn't wait, Rylie?"

***

Disoriented, Trevor shook his head, trying to clear his lust-filled haze. Trevor blinked in surprise, realizing his pants were undone. Reed's hands stayed buried inside the zipper, still lightly stroking him. He loved Reed's hands on him. The feel of Reed's smooth palm fondling him was such a fucking turn on. It robbed him of coherent thought. He brought his hands up to Reed's neck, wanting the man's lips on his again.

In the effort to turn Reed back to him, he heard someone talking briskly... But they'd been alone. He focused in on their surroundings. Reed was speaking to Rylie while never stopping the stroke of his hand on Trevor's cock. Fuck, they'd been caught.

Trevor pushed his palms forward against Reed's chest, breaking free of the hold to quickly tuck his shirttails back in. He hadn't worn underwear because he hadn't wanted to walk back into his room with Reed standing there. Now he regretted that decision as he stood exposed with the tent of his erection sticking out. Reed finally let Trevor go and turned to face Rylie.

"Well, little brother, are you going to tell me why I'm standing here looking at you instead of enjoying my balcony time with Trevor?"

"Dear God, Reed, are you corrupting my best friend?" Rylie teased, stepping further out on the balcony.

Reed adjusted his clothing while walking toward his brother. "I was doing my best until we were rudely interrupted. The sooner I get you out of here, the sooner I can get back to corrupting your friend." Reed looked back over his shoulder at Trevor as he stayed in the corner, obscured by shadows, watching the two brothers interact. Reed walked around Rylie, putting his hand on his shoulder. "What's this all about? Why aren't you in there dancing with your new bride?"

"Elise will be tossing her bouquet from the balcony. The DJ announced the throwing of the bridal bouquet after this next dance. The song's almost over, and I thought you might want to know," Rylie said, looking over his shoulder in Trevor's direction. "Trevor, I knew you wouldn't like being caught out here like this. It's the only reason I came out." Rylie didn't say anything more before going back inside.

Reed slowly wound through the tables, back to Trevor, staying a step or two away from him, running his hands through his thick blond hair.

"Are you ashamed of being with me, Trevor?"

"I'm ashamed of getting so carried away out here on a public balcony. What was I thinking? Anyone could have seen us. There are children here, Reed. We're at a hotel. We could just get a room. I wasn't considering the total embarrassment of your entire family if anyone caught us."

Trevor shoved his dick to the side, trying to smooth down his slacks in order to keep the damn thing from sticking out. It wasn't working. "Do you want me to get us a room tonight, after everything is over?" Trevor finally asked.

Reed didn't say a word more. He turned away, picking up their jackets, waiting for Trevor to finish and join him. The uncertainty of the moment made Trevor reluctant as he reached out for his jacket, but Reed mistook his action, and took Trevor's hand, dragging him forward along the balcony. Reed snaked his way through the back of the hotel to the front desk. Once Trevor realized where they were headed and what they were doing, he tried to reason with Reed.

"Reed, we can't do this now. You'll be missed. You're like the most popular guy here tonight. We need to get back to the reception."

Reed ignored Trevor, talking to the clerk instead. "Good evening, Sarah. What's available in your presidential suite series? And how long will it take to prepare?" The clerk's name tag was the only thing visible on the front of her dark suit, but Reed said her name like he'd known her for years.

"Sir, it looks like we have one suite available. It has a poolside view, it—"

Reed cut her off. "I'll take it. How long to prepare?"

"We will need about thirty minutes to prepare the room. This hotel is full—"

Reed cut her off again, pulling his wallet from the breast pocket of his suit coat. "We'll need the room much sooner. I was thinking more like ten minutes," Reed said with a wink, his sexy grin spreading across his stunningly handsome features. The front desk clerk didn't stand a chance, she stood there staring for a long moment. Her mouth opened but no words came out.

After a minute more, she closed her mouth and turned back to the keyboard, her fingers fumbling as she typed. Trevor watched the scene unfold, chuckling a little; clearly the front desk clerk was enthralled by the man standing in front of her. He knew exactly how she felt. Trevor struggled to keep coherent thought anytime Reed directed his charming smile toward him.

"Yes, sir, I will... I'll tell them..."

"Perfect! Thank you. I'll also need the Kama Sutra amenities for men." Sarah finally just shoved the key and the receipt in Reed's direction. "Ten minutes, correct?"

"Yes, sir, I've made the notes in the system. It'll be ready."

"Excellent. Thank you again, Sarah." Reed didn't wait

around. He gestured Trevor toward the bank of elevators. At Reed's insistence, Trevor walked in front of him, although he didn't know the correct elevator to use. He quickly learned why Reed had him lead the way. Every wrong move Trevor made earned him a grope to his ass or a sweep of Reed's hand down his chest, conveniently finding the front of his uniform slacks. Finally, Trevor stopped, making Reed take the lead, and all Reed did was chuckle as he walked past, that sexy grin still in place.

"You take all the fun out of things, Trevor West. I'm surprised you didn't figure out my ploy while walking through my house last night." Reed pressed the up button, turning back to Trevor with a sly grin.

"You did it all on purpose! I thought I'd suddenly become a bumbling, clumsy moron. I couldn't seem to stay out of your way." They were close to one another, face-to-face, laughing. Trevor stood no more than an inch shorter than Reed. Every time Reed stepped in, Trevor took a small step back, keeping some distance between them. They were still in public; this bank of elevators could be seen from the lobby.

"Once we're out as a couple, I won't have to conjure ways to touch you in public. I want that day to come quickly. I find it hard to keep my hands off you."

The elevator eventually pinged its arrival behind Trevor, and he turned his head to see which door opened. Reed gave him a little shove, and he stumbled back a step into the elevator right behind him. Once inside, Reed was on him immediately, fusing their mouths together in an urgent, demanding, and captivating kiss. Reed backed Trevor against the elevator wall, securing him tightly in his arms. Trevor followed Reed's lead, but it was hard to keep up. Reed was all over him.

The kiss turned aggressive and extremely hot in a matter of seconds. That rock-hard body pressed against his brought a small noise from his lips, which only urged Reed on. The elevator wall and rail pressed against his back, keeping him in place. Reed's roaming hands and heated kisses caused his body to harden. He desperately needed to slow it down. Trevor tore his mouth away from the kiss, trying to pace himself. He was on an intoxicating Reed overload, and his release was already too close for comfort.

"I want you, Trevor. I can't wait much longer." The sound of Reed's breathless plea brushed his ear and tightened his already painfully hard cock.

"You have me all messed up. I can't think straight when you're around," Trevor murmured.

"Good, that makes us even. Let's keep it that way." Reed reached over, pressed a button, and the small elevator came to a complete stop. "It will take approximately five minutes for the system to recycle itself, getting us moving again," Reed said while Trevor pulled him back in the circle of his arms, a grin spreading across his lips.

"I bet you know all the tricks. You'll have to teach me as we go."

"Mmm, you have no idea what I want to teach you, but right now, if I remember correctly, you said something about loving my hands in your pants. Let's see how much..." Reed reached down, working Trevor's belt free, releasing the button and sliding the zipper down. Trevor's cock sprung free, seeking Reed's touch. The anticipation was nothing compared to the feeling of Reed gripping his aching dick. A deep moan escaped his lips and his hips bucked forward of their own accord, chasing the friction of Reed's palm. Trevor wrapped his hand around the back of Reed's head, pulling him forward. He captured Reed's lower lip between his teeth. He sucked the plump flesh of Reed's lip, thrusting his tongue into Reed's mouth, over and over, matching each stroke of Reed's skilled hand.

CHAPTER 10

The sound of shocked gasps broke the sensual trance that held Trevor spellbound. Much to his surprise, three women stood staring at them outside the now open elevator doors. Trevor glanced up to the floor display, surprised he'd missed the elevator moving again or the ping of reaching their floor. Apparently, the haze of lust could muddle a man's brain. One of the young women stepped into the elevator, clapping her hands in a show of her approval for the show they'd unwittingly put on for them.

"No, don't stop on our account! I've waited my whole life to see something like this. God, you're both so hot," she breathed, pure joy in her deep southern accent.

Reed chuckled. "Hello, ladies. I'm sorry to disappoint you, but this is our floor. Would you hold the door for us?"

Trevor fumbled, trying to get Reed's hands out of his pants.

Reed did not want to cooperate with and fought Trevor on removing them with a gentle pinch on his sac.

"Nooooo! You can't stop. I love gay guys. Please let me watch." The blonde motioned for her friends to step in before the door closed. She pulled her phone from her small black Prada bag at her hip and handed it to her friend.

"Here, Kay, record them, hurry. I'll pay you two to keep going. I have money." The blonde rummaged through her overstuffed purse, letting the contents drop to the floor of the elevator until she pulled cash from her bag. "I can pay! I can pay, just don't stop," she begged.

Reed extended one hand out to hold the door while using the other to encourage Trevor to exit the elevator. Much to Trevor's embarrassment, his pants slipped down as he moved forward. All he could manage was to hold them up as he departed the elevator just as the door eased closed.

"Good night, ladies. Enjoy the rest of your evening. It was a pleasure meeting you," Reed said, giving the blonde a wink. Trevor could see her darting for the small opening, unwilling to let them go without her. Thankfully, she failed to trip the door sensor and couldn't make it through.

"Insistent little thing." Trevor laughed at her determination as he stood watching from the other side of the hall, still holding his pants up. "Five minutes goes by fast," Trevor said, watching Reed pull the key card from his pocket.

"Room 5612," Reed said, looking up at the ornate gold hall direction sign before turning back to Trevor, who worked at tucking in his shirt. Reed placed a hand on Trevor's, stopping him from fastening his pants.

"No, babe, why bother? They'll be coming off soon enough. Less work for me when we get to the room. I can't…" Reed didn't finish the sentence but pinned him with a hungry gaze and stalked closer. "I need another kiss. I love your lips on mine."

Reed pulled Trevor forward several steps, only to back him

against the wall again. He shoved his tongue back into his mouth, and Trevor opened for him immediately. Reed groaned loudly when their tongues met as Trevor pulled Reed's shirt free from his pants. He ran both palms to Reed's back, mapping his skin before he pressed Reed firmly against his chest, loving the warm feel of his skin. Trevor slid his fingers teasingly into the waistband of Reed's slacks before his hands trailed forward to find Reed's belt and loosened the metal clasp. The elevator doors dinged again. This time, Trevor wasn't so completely lost. He took Reed by the hand and pulled them both down the hall, searching for their room. He feared the blonde might have returned.

The torturous trip down the corridor ended at the second to the last door at the end. Reed pulled away long enough to slide the key card into the slot before pushing open the door. Reed's need to touch Trevor never faded as they made their way inside the room. Reed reached back and continued to tease Trevor's cock with decadent pressure. Trevor slipped his hands around Reed's waist to finally get the belt undone, then started on his slacks. He moaned into the back of Reed's neck, already so close to release. Slowly, he turned Reed in his arms so that he could see the feelings play out on his face. Once the slacks were freed, Trevor moved to Reed's white silk shirt, carefully working the small buttons free. He ached to feel Reed's skin against his. He craved everything being offered to him and needed it all right in this moment.

Trevor shoved Reed's shirt open and out of his way. He ran his hands over the sculpted chest, loving the feel of his muscles flexing and twitching from his touch. Returning his hands to Reed's shoulders, Trevor massaged and caressed his long neck while trailing his palms back down into Reed's slacks. He drove his fingers deep below the waistband this time, pushing the material low to allow his fingers to snake down the crack of Reed's ass. He gripped Reed's ass cheeks, pulling him tightly to him, making it hard to breathe without losing control.

Reed exhaled with a deep throaty moan. Then stayed where he was, leaning his head forward against Trevor's shoulder while skating a hand up behind his head. He tangled his fingers into Trevor's hair, pulling him into a heated kiss. The entire time, Trevor worked Reed's cock in awkward strokes, cupping, rolling, and gently pinching his sac.

Trevor pulled free with a stuttered breath. He continued the massage and whispered into the kiss. "We need to get further inside the room. I want to feel you inside me," Trevor said, gently nudging him in the direction of the bedroom, extending a foot to kick the door shut with a decidedly loud click.

Reed turned in his arms, dropping their jackets, and letting his silk shirt slide to the floor. Trevor stood momentarily stunned at the scene before him. The space was set aglow in candlelight. Soft music played in the background and rose petals were scattered across the bed and floor. A wine bucket sat close to the bed with what looked to be champagne chilling for them. The room looked to be perfectly prepared for a romantic evening.

"How did you do this?" he asked in wonder, looking back at Reed. As he gazed at the sheer romance of the room, Trevor realized he'd been unconsciously keeping his heart separate from this moment. It all crumbled down around him now, leaving his heart in serious Reed overload.

"Take off your shoes," Reed said, not answering the question, but moving them along as quickly as he could. Trevor didn't hesitate in kicking them off. Reed's mouth was pressed back against his before his own shoes hit the floor. The kiss grew hard and heated as Trevor realized they were finally bare chest to bare chest for the first time, and God, how he loved the feeling.

Reed ran his hands up and down Trevor's chest, finding and rolling Trevor's nipple between his forefinger and thumb. Trevor worked at pushing Reed's pants down over his hips. His hands gravitated back to Reed's ass, gripping and massaging the perfect globes until he yanked Reed forward, pressing their bodies tightly together and locked in each other's arms.

Finally making it to the bedroom, Reed pushed Trevor

down onto the mattress. By the time Trevor hit the luxurious sheets, Reed had discarded his pants and socks, tossing them haphazardly about the room. A sexy grin spread across his lips, sending Trevor's heart racing and his cock twitching. He'd never been more ready for anything in his life.

***

Standing by the bed, Reed gazed down at the devastatingly handsome man. Everything slowed. He stepped in between Trevor's parted legs and tenderly ran his hands over Trevor's firm, muscular torso.

He slid his palms further down to the waistband of Trevor's slacks. Reed gripped the pants and tugged, pulling them down his legs. He moaned at the sight of Trevor's engorged, tempting cock lying firm and hard against his stomach. The man looked so perfect lying there, waiting for him. Reed wanted this moment with Trevor to play over and again throughout his life.

"I'm a very lucky man," Reed said, licking his lips. He bent down, kissing Trevor's thigh before climbing onto the mattress. The first touch of Trevor's warm skin against his sent tremors burning through his body, landing heatedly in his balls. Trevor pushed himself farther up the mattress. Their gazes locked as Reed crawled in on top of him. The look in Trevor's eyes made him ache. Reed needed this man in his life; he was completely hooked. He placed one of his knees between Trevor's legs and let his eyes roam the length of Trevor's body.

"You're exquisite, Trevor," Reed whispered, lowering his full weight onto Trevor's body. He tried not to crush him as he settled between his open thighs and positioned their cocks together.

Trevor's unsteady inhale when he ground their cocks together thrilled him. He ran a hand over Trevor's hair, studying his face closely. He wanted to memorize everything about the man beneath him. Without warning, Reed crushed his mouth to

Trevor's upturned lips. Unbridled need had Trevor grinding his hips forward, holding Reed in place. A deep moan escaped Trevor as the kiss continued. Reed's tongue surged forward, probing and exploring. His hands roamed Trevor's hard body as their tongues flicked and swirled in a heated dance.

I'm yours. You have me under your spell, Trevor.

Backing away from the kiss, Reed rolled to the side, propping up on his elbow. Apparently, that was as far as Trevor intended to let him go. Trevor kept him wrapped in his muscular embrace as he swept his gaze down the length of Trevor's ripped body then back up again.

"You're intoxicating," Reed confessed. He again studied Trevor's face with the same intensity he'd used in studying his body. Leaning forward, Reed sweetly traced Trevor's lips with his fingertip.

"No, I'm not, Reed. That's you. I don't compare to you in any way." While Trevor spoke, he caressed Reed's cheek.

"The thought of making love to you takes my breath away," Reed said, and Trevor lifted his head, reaching for Reed's lips for a small, tender kiss. Turning slightly on his side, Trevor pulled him fully back onto his body, drawing his legs up, wrapping Reed in his arms.

"This feels right," Trevor whispered.

He groaned at the need building and taking over his body. Reed trailed kisses along Trevor's jaw. He nuzzled his neck, tasting with a quick caress of his tongue. The feel of Trevor's warm skin against his had his blood rushing like liquid fire through his veins, sending waves of pleasure straight to his shaft and settling heatedly in his balls.

Pushing himself up, Reed kissed his way down Trevor's chest, his body sliding against Trevor's heated skin, across that flexing chest and taut stomach, until he settled his upper body between Trevor's splayed thighs. He rolled his gaze up the length of Trevor's body and saw him in the flickering candlelight attentively watching under a hooded gaze. Reed's smile widened when he took Trevor's thick, hard arousal in his hand and stroked.

"God, I want to taste you. I want to feel you against my tongue." Reed's intense look said it all as he gazed up at Trevor. A wicked grin spread across his face. He bit his lip with anticipation and leaned in, his tongue licking at the small pearl of moisture beading at the tip.

"Mmmm... Fuck, you taste amazing," Reed murmured, bending his head forward, his mouth opened slightly, allowing only the swollen tip barely past his lips. He needed so much more of this man. He moaned at the intense flavor. Reed made slow wet circles across the broad head, lapping at Trevor's slit with his tongue.

"Damn, that feels good," Trevor groaned. He clawed at the sheets, the movement causing Reed to lift his gaze.

He wanted to watch Trevor's every reaction. Trevor's gaze was fixed on Reed's mouth, and he slowly rolled his hips, pushing his cock deeper inside. Trevor released the sheets to lightly rest his fingertips and palms on Reed's jaw, running small little caresses along his neck until he fisted them into Reed's hair.

"Fuck, your mouth feels so good. God, I love the feel of your tongue." Trevor's grip tightened in Reed's hair, grasping and holding him in place. Reed loved the possessiveness of the action. He reveled in the little sting of Trevor's nails on his scalp. Reed's mouth and tongue worked in unison as he completely devoured Trevor.

Yes, that's it, baby, let me take care of you.

He worked Trevor's base with a strong hand, stroking that hard length in time with the plunge and retreat of his mouth. He wanted to be sure Trevor was powerless against the onslaught of intense pleasure. Reed took Trevor deep and slow, then alternating to hard and soft as his tongue swirled and his teeth lightly scraped along the shaft. He slid his hands under Trevor's ass, forcing his hips up and his thick cock deeper down his constricting throat.

"No more, please. I can't take it," Trevor moaned, his breath ragged as he tried to pull back, pushing Reed's head away from him. Trevor's eyes bore into him as he whispered hoarsely, "Fuck me, Reed. Don't make me wait."

The echo of Trevor's words—Fuck me, Reed—danced in his head as he withdrew Trevor's hard flesh from his mouth with a soft pop. Reed slowly crawled up his body, strategically placing kisses and small nibbles along the way.

"You don't have to ask me twice," Reed said as he bent his head to run his tongue teasingly around each of Trevor's nipples. "I want nothing more."

Trevor shuddered under his assault, letting out a groan when Reed gave his nipple a playful bite. A satisfied smile crossed his lips as Trevor's cerulean blue eyes slowly rolled back in his head.

Reed sat back on his knees and nestled his body between Trevor's muscular thighs. Reaching across to the nightstand, he withdrew the small packet and a bottle he'd requested to be ready inside the drawer. He lifted slightly, Reed tore the packet open, quickly rolling the condom on before coating his rigid length with lubricant. He coated his fingers and very gently moved his hand down to Trevor's ass, rubbing his rim with the slickened digit.

Reed gently inserted one finger. He worked Trevor slowly, massaging as he added another, slipping into his tight channel. Reed knew by the way Trevor reacted to his touch that he was hitting all the right places. He gripped Trevor's swollen cock with his free hand, stroking him, resisting the urge to put that hard dick back in his mouth. Reed added a third finger while placing soft kisses and whispering sweet words of love and encouragement in tandem with Trevor's soft moans.

"Reed, now. I can't take much more. I'm too close. I don't want to come until you're inside me...please." Trevor gripped the duvet. He rolled his head back against the pillow, but Reed ignored his pleas.

He continued to work him with his fingers, in and out, making sure he was completely ready.

"Please…. I want this. Baby, come on. I need to feel you inside me," Trevor begged in breathless gasps. He pulled Reed's head to him, thrusting his tongue forward, deep into his mouth. Trevor's hips rocked, pushing back against Reed's hand, matching the rhythm of Reed's fingers. Trevor's kisses were hungry and demanding. Reed trembled, and he didn't know how long he could keep his own need at a distance. He'd never wanted to please anyone the way he wanted to please Trevor.

"Lift your legs for me. I need you in just the right position," Reed gasped, breaking from the kiss. Trevor lifted his legs, and Reed ran his hands up his thighs to help guide them back, placing Trevor exactly how he wanted him. A smile spread across Reed's lips when he gripped his slick, throbbing cock, dragging himself up and down Trevor's ass. He groaned before slowly pushing himself against Trevor's rim. The tight ring of muscle clenched. Trevor's body resisted his gentle persuasion. Reed moaned then hoarsely whispered, "Trevor, take a deep breath and push against me. I swear to you, it'll be so much better soon."

Reed's hips flexed when Trevor pushed against him. He needed to go slow. Reed struggled with his urges, every instinct he had drove him to bury himself balls deep, but he held onto his control. Slowly, he worked his hips, easing back and forth against the tight opening, groaning when he slipped in a little deeper.

"God…you're so tight and warm. You feel so fucking good, Trevor." Holding himself back, Reed gave another push. The thick head of his cock slid even deeper into Trevor. Lowering his head, Reed took Trevor's mouth with his, stifling the soft moans with his kiss.

Trevor dragged his hands down Reed's back to his ass, arching his hips up. Then he pushed Reed farther in as if to make his point. Reed had no choice but to slide in all the way, burying himself inside the tight heat. The movement caused Trevor to throw his head back, his fingernails digging hard into Reed's ass. A smile spread across those sexy lips, and the most erotic hiss escaped his mouth.

"So this is what it feels like? It's amazing, Reed. You're amazing."

Reed froze when he felt himself completely buried to the balls, unwilling but mostly unable to move. He was afraid the smallest of movements would send him over the edge. He panted breathlessly, whispering helplessly to Trevor. "Yes, baby, amazing. Wait, don't move...Trevor, please don't move...I'm afraid I won't last. You feel too good." Speaking through clenched teeth, Reed forced himself to take a few breaths to gather his composure.

Glancing down, he saw Trevor's beautiful blue eyes staring back at him. Trevor's jaw was clenched tight. Reed could feel the pounding of Trevor's heart in his chest.

"I'm falling for you." The words spilled from Reed's lips before he could stop them.

He bent his head and kissed Trevor gently on the lips then lifted his head. Reed watched Trevor's face as they moved together slowly, back and forth, in a steady motion.

"You feel so fucking good, love." Reed crushed their mouths together again, kissing Trevor more forcefully and deeply this time.

He tore from the kiss when Trevor bucked his hips, giving Reed no choice but to pick up the pace. "This feels right. I need it harder. I want you to really fuck me, Reed. I'm so close." Trevor bent his knees, digging his heels into Reed's ass, and lifted his hips to meet Reed's thrusts. Their bodies moved in perfect sync with one another, creating a beautiful friction.

"I'm drowning in you. The feel of you, the taste of you... Never before...have I ever felt this," Reed whispered into Trevor's neck, hair, and ear. Reed anchored himself on one arm and drove into Trevor's body. Reed took Trevor's hard cock in his hand and lovingly stroked. Trevor threw his head back against the pillows, arching his body up, bucking into his hand. All the while Trevor begged Reed to finish him. Reed held off, stroking Trevor with the rhythm of his own thrusts, taking them to the edge.

Reed looked into those beautiful blue eyes and watched intently, knowing he was about to come undone. Unable to hold himself back any longer, Reed threw his head back and pounded into Trevor even harder.

"Oh, yes, Trevor... I... Yessss." The base of his spine tingled. His balls tightened excitedly as he pumped deeper. The heat roiled through his veins. His hips thrust forward with a steady pounding, and he never stopped the constant stroking, matching the movement of his hips. "Mmmm...yes ...oh... yes... Trevor, come with me, baby." As if on command, Trevor's hips thrust forward. His body shuddered and his cock jerked in Reed's hand, shooting wet, creamy ribbons across his stomach and chest.

Reed's release erupted on a shout. His body arched, pushing him deeper into Trevor. He shuddered while Trevor spasmed around him, milking every last drop from him. Reed drew in a breath and collapsed, nestling his face in the crook of Trevor's neck. It had never been this intense before.

"Thank you, Trevor," Reed gasped out in a breathless whisper against his neck after several long minutes passed.

Trevor's eyes remained closed, a sigh tearing from his lips. When Reed pulled his head up, Trevor tightened his embrace. He seemed unwilling to let him go. Reed placed his lips against Trevor's for the softest of kisses, and Trevor's eyes blinked open.

"What're you thanking me for?"

"You were perfect," Reed said, slowly withdrawing from, before sliding his body alongside Trevor's.

He kept Reed locked in his tight embrace.

"Thank you for sharing your first time with me. Thank you for sharing yourself with me." Reed brushed the hair back from Trevor's brow. He stopped talking, not wanting to confess every emotion coursing through him, afraid he would scare Trevor away.

"This was right for me. I should be thanking you for making

it so special." Trevor tenderly traced the outline of Reed's lips before caressing his jaw.

"I've never had these feelings before with anyone. This is all completely new to me." Lowering his head, Reed trailed soft kisses up Trevor's neck and down his strong jaw.

"You don't have to say that," Trevor said, repositioning himself on the pillow as he spoke. He smiled at the frustrated look no doubt on Reed's face and placed a finger on his lips to stop him from responding. "Then we're both in unfamiliar territory."

"Have you worked up an appetite? We should probably go back down and tell the family goodnight." Reed continued with the small soft kisses, holding Trevor tightly. "What kind of best man would I be if I just left for the night? It'll only take us a minute to take our leave. The night's still young. How about breakfast in bed in the morning?" Reed asked. Trevor's hand caressed him softly on his back. "A quick shower perhaps before we go back downstairs?"

Trevor softly kissed Reed and closed his eyes again. "Reed, food and a shower would be good, but a few minutes of sleep would be better." Within seconds, Trevor drifted off to sleep as Reed continued to gently nuzzle his jaw.

Pulling Trevor closer, Reed stayed tight in the circle of Trevor's arms while he slept. All of these feelings of wanting to take care of someone were so new, but he wanted exactly that with Trevor. I think I'm in love... A small smile spread across Reed's lips as he trailed kisses along Trevor's jaw and neck. His entire world seemed to settle in around the man softly snoring in his arms. After a long moment, Reed continued the conversation aloud, more secure now that Trevor wouldn't bolt if he heard the directions of his thoughts.

"I've never been so taken with someone. We've only known each other for a few days." Reed looked down, smiling at the peaceful look on Trevor's beautiful face. He reached out to lightly trace Trevor's full lips with his fingertip, and softly whispered,

"I'm afraid I've already fallen in love with you." The confession again made him grin. "You've captivated me completely, Trevor West." Tenderly brushing Trevor's hair from his forehead, Reed continued, "No matter what the future holds for us, I'll be forever yours."

Reed's phone went off at the same moment an alert came from Trevor's phone. Trevor jerked awake, confusion crossing his brow as he pulled Reed tightly to him. The embrace became one of protection.

"It's okay, beautiful. It's just our phones. I think we've been missed downstairs." Reed pulled free, rising from the bed. Trevor tried to follow, but Reed kept him down. "Let me grab a towel." Reed quickly cleaned himself then grabbed a towel for Trevor.

Heading back, Reed dug through their clothing to find their phones before wiping the towel across Trevor's stomach. The alert on Trevor's phone sounded again, giving the official military ringtone this time. Trevor didn't hesitate then, rising and reaching for his phone.

"Shit, we've been called in."

"I see that. Rylie's asking me to come to the front. He wants to know if I'm with you. Cars are on their way," Reed read from his phone, sending a quick text back.

"Damn, poor Elise. This is gonna be hard on her." Trevor rose quickly, going to the bathroom. Reed followed behind him, picking up their clothes as he went. They dressed together. All the romance faded into the reality of what faced them. Reed finished first and stood by the door, buttoning up his jacket. Trevor stopped in front of the mirror, finger-combing his hair back in place before going to Reed.

"I don't think you want our goodbye to be in front of the others," Reed said and tenderly pressed his lips to Trevor's. Reed broke from the kiss, his brow furrowing as he focused on Trevor. "I find it very difficult to pull myself away from you. When will I hear from you?"

"I don't know. You know the rules. I have no idea why we're being called in. I'll contact you as soon as I can." Remorse sounded in Trevor's voice as he spoke. "If it's too long for you to wait, I'll understand. Thank you for tonight. It means everything to me. It'll always mean everything to me."

"I'll wait for you no matter how long it takes. I meant everything I said to you. Even the parts you slept through." Reed gave a small grin while lifting his hand to Trevor's cheek, caressing him with his thumb. Reed never broke eye contact and hoped his eyes spoke of the love coursing through him for the man standing before him.

"I've gotta go," Trevor spoke softly, kissing Reed quickly. They walked to the elevator, hand in hand. They stayed quiet for the ride down. Reed's heart was breaking; he'd only just met Trevor, but his whole world was being ripped away from him at this moment.

When the doors opened to the lobby, Reed released Trevor's hand, not wanting to out him to his team. Two vans sat ready to go as members of his team prepared to leave. Elise stood in her wedding dress, wrapped in Rylie's arms, crying her heart out.

Reed broke out into a jog across the crowded lobby when he made eye contact with Rylie's anguished gaze. Reed took Elise from Rylie's arms, bringing her to his chest. He ran his hands up and down her back in a loving gesture, trying to soothe her.

"Go, brother. The sooner you go, the sooner you'll be back to us."

He watched, feeling a deep loss as Trevor piled into one of the vans. Rylie went in behind him, sitting on the seat with him. Both men stared out the window, watching Reed hold a sobbing Elise as they pulled away.

CHAPTER 11

Tugging his pack forward, Trevor dropped to one knee to rummage through the heavy backpack, pulling out the few necessary items he needed to stay alive. He had been instructed to lighten his load, and after twenty-one miles of running through an overgrown jungle in the dead of night, the idea of lightening his load sounded like a great plan. Rylie, his newly appointed team lead, wanted to get back home to his new bride, which turned out to be a good thing for all of them.

Sweat trickled down the side of Trevor's face. The jungle temperatures soared, and Trevor wore full combat gear. Most of his weapons were strapped to his body. The backpack held mostly luxury items to help in a long-term stay in the jungle. Trevor had no desire to make this an extended trip, and forcefully tossed the pack into the dark, dense foliage of the jungle. He watched it disappear as it spiraled through the air a few feet away from him.

Trevor tilted his head forward and touched the side of his specialized helmet. The shield connected with his right eye. The night vision scanned the area, pulling a grid forward for Trevor to see. The run had been difficult, but the helmet ensured he knew of jutting logs, or pending quicksand patches while he ran full out. The helmet also showed the large snake, hanging like a vine, about fifty feet to his right. Damn, he hated snakes.

He took off again, focused on the layout of the jungle, jumping and turning as he watched through his shield. Trevor relied completely on the face mask. The tangle of vines in the tropical jungle was pitch black to the human eye. He couldn't see his hand in front of his face without the device.

Trevor was roughly thirty hours into this mission. Thirty-one hours since they left the wedding, and he'd left Reed Kensington behind. Each member of his team vowed to have Rylie back home and in his bride's waiting arms as soon as humanly possible, but all Trevor could think about was getting back to Rylie's older brother. But right now, Trevor needed to clear all the jumbled thoughts of Reed from his head and concentrate on his assignment.

This mission consisted of bringing in Birdseye, an international terrorist on the United States' most wanted list for the last twelve years. The target had shifted to the number one most wanted spot after recent terrorist attacks throughout the United Kingdom and the discovery of plans targeting the United States. Birdseye's crimes also included wide, sweeping acts of genocide throughout his country and several others.

Reportedly, communist leaders paid and hid him well, always keeping him just out of reach every time the United States got too close.

None of it really mattered though. Trevor's team had been sent to bring Birdseye in, dead or alive, and if their intel proved true, they would achieve their mission. They always did. The only complicating factor was reports of women and children in

Birdseye's compound. It was suspected they were being held against their will.

Staying low, Trevor ran in the direction his screen indicated. He checked his wrist compass and calculated approximately three more miles to reach the compound. Trevor's entire team was in this jungle, but they were spread apart over several miles, circling the compound as they converged on their target. Only eight of the thirty or so men were breaching the walls tonight. Brody was Trevor's partner as usual, but their relationship had been strained since the moment Brody watched him walk through the front lobby with Reed. He didn't know what the man's problem was, but that was something for another day. They had to put all that aside and focus on the mission, on having each other's backs.

"Trev, two point four miles east, southeast," Rylie said into the headphones of his helmet. "It's recalculating the coordinates on your screen now. Birdseye's currently located on the second floor, northeast corner. It's your corner, Trevor. The gate will be secure, two guard posts. I'll give you the heads up upon entry. Trev, you'll take the second guard post. You and Brody enter together. Six females are being held in the room, eleven children ranging in age from three to thirteen are also present. The older children are suspected to be armed, but no visual on that. Still no sign they know of the impending strike."

Trevor picked up the pace, following the coordinates. It took less than twelve minutes to reach the first stop point. Trevor stayed hidden, waiting for further instruction. The signal came quickly from the small guard shack his team had overtaken. Rylie gave the command, and Trevor raced forward with his weapon palmed, staying out of the moonlight. A second small guard shack in the back of the compound held one occupant. Trevor dropped behind the first post, took a knee, and aimed. The shot was quiet and deadly. The guard dropped quickly as he never saw it coming. Brody came from the south, disarming the gate, allowing several others, including Trevor, to rush forward and enter the compound. The team raced to their designated areas before the next sweep of the floodlights could catch their movements.

The plan outlined during their briefing had all gates opening simultaneously. Based on the lack of noise, or notification, Trevor assumed it'd worked. The compound was a three-story fortress. Reports indicated a possible basement, but no visual to confirm. The structure appeared to be constructed of concrete and steel, making one giant square with six windows on each floor, eighteen total per side.

Reaching the back of the building, Trevor counted off the windows, finding the one flashing in his helmet. Command post gave him the green light to move into place. Brody stayed beside him. They were now pressed against the compound wall. Trevor reached out, tossing a thin microfiber rope into the air. His aim was perfect. The small metal clasp connected securely to the ledge. Trevor gave a quick tug on the rope, satisfied it could hold his body weight, relieved he made it on the first try. He attached his rope to his chest armor harness. Trevor stood ready to reel himself up.

With a press on his earpiece, Trevor gave a silent code that he and Brody were there and waiting. Brody focused on surveillance, and when gunshots sounded, Plan B came into full force and effect. Command center no longer dictated their moves; they were now in survival mode. Nothing more to do than accomplish their mission and get the hell out.

Brody rounded the corner where the gunfire originated, firing off dozens of rounds. Trevor moved forward, scaling the building within seconds.

The small concrete ledge held, allowing him to swing. He landed easily on the side of the small ledge hidden by a thin wisp of a curtain. He pulled a pen-like device from his jacket, his helmet's electronics automatically connected. Trevor extended its size by about a foot. The tip held a lens, showing the images of the room across the mask of his helmet.

Trevor tuned out all the gunfire going on around him, trusting

Brody to have his back, while quickly surveying the room. Birdseye stood with his back against a far wall, away from all the windows. Women and children were positioned at every opening, making it more difficult to hit his intended target.

Counting the heads, there was double the number of children than had been indicated. The small lens caught Grigsby, the soldier on the other ledge, just caddy corner to where he stood. Trevor touched his earpiece, giving them the signal that he was ready, knowing Rylie and his commanders could see through his helmet. He carefully placed his lens on the ledge. Trevor angled it to still see most of the room.

He pulled his weapon from his vest and positioned himself. Birdseye grabbed a very pregnant girl, using her as a human shield. She screamed out in fear, and Birdseye gathered his fist, punching her in the side of the head. She fell as his foot connected with her belly, kicking her to push her away. He caught the action through his helmet and that completely pissed him off.

He knew the reason they had picked him for this mission. This guy was going down by his hand. Trevor took aim. When he fired off his shot, Grigsby fired mere seconds later. Birdseye was hit with perfect accuracy in the middle of his forehead, dropping to his knees. The sounds of gunfire filled the small room. Trevor's helmet showed an unidentified insurgent charge forward after seeing his leader lying lifeless on the floor.

Instinct told Trevor this wouldn't be good for those inside the compound, so he ripped the rope from his chest harness while trying to take aim. The insurgent screamed and began firing on the women and children. Mass chaos ensued. Trevor didn't hesitate. Unable to get a good shot, he barreled through the window, landing on his feet. A searing burn lanced through his shoulder from the bullet meant for the small child under his window.

Running backward, the insurgent grabbed a child to his body before ducking away from the door. Trevor followed, dodging screaming women and children, not letting himself be distracted by the injured. The other soldiers would render aid where needed.

When he made it to the doorway, Trevor fired off several rounds, using his lens to gauge distance. There were many cover points along a narrow hall. The sounds below indicated more gunfire, but Trevor wanted the fucker who'd opened fire on these children.

Firing his rounds again, Trevor bounded out of the room. Across the stairs, several shots were fired back at him. Trevor didn't slow down but fired in their direction while sliding behind a banister. Slowly he picked off everyone he could find hidden.

The floor was quiet again. He ran in the direction the cowardly insurgent had fled. Coming to a door, Trevor kicked it open, jumping aside. Bullets flew past him, missing him. The blood from the bullet wound in his shoulder dripped down to his hand. The weapon slipped in his grip. After another moment of quiet, Trevor used his lens to find the insurgent. The man stood ready to fire. The child sat crying between him and the door.

Trevor knew he would be faster, hopefully able to grab the child crying just a few feet away. He quickly shot out, turning the corner. Trevor fired, hitting the insurgent square in the chest. He dove for the child, grabbing the little one to him as he saw the live grenade lying in the man's hand. Rylie yelled in his helmet. Trevor took off running, but only made it a step or two before the grenade detonated and the floor crumbled underneath him.

From the corner of Trevor's eye, he saw the soldier from the window rounding the corner. He threw the child in his direction, praying for the catch. There was no time to know for sure; the floor collapsed out from under him, hurtling him down through the three-story building. Shots whizzed past him as he fell, some making contact with his leg, shoulder, and arm. The pain blazed through his body with each bullet, but Trevor forced it all away. There was no time to let it register, because he needed to brace himself for the fall.

The impact of each floor slammed his body hard, but slowed him until that floor gave way, sending him falling through another. The floors caved in like a house of cards. Trevor landed hard in a basement room. His back and right leg landed on a mattress; his left leg slammed to the ground. Debris came crashing down on top of him. Trevor tried to shove himself away from the gaping hole in the ceiling but was helpless as flying chunks of wood and boards struck him over and over again.

When he realized his weapon was still in his hand, he lifted it to the ceiling, trying to protect himself from the insurgents. The house trembled. The floor underneath Trevor quaked. The entire side of the compound crumbled down around him.

Concrete and steel beams fell, burying him in rubble.

CHAPTER 12

"Trevor, man, wake up! Can you hear me?"

Jarring himself awake, Trevor's vision blurred, but he could make out several members of his team looming over him. His body hurt like a son of a bitch. His leg felt like it was on fire. Nausea nearly overwhelmed him, and he couldn't shake the haze from his brain. Rylie's face came into his line of sight. For the first time, he realized how much Rylie looked like Reed. What a strange thought to have at a time like this.

"He's lost a lot of blood," someone said. Pain shot through him when he tried to move from the awkward position he lay in.

"It'll take too long to get this shit off him. The leg's shattered. We have to move out before their reinforcements descend on us."

"Get medic help now," Rylie yelled. Turning back down to Trevor, Rylie lowered his voice. "Trev, we'll get you out of here.

I promise. I won't leave you."

Trevor nodded, but the pain remained too intense, and lightheadedness caused his vision and thoughts to swirl. "Did he catch the child?" he managed to ask before his eyes involuntarily closed and everything went black.

***

"Fuck! Goddamn it. Fuckin' hurts." Trevor woke, ready to fight. Brody and Rylie were there, holding him in place. Brody pinned his arms down. Rylie lay across his legs, trying to hold him still. "Get the fuck off me! Goddamn, it hurts."

"Trevor, you have to stop. Don't move. You're making it worse." Tears streamed down Brody's face.

"Keep hold of him. We're almost done." The sounds of saws and drills sent unbelievable agony pulsing through his body, clouding his brain. It was too much. Trevor vomited before his world went dark again.

***

"Dad...it's Trevor." Tears clogged Rylie's throat, making it hard for him to talk. Rylie dropped the phone to his thigh, rubbing his hands over his face, wiping his eyes.

"What?" Concern laced his father's voice. "Son, are you there?" Rylie could hear his father calling for his mother to pick up the other line. "Tell us what's happened."

"Dad, it's bad. He's been hurt really badly." Rylie cried openly as he spoke; grief tearing at his heart. Hearing his father was all it took to finally push him over the edge. He could hear Reed asking questions in the background.

"Who's been hurt? Has Trevor been hurt? What happened? Hold on, your mom's getting on the phone."

"Rylie, what's happened?" his mother asked.

"Trevor's been shot, multiple times. And he lost his leg. They had to take it in the field. He was awake when they did it." Rylie sobbed harder, remembering how he held Trevor down, allowing this to happen to his best friend.

"Oh, Rylie," his mom wailed, further decimating Rylie's ability to maintain some emotional distance and relay the terrible news.

"Where are you now? Where's Trevor?" His dad took over the conversation again, asking Rylie for facts.

"Trevor's in Germany. They got him stable and transported him today. It was the closest place. He's in surgery now, but he's lost a lot of blood. Please pray for him."

"We will. Reed's here. He wants to talk to you."

Reed's voice was intense, anxiety filled, desperate. "What happened?"

Rylie paused to control the memories that threatened to overwhelm him. "He lost so much blood... Trevor's hurt bad, Reed. They thought he was dead. They made me hold him down." He couldn't get the story out, the emotions too much to deal with at the moment.

"Tell me exactly where Trevor is, Rylie."

"He's at Landstuhl. They won't let me go to him yet. It'll be a day before I can get there." God, how he wanted to be there with his friend, his brother.

"Dad, get me whatever clearance I need," Reed said. "Rylie, I'm on my way."

CHAPTER 13

Trevor's eyes fluttered, but it took several attempts to get them to stay open. An annoying beep kept sounding off in the background. Who would pick that for their ringtone? His mouth rivaled the damn sands of a desert. He tried to lick his lips, but his tongue couldn't muster any liquid, like sandpaper dragging over his chapped lips. Unable to wrap his mind around why he felt this way, Trevor fought to drag in memories from the night before. That wasn't his ceiling. How much had he drunk to put him in this condition?

He turned his head and pain radiated through his brain, blurring his vision even more. Cords touched his face, and he looked around finally recognizing the sterility of a hospital room. An ugly hospital room, so that meant it was probably a military hospital, which would make the drunken night out such a better option than anything that could have landed him there.

Something was in his right hand. Trevor lowered his gaze, focusing on the blond head. The pain in his head didn't help his confusion. He furrowed his brow. Why was Reed here? Reed lay there, sleeping, his head tucked on his arm. Their hands were linked together even as he slept. The connection somehow reassured Trevor, but the position Reed slept in looked incredibly uncomfortable, as did the chair under his butt. Trying to rise, Trevor stopped short. The pain in his shoulder, leg, and arm were excruciating. Bile rose up his throat, making him reevaluate his effort to move at all.

Rylie came into his view from the left, placing a hand on his arm. "You're awake. Thank God. Stay down. You've been hurt. Do you need a drink of water? Reed tried to keep ice on your lips and tongue, but you didn't make it easy." Rylie spoke slowly and quietly, but Trevor's mind seemed unable to focus on the words being said to him.

Start with the basics.

"Where am I?" he asked hoarsely, not much louder than a whisper. God, had he swallowed a cactus? Rylie brought a small cup forward with a towel, drizzling water into his mouth, wiping away the wayward drops running down his chin.

"You're in Germany. You've been out for a few days."

"What day is it?"

"Tuesday, around two in the morning," Rylie said, letting a little more water trickle past his lips. "They had you out for several days to give you time to heal. Then you took your time coming back to us. You've been here about a week and a half."

"I was at your wedding." Trevor tried hard to remember something, anything more than the big wedding weekend. It was all so fuzzy. Confusion caused his brow to furrow again. Rylie gave him another drink.

"Yeah, we got called out. You were hurt trying to hero up." Rylie wiped Trevor's chin; all the water in the cup was gone.

"That doesn't sound like me."

"Whatever, man. You saved a room full of children."

Trevor wet his lips with his tongue, while Rylie filled the small cup again, drizzling more water into his mouth.

"What happened after that?"

"You got shot a bunch of times and fell a few stories. The building thought it should fall with you to keep you company." Rylie tried for lighthearted, but his eyes said something different.

"That's what hurts like hell. I don't think that was probably part of my plan. I don't remember any of it." Trevor looked over at Reed who slept through their quiet conversation. "Why's he here?"

"Reed came right away. It didn't look good for you. You lost a lot of blood, and they were worried about an infection. I called Mom and Dad. Reed was there and arrived here twelve hours later, before they even allowed me to come. He's been by your side ever since. I think this is the first time he's really slept since I've been here."

Trevor watched Reed while Rylie spoke. He looked so handsome lying there. Trevor wouldn't mind waking up in a hospital every day if he woke to Reed's face every morning. After a moment, he lifted his eyes back to Rylie.

"So I guess everyone knows now?"

"Yeah, pretty much," Rylie said, looking him straight in the eyes.

"Does it change anything?" Trevor asked, holding Rylie's gaze. His mind began to clear; flashes of memory made his head hurt. The hotel room came flooding back to him, and he could feel the stain of a blush crossing his cheeks.

"Nah, man, not for me. I've known for a while," Rylie said, looking down at his sleeping brother.

"How?"

"I don't know. Reed just never hid it. You two are a lot alike, in many ways. I'm glad you're together. I didn't realize it got so serious, but Reed needed someone. He needs to settle down. We were beginning to think he'd be a player for the rest of his life." Rylie gave a quick smile. "I'm glad it's you. I couldn't have asked for a better man for him. I wish I would've thought of it. I'd've done the hookup before now. I need to tell your nurse you're awake." Rylie turned away then came back, leaning closer to Trevor. "You should know, Reed's been a bear where your care's concerned, throwing around Dad's connections and all that legal jargon he's so good with. He required second and third opinions on everything and made calls, conferencing with doctors from Walter Reed. It didn't matter that he wasn't your family. If you didn't make it through this, it would've destroyed him. You should've seen him. I'm sure they're past ready to get rid of him around here. I'll be back, but I know he would rather be awake now that you're awake."

Rylie reached down to clasp Trevor's left hand, giving a tight squeeze. It was then Trevor realized the bandages around his chest kept his arm secured to his side. He couldn't lift his arm at all. Quietly, Rylie left the room, making sure the door click didn't wake Reed. Trevor looked down at the sleeping man. After a second of staring and memorizing Reed there with him, he pulled his hand out of Reed's and lifted a finger and gently ran the tip over Reed's full lower lip. The movement caused Reed to jar awake, lifting his head in a rush. Reed's eyes were swollen red, sleep-deprived, and swept up to his immediately.

"You're awake. Thank God. Are you in pain?" Reed leaned over the bed, running his fingers through Trevor's hair then down his face. Relief flooded his features as he lowered his head, gently kissing Trevor's lips as if it were the most natural thing in the world.

"A little. You're here," Trevor replied, his voice coming out a little stronger than before.

"I am. I've been waiting for you to wake. I'm sorry I fell asleep." Reed stayed over him, resting a hip on the side of the bed while he continued to caress his fingers through Trevor's hair.

"Don't be sorry. Rylie told me you've been awake for days. You shouldn't have come all this way."

"Here, take a drink. I've been trying to keep your lips and mouth moist. I read it helps. I don't know if I did a sufficient job though." Reed's relieved gaze met his. "I didn't want you to be alone. You agreed to a relationship with me." Reed's hand swept to his heart. "It means something to me. I had to be here with you, taking care of you."

An unsteady breath escaped from Reed's full lips, the only crack in Reed's confident certainty. He looked away to pour a small amount of water into Trevor's mouth, wiping away the droplets. "At least I've told myself you agreed to a relationship with me. It might be that I haven't formally asked you yet, and just made it up in my mind." Reed's piercing gaze lifted to Trevor's again. "Regardless, I needed to come to you."

"Rylie said you've been managing my care. What're they saying?" Trevor watched pain slice across Reed's face.

"There's more—"

The nurse walked in, cutting Reed off. Rylie, followed by Brody, trailed along after her.

"Good, you're awake," the nurse said. Reed rose, standing close to the front of the bed, taking Trevor's hand in his own. "Sgt. West, I'm Alice, your nurse. Dr. Willis is on his way. Are you in pain, sir?" She carried a small tray with a syringe lying across the top. As she spoke, she sat the tray down and scanned the different monitors above Trevor's head before picking up the needle and removing the cap.

"A little," Trevor replied, looking at the nurse, who wouldn't really look him in the eyes then over to Brody and Rylie. Brody wouldn't look him in the eye either. Instead, he kept his gaze downcast, focusing somewhere along Trevor's chest. Trevor remembered the anger he saw on his buddy's face when he exited the elevator back at the hotel, but somehow, he didn't think this had to do with that.

"This will help, sir. It's a mild pain reliever. It also acts as a sedative." Thumping the syringe a couple of times and removing any air, Alice then inserted the needle into the IV. A doctor entered the room at the same time, making the already small room packed.

"Hi, Sgt. West. I'm Dr. Willis. I've overseen your care while you're here. We're glad you're awake. How are you feeling?" Dr. Willis picked up the chart at the end of the bed and flipped it open.

"I'm sore," Trevor answered and kept watch over the faces of everyone in the room. Brody still wouldn't quite make eye contact with him, and Reed looked tense, tracking every movement the nurse and the physician made.

"I'm sure you are. You've been through quite a bit. Simply stated, we've removed four bullets from your left shoulder and arm. From your hip and another in your left thigh. Miraculously, the tissue damage appears to have made minimal disruption, and no infection to this point. You were lucky. Nothing hit any major arteries or organs. We're encouraged that there's no fever. Your care has been extremely aggressive. Your young man here made sure of it." The doctor stood at the end of his bed, pausing for a moment, looking at Reed as if he needed to find his words. After a moment, he took a deep breath and continued, rubbing his palms down the front of his lab coat as he spoke.

"Son, field triage made the decision to remove your left leg, and from what I saw when you arrived, it was just in time. You would not have lived much longer with the significant blood loss you experienced."

"I'm sorry," Rylie burst forward to say. His voice cracked, tears formed in his eyes, and desperation filled his words. "I'm so sorry. If I'd had more time, or better medical training, I might have been able to do more."

Trevor watched Rylie, and then looked over at Brody who still wouldn't look at him. His muddled mind forced him to try harder to register everything coming at him. The new round of pain medicine acted fast, already flooding his system, numbing his thoughts even more. Finally, Trevor turned his gaze to Reed, who looked at him with deep pity. Trevor didn't like that look at all. Reed gripped his hand tighter, not letting him go as he tried to shake free of the hold. His eyes drooped as the realization of what they said rattled around in his groggy brain.

"I've lost my leg? Where?" Trevor focused only on the physician.

"Below the knee."

"And my shoulder and arm look good?" Trevor asked, fighting to keep his eyes open, his mind working. Assessing the situation. Analyzing the facts. Something he was trained to do.

"Right now, they do, yes. It's miraculous as I said, but I can see a full recovery on your upper extremities with physical therapy."

"What's next for me?" Trevor kept his eyes on Dr. Willis, not wanting to see any more pity or tears on his behalf.

"Well, if everything stays like it is, you should be able to be transferred stateside as early as tomorrow for physical therapy and prosthesis fitting and care." Dr. Willis placed the chart back at the end of the bed.

"Will I be allowed to stay in the military?" A yawn tore from Trevor's lips, and he forced his eyes open to get all the information he could.

"Sir, that's a conversation to have with your superiors. I don't have those answers. You need to rest. Your recovery will require all your strength."

Trevor furrowed his brow, attempting to process everything. "They aren't going to let me stay with my team without a leg. What am I gonna do now?" Trevor tightened his hold on Reed's hand as if it were a life preserver thrown in his direction in a stormy, turbulent sea. Before too much fear could grip his heart, his eyes closed and sleep took over.

CHAPTER 14

Startled awake, Trevor looked around the small hospital room, finding it still ugly as hell. But thankfully, he was alone this time. He lay there several minutes, looking up at the ceiling, trying to remember everything they'd told him before the pain meds kicked in and he passed out again. That was a bold move on their part to dump everything on him when his mind was too groggy to properly process.

How long had he been asleep? A glance out the window at the position of the sun made him guess the time to be somewhere around noon. So, he'd slept through the night and into the morning.

Trevor did a quick assessment of his body. He could feel the tightening in his shoulder and arm, but the pain wasn't terrible. Taking it as a good sign, he used his right hand to flip the blanket and sheets back from his chest. Under nothing more than sheer willpower, he gritted his teeth and used his right arm and the armrest on that side of the bed to pull his body to a sitting position. It took a considerable amount of time, but he made it. Trevor's initial thoughts about the pain being bearable were banished. Every muscle in his chest tensed under the excruciating pain searing through his left shoulder. He looked down, surprised nothing was torn open and bleeding out.

He sat there for several minutes, preparing himself mentally. Every emotion played out in vivid detail through his mind. Moments of deep self-pity kept trying to slip in, but he fought against them. Finally, he pushed the covers away and manned up, looking down at his leg, seeing for the first time that his foot was no longer there. It was severed below his knee. The sight startled him. His stomach churned, threatening to revolt. His heart pounded in his chest. He couldn't stop staring at the stump. It was just…gone. His lower leg was gone, and his life would be forever changed.

How could he continue his military career? It was all he'd ever wanted. His team had become his family. Trevor hated weakness in himself, but he allowed this moment to let sorrow fill his heart. They would never let him stay with his team, and his team was everything to him. Running his hand over his face, then through his hair, Trevor forced himself to buck the fuck up before the unshed tears threatened to fall. Shit happened for a reason, at least that was what he'd always heard. He'd figure this out. He had to.

Never taking his eyes from his leg, Trevor's thoughts went to Reed. And wasn't that just something, the way his heart reacted to the man? Throughout this dire situation, Reed gave his heart hope. Absently, he rubbed across the bandages covering his heart, the images of his leg faded, and the way Reed looked sleeping on this bed came to mind. He'd looked so handsome. Drop dead gorgeous in every way, but while he slept, those few hard edges softened, and his full lips pouted. Trevor fell completely in love with Reed in that very moment.

A grin tugged at his lips. Like he wasn't already head over heels for the guy. But at the first moment of seeing Reed asleep— even though he didn't know why Reed was there—he knew without question the man would forever be the one true love of his life. Rylie had it completely wrong. He wasn't anything like Reed. Reed was strength, love, and goodness. Compassion and caring, all wrapped in an extraordinarily handsome package. Trevor could never live up to half of what he already saw in Reed.

Trevor's brow furrowed and his heart filled with unimaginable anguish. For the first time since his mother died, small involuntary tears slipped from his eyes. Reed needed to go. Trevor couldn't allow Reed to be strapped with this. The longer he allowed this connection, the harder the end would be. Tragedy always faded for those not directly living it. Those supporting and helping always slipped away and lived their lives again. If Trevor let this continue, Reed would move on when he'd had enough of him. It would destroy his heart, forever.

Trevor's stump came crashing back into his focus. Stump... he had a stump. And Reed needed to go. He had to focus on his recovery and finding a new game plan for his life. He couldn't afford to have an injury of this magnitude along with a completely broken heart. People didn't recover from shit like that, and the double whammy carried the potential to demolish him. His resolve built as he squared his shoulders. He could do this. He didn't need anyone's pity or help. He pulled the IV from his arm. Trevor released himself from the tubes stuck inside his body. Carefully, he moved to the side of the bed. He needed a drink of water and to brush his teeth.

Placing his right foot on the floor, Trevor looked through the room, judging the distance and available path to the bathroom. He wasn't sure he could hop his way there without tearing open some of his incisions. Instead, he edged Reed's chair closer to the bed. Trevor gripped its armrest and slowly rose. He lowered his weight onto his right arm and leg, using both for complete support. His muscles flexed and strained from his neck down. Trevor's right knee immediately gave completely out, buckling under him. His natural instinct was to balance himself with his left leg. The movement made him awkward, pitching him forward. Trevor clutched the chair. He used every muscle in his arm to keep the chair in place, only to land in a hard thump on the soft fabric. He panted. Pain ripped across his body in wave after agonizing wave. He gripped the side of the armrest, digging his fingers tightly into the plastic. Trevor hung his head, breathing through the pain, trying to gather enough strength to try again.

"What are you doing?" Reed came into the room, panic filling his voice. "Why the hell are you out of bed?"

Trevor didn't look up at him nor did he speak. He just sat there with his head lowered, trying to find the distance he needed to put between them. Reed came straight to him, dropping to one knee.

"Trevor... Hey, what's going on? What're you trying to do?" Reed placed his thumb under his chin, and a small struggle began. Finally, Trevor lifted his eyes to meet Reed's.

"I wanted to brush my teeth. I thought I could manage it. I probably could have, but my shoulder's too fucked up, and I can't move my fucking arm. Why's it so tightly bound to my chest?" Anger filled Trevor's words. He started to rip the bandage from his chest to free his arm, taking all his frustration out on the adhesive and gauze covering his wounds.

"Stop. They're there for a reason. Come on. I'll help you," Reed said, moving to Trevor's right side to pull him up.

"You've done enough." Trevor refused the immediate help and tried to look Reed in the eyes but couldn't, casting his gaze away. "Look, I think you should go."

"Come on, handsome. Wrap your arm around my shoulder. I'll get you in there. You can handle the rest once you get there." Reed never acknowledged the words Trevor said but bent toward him and tried to wrap Trevor's free arm around his shoulder.

Trevor looked at Reed for several long moments, trying to

decide what to do. Reed stayed bent, looking directly at him, Trevor's arm in his hand. There was a standoff between them. Trevor desperately wanted to be able to get across the room by himself, but he finally gave in. He reached up, wrapping his good arm around Reed's strong shoulder.

Reed smelled incredible; not the scent he wore the entire time they were together at the wedding, but something else just as nice. His stomach clenched, his body stirring to life even under all the pain and medicine. With an inward groan, he did the one thing assured to take his mind off Reed. Trevor anchored his good arm and pulled himself up. His weakened leg started to buckle again, and pain shot through his left shoulder and chest.

Reed struggled to find a good holding point along the left side of his body. Bandages were wrapped around Trevor's shoulder, chest, hip, and leg. More bandages reached lower around his hip and all the way down to his stump. After several attempts, Reed found a good spot, but the steps were awkward and difficult, causing immense pain with every slide of his leg. He had no idea what he was thinking by trying to get out of bed at all.

Reed finally wrapped both his hands around Trevor's waist, pulling him tightly against his body, gently tugging him across the floor. Even then, it took time to get to the bathroom.

If there was even the smallest hope of a possible relationship between them, this move across the floor killed it. This whole scene strengthened Trevor's resolve: Reed needed to go. As much as he might want a life with Reed, it wouldn't be fair to continue a relationship with him. He had to make Reed understand.

Reed got Trevor inside the small bathroom, leaving him at the sink. He pulled Trevor's toiletries out, placing them and a towel within reach, before stepping from the bathroom. The door was left open a crack, and he stood just outside, waiting.

"I've been talking to my dad. There are great rehab hospitals in the States. I think you would do well there. Your shoulder's healing nicely. They think it should have a complete recovery with some hard work, and you're used to hard work. Your body wouldn't look like that if you weren't a hard worker. Rylie had to go back to deal with the paperwork. Brody left to deal with something, but I really don't remember what. You all are being called heroes for taking Carlos Mendez down. Every news station around the world is covering it. Your name hasn't been released, but everyone's trying to find you. The president and his office were watching it all happen. They got to see you dive into the room. The president wants to talk to you. He's already talked to Dad."

Trevor looked at himself in the mirror while Reed spoke. He looked like hell. His hair stood on end. His complexion was pasty white. His eyes had deep, dark circles underneath. A clammy, cold feeling rippled through his stomach and showed on his skin. While standing there, Trevor looked to be paling by the second as he tried to balance himself on one foot. Leaning on his good arm, Trevor bent, quickly turning on the water. He ducked his head, attempting to splash his face and hair with the limited reach of his hand. A towel lay folded on the sink, and he managed to dry himself. The cool water did little in making the color of his skin more natural. Trevor continued to lean on the sink to brush his teeth and run a comb over his hair before reaching to open the door. The throbbing in his shoulder and leg began to take its toll on his stomach. He felt queasy as hell, and after everything else, he didn't want to vomit in front of Reed.

Stepping up, Reed grabbed him, watching him closely. Trevor didn't make eye contact but concentrated on making it back to the bed. His muscles were sore as hell. His right leg shook and twitched under the strain. Reed tried to help him back into bed, but Trevor resisted; he wanted to do it on his own. He pushed himself up, bracing his right arm on the soft mattress. His body was too weak, and his arm gave out, forcing him to fall backward. Reed stayed back, giving him a minute, before breaking down and forcing his help on Trevor.

"Trevor, it's too early for you to be out of bed, and you're being too stubborn for no good reason." Reed stood back after moving Trevor's legs under the blanket. His brow furrowed in annoyance. Concern filled his voice.

He took several deep breaths, mentally trying to ease the pain and remember his convictions.

"I don't want to sound ungrateful, but you should go back home." Trevor refused to look in Reed's direction. He just stared up at the ceiling. His heart resisted his words, but he pushed through them, getting them out there between them.

"And why is that?" Reed came closer, anchoring his hip on the side of the mattress.

"I'm out of the woods, but I'm a mess. It's a long recovery, not something you need to strap yourself with. I appreciate you coming. Rylie told me you fought for me, and I thank you. But this is too much. I'm not even sure I'll be employed much longer. I don't have any skills except being a marksman, and there isn't much need for a one-legged sharpshooter in the real world. You should go. I'm not your boyfriend, not really. You barely know me. It was three days; that's all we had. You need to go home. You should go." Trevor never took his eyes from the ceiling, knowing if he looked at Reed, he would risk his heart winning over and begging Reed to stay.

Reed responded by entwining their fingers and resting more of his weight on the side of the bed. He pushed the covers back to brush his fingertips along the inside of Trevor's right calf, going up to his knee under the standard issue hospital gown he wore.

"It was an excellent three days, wasn't it?" Reed replied. Trevor stayed quiet and closed his eyes. "So, you're saying you want me to go, so I'm not stuck with you once I figure out how hard this is going to be?" Reed asked, lowering his voice.

"Yes. No. Yes," Trevor said, his eyes opening as he stuttered around his words, trying to decide what that sentence really meant.

"Well, you're in luck then...for now. I've been waiting for you to wake. I need to get back home. I've got some things to take care of, and there are important deadlines attached." Reed ran his hand up the inside of Trevor's thigh. His traitorous cock slowly hardened with every sweep of Reed's fingers. How was it even possible to be so turned on under the flood of emotion and pain he'd been dealing with? In fact, the only thing he could concentrate on was the warmth of Reed's fingers inching closer to his now rising cock. It felt so good to be touched. God, he wanted more. When Reed's hands were on him, he forgot about the pain and everything else that held him hostage. Reed must have sensed Trevor's need to be touched. He slowly pulled up Trevor's hospital gown. His hard-on grew even harder with each tug of the material.

"I would just like you to tell me if those days we shared meant anything to you," Reed said, his voice startling Trevor.

"No, they didn't. It was just a fling." Trevor didn't hesitate to lie, trying but failing to keep eye contact. He tried to lie there, looking tough and uncaring. Trevor needed Reed to leave before he completely caved under the heated touch.

"You're lying. I'm an attorney; I'm paid very well to know a lie when I hear one. So let me get this straight, what you're now trying to say is that everything you said to me in the hotel room was a lie? Is that what you want me to believe? You have casual flings all the time?" Reed's eyes narrowed and a sly smile lit his face. "I don't think so, handsome. I think you're just trying to play the brave soldier, always doing what's best for others. What you don't seem to understand is that those three days were life changing for me. I meant everything I said to you on the balcony and in that hotel room. I'll forever remember everything you said to me."

Reed moved the gown up past Trevor's hips and gripped his engorged erection in the palm of his hand. He wrapped his fingers around the swollen length and stroked. A hiss escaped Trevor's lips. He fought the urge to push up into that tight fist. He tried hard to ignore the warmth of Reed's palm against his sensitive skin, but his efforts were useless. Reed's smirk grew as he watched

Trevor watch him. Reed continued to stroke while he spoke.

"I remember clearly. You said you wanted to be in a relationship with me. I agreed. In my book, that means you became my boyfriend. I'll abide by your wish for me to leave, for now. But know I'll always consider you to have said you were mine, Trevor." Lowering his head, Reed swiped his tongue across the broad head of Trevor's cock. "I washed you while you were sleeping. Rylie told me how you would hate not bathing every day. I noticed that when I was in your room the night of the bachelor party. While bathing you, I paid special attention to this area." Reed's hand tightened around Trevor's thickness. "They've told me your sexual health is important. God, I want to taste you again."

Trevor trembled helplessly as his throbbing cock slid past Reed's lips into his sweet mouth. He'd never in his life felt anything this amazing. Lowering his eyes from the ceiling, he watched as Reed lapped and sucked him lovingly. His body betrayed his words, reacting so readily to Reed's touch. Deep down, he knew the truth of the situation. Sure, Reed said these things now, but when they returned home, Reed would resent and pity him. He didn't want to be pitied. Trevor tangled his hand in Reed's thick blond hair and fought with himself.

He concentrated hard, needing to remember everything about this moment to get him through the rest of his life. His resolve was set. Reed wouldn't be in his life any longer; he couldn't allow it. But he needed to be able to pull this moment from his memories during the lonely times in his life when he missed Reed the most. Trevor's heart pounded hard in his chest. His breath hung in his throat as pleasure edged out any discomfort and every logical argument that had formed in his brain. His eyes tried to roll back in his head. He didn't want this to end. It felt so good.

Not knowing how long he could hold off, Trevor's jaw clenched as he fought his release. Reed worked him effortlessly, building his pace to a delicious rhythm. He strained to keep his body at bay. Reed's words, with his bold actions, caused his carefully laid resolve to fracture. Lord, he had it bad for this guy.

Letting his thoughts go, he settled into the moment. He pushed himself deeper into Reed's hot mouth. Reed rewarded his slight thrust with an approving moan that vibrated deep from his throat. Reed's throat constricted around his swollen dick, making his toes curl. The sensation almost made Trevor shout out Reed's name in gratitude. If that wasn't enough to send him over the edge, he felt Reed's warm palm cup his sac and gently roll his balls in time with the rhythm of his wicked mouth.

Forcing his eyes to open, his breathing grew ragged as his hips rolled forward eagerly seeking the delicious strokes of Reed's tongue. The silky strands of Reed's blond hair slipped through his fingers when he tightened his grip. The pain of his physical and mental wounds had completely vanished, lost in the pleasure Reed gave him. Trevor let himself go. He let it all go, and the only thing existing in this moment was the way Reed made love to him with his mouth.

"Reed, I can't last. I'm going to..." His body convulsed, and he cried out against the onslaught of pleasure.

Reed continued to stroke him, paying special attention to his sensitive, tightened balls and thick base as he devoured Trevor, swallowing his essence. All Trevor could do was shudder as he watched Reed's tongue lap the last of his spent seed. Reed lifted his head, pegging him with a hungry, sexy stare, sending another shock wave through Trevor's pulsating body. He ran the back of his hand across his mouth and lifted from Trevor before licking his lips.

"Mmm, I could feast upon you all day, but you're right, I must return home. I have a lot to do. I'll call you when I get there. We need to talk about the future." Reed ran his fingers lightly over Trevor's face while looking him over closely.

Trevor did the same with Reed, memorizing everything about him. His heart ached in his chest.

"I'll call if it's not too late here. Otherwise, I'll call you tomorrow. You need your rest and stay in bed. No more trips to the restroom by yourself. It's all going to be okay, Trevor. I promise. They'll take care of you here, I've been assured. Don't be worried, and do not fight the medicine. They'll be here any minute with your pain meds. I expect you to take it. You have to give yourself time to heal." Leaning in, Reed captured Trevor's lips. Reed didn't hold back, and Trevor returned the gesture in a long, slow kiss.

It felt very much like the goodbye it was intended to be. It broke Trevor's heart, and he kissed him back with everything he felt so deeply in his soul. Reed pulled away first, touching Trevor's face one last time before turning and walking out the hospital room door.

Reed didn't look back. Trevor knew with all certainty because he watched him leave until the door clicked shut behind him.

CHAPTER 15

"Sgt. West? Good morning, sir. It's early. I'm glad you're awake. We're transferring you to the States today. Your flight will leave in an hour and a half. I'm the nurse scheduled to make the flight with you. I'm Anthony. Nice to meet you." Anthony came through the hospital door at a quarter to seven in the morning, pushing a huge, oversized wheelchair almost too big to get through the doorway. He hadn't thought they'd get his transport back Stateside arranged so quickly. All hospitals might look the same, but he was ready to be somewhere closer to the place he considered home.

The nurse wore bright, yellow-colored scrubs across his at least six-five frame. His physique could only be described as a solid brick wall of muscle. Tattoos ran up both dark arms and his head was shaved bald. The grin Anthony wore covered his entire face. He stuck out his hand to Trevor when he got close enough, and Trevor didn't hesitate to return the shake.

"We need to check your wounds before we leave. Nurse Alice Hatchet is on her way down with some supplies to do a quick bandage change." Anthony stepped closer as if he were about to impart some great secret. "I don't know about you, but she just gives me the creeps. She only ever smiles when she's about to give someone bad news. Let me get these bandages off you. I swear, she purposely tries to take skin with the adhesive bandages when she peels them off."

Without gaining any sort of permission, Anthony unwrapped Trevor's arm from his chest, carefully pulling the bandages free of each wound. It took some time, but Anthony got him completely unwrapped.

"Damn, man. These look great. You got some big luck inside you, my man. I can't believe how good they look. I bet these staples can come out real soon. Look at this light pink scar. No sign of infection at all." Anthony talked the entire time he worked, even when Nurse Hatchet had arrived. Trevor never had to utter a single syllable the entire time Anthony and the nurse worked on him. He even laughed a couple of times when Anthony goaded Alice about her bedside manner. Even with all the commotion in his room, Trevor kept one eye on the clock above the door. They were starting the next day and Reed still hadn't called like he said he would.

"Your leg's healing nicely too. The swelling's down. I hope it stays that way through the flight. I don't think it will though. It'll have to be a smooth flight, no banging around, and still, it'll be hard to keep it from swelling up. But once you're relocated, physical therapy and the prosthesis fitting will begin right away. It's all super-fast now. They'll have you up and running, as good as new, real soon. You're a strong dude." Anthony's finger tapped against his own temple. "I bet you'll be up on a prosthesis in a few weeks, month tops. I heard you were the one to take that Carlos guy down and saved a kid in the process. It's just a rumor here, but it's spreading like wildfire. Do you have any questions so far for me, sir?"

Anthony was a lot to follow along with, but he seemed like a nice enough guy.

"Am I traveling in this gown?" Trevor watched Anthony as he handled him with skill and ease. Anthony was strong. He lifted and moved Trevor with no problem, and little to no discomfort on Trevor's part. There had been no pain when he changed his bandages either.

"Nah, man, I brought some loose-fitting clothing for you." Anthony handed him a pair of sweatpants, a T-shirt, and a flip-flop. Again, he didn't ask for permission before he started to help Trevor dress. "So much with you is a secret, but I'm gonna tell you, you got into one of the world-renowned rehab facilities in the States. They'll get you going quick, I promise. They're the best. I put your discharge folder in the chair. I'm supposed to tell you it has all the military contacts, including telephone numbers for counseling services to help with each stage of depression people with this type of injury go through. And please don't hesitate to use them if you need it. There's more I'm supposed to say, but honestly, it's a bunch of major boring bullshit that you really don't need."

Trevor pulled on the T-shirt. His bandaged left shoulder and arm stayed on the inside of the shirt. It took time to get dressed, and about once a minute he looked over at the phone. Reed still hadn't called. Trevor supposed it meant Reed took his warning to heart. Which was for the better, but his heart ached watching each minute pass without a word.

"I'm ready," he finally said, moving his right leg over the bed onto the floor.

Out of nothing more than sheer desperation, Trevor reached out and picked up the phone by the bed, listening for a dial tone. Damn it. Everything worked. While the nurse stood by the bed, watching him, waiting for him to rise, Trevor thought of calling

Rylie to get Reed's number just to let him know he was leaving, so he wouldn't call and think Trevor was ignoring him or that something had happened.

"Sir, are you ready? I already told you I'm your nurse for the flight. Hope you weren't planning for some short, tight, hot number to accompany you today." Anthony stood there, eyebrows raised, a big grin spreading across his face.

"I'm ready and you'll do fine. I'm sorry you have to make the trip." Trevor dropped the phone back in place and moved his body off the mattress. The searing pain he'd expected in his shoulder held off when Anthony came to his right side to help him into the chair.

"I'm being paid well for this flight; it's all good for me. I'm afraid though this chair's as comfortable as it gets. Keep your left leg raised here, sir. Yeah, just like that. I'll strap it in, but it has to be raised to help keep the swelling down. Is there any luggage you brought for your resort stay here with us?"

"I travel light," Trevor quipped, adjusting himself in the chair, trying to get comfortable before running his fingers through his hair. "I hate the up-charges for extra luggage."

Anthony barked with laughter at his joke and reached down to give him a quick fist bump. "Now hang tight, sir. I assure you, by the time you reach home, you won't ever want to see another wheelchair again."

"Yeah, I'm already there." Trevor reached out to push the hospital door open. They banged their way through the small opening.

"I know, buddy," Anthony replied, patting Trevor's good shoulder as they made their way to his flight.

CHAPTER 16

Nothing had gone smoothly since Reed returned last night, and now Trevor's flight was on a delay. The flight crew reported in regularly, and from what they told him, the turbulence was a bitch for a large portion of the flight. The on-flight nurse reported Trevor denied pain meds for the first few hours, only to give in during the worst of the storm. Reed was learning his Trevor could be a stubborn one. Even under all the tension of the last twenty-four hours, the thought of Trevor being his made him grin.

The Escalade Reed had rented based on the suggestion of the rehab center was parked close to the small private airport's runway. He stood outside the SUV and dropped his sunglasses in place. The warm early May sun beat down on his face, warming his skin. The signs of an early summer were already starting, giving them a record-breaking heat wave for the first time in years.

Leaning back against the truck, Reed checked his watch again, mentally going over everything on his to-do list one last time. There had been so much to plan for, so much to do to prepare for Trevor's arrival. This was his best attempt at being a knight in shining armor. He sure loved being in a position to help in Trevor's recovery.

Reed didn't get to talk to Trevor before he left the hospital this morning. He could only imagine what Trevor thought about him not calling. Well, he knew exactly what he thought, and it made his grin widen thinking of the surprise he hoped to have pulled off.

His cell phone rang in his hip pocket. He palmed his phone quickly, running a finger over the touch screen. Preparations were still underway, and this message was from his contractor who had just finished the additions to the guest room he'd planned for Trevor's long-term stay. Another message came in shortly after from the public affairs officer at the rehab hospital. They were letting him know they would accommodate any of Trevor's needs.

Reed had counseling ready for Trevor. He had tried hard to think of everything Trevor might need. Rylie would be home in the next day or so and would bring Trevor's personal items, but until then, he would need clothing and toiletries…

At the last minute, Reed had gone shopping to pick up a few things to tide his Trevor over. A chuckle tore from his lips at the ridiculousness of how accustomed he was getting to referring to Trevor as his. One store he stopped at earlier, he kept the young salesclerk with him for several minutes, just telling her in detail how he'd met his Trevor. She stayed attentive through it all, only glazing over once or twice as he spoke. She'd been such a trooper he'd ended up spending way more than he should have just to give her a better commission as a thank-you for letting him prattle on and on. He couldn't seem to help it at all. It was just what he felt so deeply in his heart. Every one of Reed's thoughts stayed centered on the guy.

Reed had worked out taking a couple weeks off work. He'd stayed up most of the night transitioning files to his staff. Even then, he would have to be available to answer any questions, and his staff took full advantage by texting and emailing him several times an hour. All things considered, Reed's excitement level soared. He couldn't wait to spend this time with his new Trevor, even under such a dire situation. Reed absolutely loved the idea of Trevor coming to stay in his home.

Finally, hours later, the plane emerged from the clouds. The private jet belonged to his father's firm. Reed had chartered it for a small fortune today, but the powers that be from the United States government got wind of the trip and sent his father a message, letting him know they would be picking up this tab. Every political leader wanted to meet the hero who'd saved so many at his own risk.

As he watched the plane descend, Reed hoped Trevor still found the flight more comfortable than being handled like cattle on a normal military flight. Even with the weather delays, Reed wanted this to be a better experience. He waited for several minutes after the plane landed and the airport personnel secured the ramp they'd use to exit Trevor from the plane. He took a deep breath, trying to calm his nerves and slow his pounding heart as he took long strides across the runway to the bottom of the ramp.

He was a man on a mission. Reed stood to the side of the ramp, watching as Trevor was carefully wheeled down. Trevor hadn't seen him yet. Reed had given strict instructions not to tell Trevor of any of these plans.

"Sir, I think this is your next ride," Anthony, a friend of his father's, said loud enough for Reed to hear. Trevor looked up at the male nurse, but the bright sun hit just right causing Trevor to squint while quickly looking down.

"Thank you. Where do I go from here?" Trevor asked. He reached down with his right hand to push the wheel.

"You're coming with me. I can take it from here, Anthony." Reed's voice startled Trevor. He flipped his head around, shading his eyes with his right hand. Reed stood proudly at the end of the ramp. He kept the sunglasses in place to help hide some of the emotion he knew churned through his gaze after seeing Trevor.

On impulse, Reed reached down and quickly kissed Trevor's stunned lips.

"I can help get him to the car for you, sir," Anthony said.

"I've got him. Thank you again." Reed reached out to quickly shake Anthony's hand but kept his gaze on Trevor. Trevor didn't even seem to notice the kiss. Reed didn't give either man a minute to respond before taking the back handles of the chair.

"What're you doing here?" Trevor finally asked, looking back over his shoulder.

"I'm taking you home, not to the hospital. They'll handle your care as an outpatient. I'm sorry I missed you this morning. The nurse on duty said you had just left when I called. I didn't realize the flight would leave so early."

Anthony stood at the end of the ramp. Trevor turned to shake Anthony's hand, but they were already several feet away. All Trevor could do was wave over his shoulder. There was no way Reed would go back to let Trevor say a proper goodbye at the risk of Trevor deciding not to go with him.

"Good luck, buddy. It was an honor to ride with you, sir," Anthony called out from the end of the ramp.

Trevor lifted his hand again for a wave, but quickly turned his gaze back to Reed. "What's going on?"

Reed never stopped his purposeful steps to the SUV parked a few hundred feet away. Trevor's head stayed cocked toward his. Reed couldn't resist leaning down to give Trevor another quick kiss on the lips, never breaking stride. "After staying by your bedside for so many nights, I found I missed you terribly. You've really got me hooked."

"Reed, really, what's going on?"

"I've done some arranging, called in some favors. You'll be staying with me to help with your anonymity. Hopefully that stay will be indefinite, but that's your call. We can work together in getting you back healthy…

"Reed, this is too much for you to deal with. I can't let you take—"

"No," Reed said firmly, interrupting him. "I want to do this. Please let me. It's important to me. I've made many arrangements, but anything you're uncomfortable with can easily be changed." They reached the SUV, and Reed helped Trevor into the back seat on the passenger side. He never really gave Trevor the option he planned to.

Reed positioned the pillow the way the hospital instructed before making sure Trevor was tucked in tight. Once Trevor was secured in the back seat, Reed lifted his gaze, just staring at his sexy as hell albeit exhausted boyfriend. Something about having Trevor in the car made Reed feel like he may not fight him on this.

Under the shade of the back seat, he lifted his sunglasses. His gaze swept over every inch of Trevor's stunning face. Reed reached out to brush the hair from Trevor's forehead.

"This is all new to me. I hated leaving you at that hospital. It tore me apart having to step on that plane without you. If you'll let us, we can get through this together. I want you to stay with me, at the very least until you get your strength back and your shoulder and arm are usable."

Reed watched the confusion pinch Trevor's face.

"Say yes." He leaned in and kissed Trevor tenderly on the lips again, this time using the tip of his tongue as he sucked his lower lip into his mouth. "I feel settled now that you're here with me."

"Reed, I just don't want to put you out—"

"No, please. I see the doubt in your eyes. We can do this. I can do this. Let me. Let's get you home. It's been a long trip. No decisions have to be made right away." Reed didn't wait for Trevor to respond; he closed the door with a soft, secure click.

He darted around the back of the SUV, putting the wheelchair away. Anthony still stood at the bottom of the ramp, waiting as Reed had instructed him to. If Trevor wanted no part of this, he wanted Anthony to get him directly to Walter Reed. He gave a thumbs up, and Anthony's grin spread further across his face. He raised both his hands in return, giving Reed the double thumbs up back.

"Good luck, man," Anthony yelled across the tarmac.

"I'll need it. He's a stubborn one. Thank you!" Reed called back, before climbing into the front seat. With a quick look over his shoulder, he gave Trevor a grin. Relief finally eased his heart, making his own grin wider. Reed had Trevor tucked securely away in the back seat, heading to his home. He let out a pent-up breath he didn't know he held and started the engine.

***

If it were any other time, the drive to Reed's house would almost be comical. Reed took every back road he could find, never daring to venture out on a main road. If he tried to say he ever went over thirty miles an hour, Trevor would have called it out as the lie it was.

As he'd come to expect from Reed, he kept a steady stream of conversation going, talking about nothing of consequence as Trevor's thoughts strayed to his surprise at seeing Reed standing at the bottom of the airplane ramp.

Reed Kensington had totally shocked the shit out of him. He was the last person he'd expected to see waiting for him after such a torturous flight.

In Germany, traffic had been a bitch. They had arrived late to the airport; so late, he expected to be taken back to the hospital for missing his flight. To his utter surprise, Anthony wheeled him straight onto a private jet. Disbelief couldn't even begin to describe those first few minutes of realizing he would be alone on the flight. Trevor couldn't quite wrap his mind around it, and the questions flowed, but Anthony brushed it off with some drivel about how all officers and VIPs got this treatment. Anthony had effectively moved his mind away from his doubt by showing him all the cool gadgets he found when preparing the plane for the flight.

A young female flight attendant came out of the front cabin to help secure his chair in place before liftoff. During introductions, she mentioned Mr. Kensington's name, helping everything fall into place. Trevor assumed she spoke of Rylie's dad. Mr. Kensington was an ambassador and well-connected enough to pull together a hookup like this one. Both the attendant and Anthony tried to cover her mistake, and he let it stay hidden. It was such a nice gesture; Trevor hadn't wanted to ruin Rylie's father's surprise.

Almost immediately after takeoff, Trevor's leg had begun to throb. Anthony told him something about the pressure of the altitude and it all being normal. Hours into the turbulent flight, the outgoing Anthony, who was strapped securely into his seat, began to pray openly. The flight attendant stayed belted down, locked in her seat too. The weather raged and they couldn't seem to get high enough to get out of the storm. The turbulence kicked Trevor's ass, slamming his leg and shoulder hard against the seat, jostling him over and over. Trevor had tried to man up, gritting his teeth, and refused to take the pain meds. An hour later, he caved and took the pills. It wasn't quite strong enough to block the mounting heartache of Reed not calling, but it took the edge off the pain ricocheting through him with every bounce of the plane.

All these hours later, his leg lay carefully propped on pillows that Reed had placed underneath him. The relief of seeing Reed at the end of the ramp had been staggering, making it hard to see anything more than the stunning man and all the effort Reed had gone to on his behalf.

How the fuck was he already so attached to Reed after such a short time?

His life was literally falling apart around him, and all he could think about was the man driving twenty-five miles an hour in order to make sure he was safe... Reed barely knew him yet had carefully and completely orchestrated every bit of his care, giving Trevor hope during such a dire time. How was that even possible? He'd never experienced this magnitude of feeling for another person. Reed had taken away both his worries and his breath. Of course, he was forever devoted to this man. A staggering amount of love poured through his heart.

Fairy tales were real. Trevor had his knight in shining armor.

Reed reached back to take Trevor's hand. He brought his gaze back to the front, meeting Reed's stare in the rearview mirror. He ran his thumb over the palm of Reed's hand. If his knight wanted to hold his hand, it was the least he could do in return.

"I like touching you," Reed said with a comforting wink in the rearview mirror.

Reed watched him through the mirror for the length of the stoplight. Heat crept up Trevor's cheeks, holding Reed's hand tighter while he spoke. "You didn't listen to me at all when we were in Germany, did you?"

"I hear everything you say. I just retain the parts I like." Reed grinned and kept one hand on the wheel, the other in the back seat holding Trevor's. If it were possible, Reed went even slower as he drove on. "Truthfully? I feel like I seem controlling, and I guess I am, but I can help you. I want to help you. I feel like this is something we're doing together...I don't want you to be uncomfortable with what I've done." Reed glanced into the mirror, quickly catching Trevor's eye. "I'm into you. Really into you."

After a time, Trevor lowered his head, bringing Reed's hand up for a kiss. "Thank you for this. I didn't realize how much I would miss you. I stared at that dumb phone all night. I was so afraid."

"Afraid of what?"

The rearview mirror showed all the secrets Trevor held securely in his heart. The truth was right there in his gaze, and he moved his eyes, looking out the passenger side window. After a minute, he finally answered. "I was afraid I ran you off. I didn't like it." It came out in little more than a whisper. Trevor was surprised Reed heard him at all.

Reed's hand tightened over his. "I want you too."

CHAPTER 17

A soccer ball flew across the windshield of the Escalade, forcing Reed to jerk the steering wheel to the right to avoid hitting the ball and any children running after it. He refused to go over ten miles an hour on the neighborhood street, but he lifted his eyes up to the rearview mirror, silently praying the sudden movement hadn't jostled Trevor too much.

After running a concerned gaze over every part of Trevor's tempting body that he could see in the small mirror, Reed looked over his shoulder to see firsthand if he was hurt. All he saw was a small wince, but Trevor's face quickly relaxed when their eyes met. If Trevor was hurt, he hid it well, but stayed braced with his right arm on the passenger side seat, holding himself in place. After the minute-long assessment, and feeling reasonably sure Trevor wasn't hiding the pain, Reed looked back out the front window over toward the children. He let the SUV idle in place while he calmed his nerves and settled his pounding heart.

Many young faces stared back at him. One grabbed the ball that came to a rolling stop in the middle of the street. The little one scurried to the sidewalk with their other playmates. One side of the street looked happy, jubilant, and ready to keep playing, waving Reed on with a sense of urgency. The other side all glared at him with deep disdain. All Reed could do was chuckle at the intensity of their disappointment. Rolling down the driver's side window, Reed yelled a quick apology and a wave before driving through the Saturday morning kickball game. He gave an apologetic smile to the disappointed children standing on the other side of the street as he drove by.

Yesterday morning, when first arriving home from Germany, Reed had been met at his front door by the captain of the underdog team, the ones who now stared Reed down with their sad, dejected faces. Every stare made it clear their defeat rested on his shoulders. They came to him prepared, using all possible tactics to draw him into their desired result, including having one of the girls carry a cute little puppy. Their worried faces and sweet voices begged him to play with them in today's game, like Reed had done on one previous occasion. They'd explained how they'd strategized for days. They followed him inside his house and pulled out pads with pages of playbooks they'd created throughout the week.

They showed Reed very clearly how they needed him to be their secret weapon in winning this week's contest. They even pulled out a half used ten-dollar gift card to Starbucks—one of their mother's had donated to the cause—because they knew how much Reed liked his morning Caramel Macchiato.

The children were completely convinced Reed would be their only hope. But their eager little faces became increasingly dejected and disappointed when Reed told them he couldn't play this weekend but promised to make it up to them the following Saturday. By the looks Reed received now while driving through the game, he assumed they were correct in their assumptions about this game and were losing badly.

Slowly, he continued to drive down the treelined street. Reed brought his eyes up to the rearview mirror every few seconds, watching Trevor much as he'd done the entire ride from the airport. Trevor stayed more quiet than usual, staring out the passenger side window. His face was masked, showing little emotion. Reed wished he knew what might be going on inside that handsome head.

Making an exaggerated wide right turn, Reed navigated the massive SUV into his driveway. Pulling forward up the long drive, he came to a stop at the sidewalk leading to his front door and lifted the gear shift into park. He didn't move from the seat right away. Instead, he looked out the front window, observing the construction crew in his yard. Several men of various ages and races were in their jeans and tool belts, just finishing the ramp leading to the front door.

The crew looked to be in the cleanup stage, loading their equipment in the back of a couple of pickup trucks sitting out along the street, preparing to leave. The projects this construction crew were hired to do today had cost a small fortune, but they were good to their word. Not an inch of the landscaping looked harmed or out of place in the process of building the outside ramp. Reed hoped the inside looked as good.

His mother, Olivia, stepped out the front door, dressed in her tailored suit. She walked down the wraparound front porch, and he imagined her high heels clicking on the wood as she made her way toward them. She waved with a big smile on her face. Reed grinned back at her and pulled himself from the SUV.

He opened the passenger side door, stuck his head in, and whispered quietly, "I couldn't hold her off. I hope you don't mind. She's been here for hours trying to help get everything ready for your arrival. Dad could barely keep her from coming to Germany."

Reed didn't wait for Trevor to answer but disappeared only

to arrive back in just a moment with the wheelchair from the back hatch. Getting Trevor out of the car was a little trickier than getting him in.

Slowly, they worked together to get him out of the vehicle. Reed's mother stopped at the end of the ramp, watching them closely with her hand shading her eyes from the bright May sun. Once settled in the chair, Reed came to the front, leaning in to look directly at Trevor to assess his pain level. Only the smallest of tics in Trevor's tightly clenched jaw indicated there might be discomfort.

"I think future trips should be with me riding in the front seat," Trevor finally said, adjusting himself in the chair.

"The hospital advised that to be a rather bad idea. If we were to be involved in an accident, you could be further injured. Not a good idea until you're fully healed," Reed said while locking all the pieces of the chair in place then going to the back of the chair and pushing Trevor up the walkway to his waiting mother.

"Yeah, I'm not sure a car accident's possible. You drive like you're ninety. I think if you're the driver, I'm certain we're safe from any future injuries there, Grandpa." The smile carried in Trevor's voice, his words ending in a chuckle as he looked over his shoulder, giving Reed a clever grin.

"Say what you will about my driving, but I think the back seat is the safest place for you. Regardless of what that smile does to the pitter-patter of my heart." Reed looked down at Trevor's smiling face and checked the urge to run his fingertips along his jaw and cheek.

Trevor would be uncomfortable with the PDA in front of his mother. Instead, Reed just returned the smile with his own cocky grin.

"Mom even cooked for you. I can't remember her ever cooking for me. I think that definitely means she likes you better than me," Reed said loudly, ensuring his mom would hear.

"Reed Kensington, you know that's not true. I cooked you

a special grilled cheese sandwich when you came home from camp with a broken leg when you were twelve years old. I can't believe you don't remember me slaving over the stove for you. How ungrateful of you, young man. I taught you better than that," Olivia remarked in her cultured southern accent as she hurried toward them. "Trevor, I'm glad you're home," Olivia said, bending down to take Trevor in a careful hug. He lifted his right arm and held her tightly. "You scared me to death, son. Please don't ever do that again."

"Yes, ma'am. I'm sorry for the trouble I caused," Trevor whispered against her ear as he held her a moment longer while she kissed his cheek. Before she rose, she used her thumb to wipe away the pink lipstick left behind. Tears swam in her eyes.

"Trevor, honey, you're no trouble at all. I'm so proud of you. Rylie said you saved dozens of women and children. I've been watching the national news about it all, talking to Reed and Rylie when they called. Everyone's calling you a hero. Of course, they aren't saying your name, but I know who they're talking about. I'm so proud of you. You were brave and selfless and very fearless." Olivia ran her fingers through Trevor's short military cut then along his shoulder. Emotion played across her face while she tried to keep herself together. Finally, she reached down to kiss his cheek again. This time she left the evidence behind.

"I didn't do anything more than anyone else did that night. Every member of my team would have made those same decisions if they'd been in my shoes. I'm no hero," Trevor responded.

Reed could see his mom ready to argue the point. Not wanting any reminders of what his soldier had gone through that fateful night, Reed pushed Trevor forward again, up onto the ramp. The construction crew had done a superb job. There wasn't even a jostle when the wheels hit the small incline.

"Mom, is Dr. McBride on his way?" Reed asked, making his way up onto the front porch. Olivia took Trevor's hand, walking along with them.

"Yes. I talked to him a little while ago. He'll be here soon. Trevor, I made your favorite chicken enchiladas with that special Spanish rice you like. Everything's in the fridge, ready to pop in the oven to warm. I hope you're hungry. I made enough to feed an army, but I have to run now. I just wanted to see you home. Dad and I will be back tonight when he's off. We love you two." She bent again and kissed Trevor, this time sweetly on the lips, giving him a tight hug before turning to hug Reed, whispering as she held him, "You make me very proud."

"Thank you," Reed said as she turned to leave.

"Thank you for the food and for being here, Mrs. Kensington," Trevor added, watching Olivia's retreat.

"Honey, I've told you to call me Mom—Olivia at the least—and there's no place I would rather be," Olivia called back. "Rest, Trevor. We'll see you tonight."

Reed pushed Trevor through the front door, eyeing the changes to his home closely.

Everything in the entryway had been moved out of the way, as per his instructions. Furniture, tables, and plants all shifted to make room for Trevor's wheelchair. From the corner of his eye, he could see into the guest bedroom off to the left of the entryway. A new ramp covering the few steps down into the room looked completed and natural to the room.

Pleased, Reed looked around his newly designed entry. He had wanted a seamless transition for Trevor; nothing that would jostle the chair as he entered any room, including the front and back doors. The contractors did excellent work, even matching the hardwood throughout the house.

From this vantage, Reed could see the room looked ready for his guest. Originally, Reed had every intention of giving Trevor his own space, but things changed when he saw Trevor exiting the plane. Reed wanted Trevor with him, in his bedroom, hopefully forever. He didn't even want to offer the guest bedroom to Trevor for fear he might accept.

All his newfound nurturing instincts slammed forward. How could a chance meeting have changed his heart and life so drastically? He knew the stories about how the men in his family fell hard and fast—hell, he'd seen the evidence with the love and devotion he'd witnessed over the years—but he never thought that would be him. He'd never anticipated that sort of feeling in his own life, and how it shifted all his desires and thoughts for the future. Now, an overwhelming need to please Trevor drove him. He wanted to keep Trevor close so he could protect and care for him.

"You went to a lot of trouble, Reed. Building ramps, moving your house around. You shouldn't have done all this. I could have stayed at a hospital." Trevor craned his neck, looking into the guest room. Reed went with his instinct and bypassed the room all together, heading for the hall separating his bedroom from the rest of the home. He stopped momentarily in front of the doorway.

"We needed to make the house easier for you to use until you're back on your feet. I won't dominate this decision, it's too important. I'll let this be your choice. I prepared the guest bedroom for your stay. I didn't want you to feel like I was pushing you into my house, or my bed." A thoughtful smile slid across Reed's face as he looked down at Trevor's upturn face. "But I find now that I really want you in this room with me. I want to be there if you need me. And yes, although that's the truth, I would also just like you there with me even if you don't need me. So you decide which room."

The uncertainty in Trevor's gaze melted Reed's heart. It seemed they were both in the same place with their feelings.

Reed couldn't help but lean down to brush his lips softly against Trevor's in a tender kiss. "I've been waiting to do that since we got home."

"I'm going to need help, but I don't want to be in your way or be a burden. It's my biggest concern about this whole deal." Trevor kept his serious gaze intently focused on Reed, waiting for his answer.

"I can honestly say I don't think you can ever be in my way. I want you here with me. It's my choice to have you here. Now, you decide. Forward into my spacious and beautifully decorated bedroom with the softest mattress you have ever laid on and a large television with all sorts of features I don't fully know, or back to the smaller, conservative, but still very nice guest bedroom."

"It's your home, Reed," Trevor said with a yawn. "You decide."

Reed didn't say another word, just pushed him forward into his room, moving directly to the bed.

"I've been told you need to lay down and rest to let any swelling from the flight resolve. Dr. McBride will be here to change your bandages and check your wounds any time now. He'll also leave us antibiotics and pain meds for you. I've known him most of my life. He's a physician from Walter Reed and has spoken to the treating physician in Germany. And as I say this all aloud, I feel like I'm being controlling instead of helpful. If there's anything you're unsure about..."

"Reed..." Hesitation more than concern laced Trevor's voice. Reed didn't pay him any attention but went to help him from the chair into a sitting position on the bed.

"I bought you a few things. Rylie helped me with the sizes. We can get you more when you can go with me and pick what you like yourself. Rylie's bringing your belongings home when he comes in the next day or two."

"Reed, listen to me." Trevor hissed and held in a breath. Reed could see the jerking in his left shoulder and arm while lowering his body onto the bed. After a deep breath, Trevor lifted his pain-filled eyes, looking directly up at him. "I have some money saved. I can pay you back for this. And when you've had enough and want me to leave, I'll be okay. You need to know that."

Reed smiled down at Trevor, running a finger along his jaw. "I knew you were going to say something just like that, so I was ignoring you on purpose." After pulling Trevor's shoe off, Reed worked the T-shirt over his head. "I don't have any experience in this relationship business as I've never had one before, so I've been watching happily married couples almost since first meeting you. It's interesting how much I want to be one someday. One thing they all seem to share is that they blissfully ignore each other when they don't want to hear what the other is saying. Who am I to doubt the strategies of all those happy couples? I'll work your sweatpants off next so you can get comfortable in bed. Now lift your arm so I can get this shirt off."

"Just tell me you heard what I said." Trevor gave a low rumble of a chuckle when Reed tickled his chest and under his arm with his fingertips while removing the shirt. "Okay, I see you heard me, and you don't play fair."

"Handsome, fair is a relative thought. I think it's completely fair to get to run my fingers over those tight, hard stomach muscles of yours, which continue to invade all of my thoughts and most of my dreams." Removing Trevor's pants became a whole ordeal. Reed's voice lowered as he spoke. He focused on Trevor's cock, grinning as it grew plumper each time he touched Trevor. "Are you teasing me, Mr. West? You should know I'm incredibly happy having you here in my bed."

It excited Reed to know that just his touch brought on such a visceral reaction. Trevor tried to cover himself, tried to keep his hard dick lowered, but there was no way to hide it. Reed slowly continued to tease Trevor's black sweatpants off his body. Finally, Reed's restraint broke. He slid his hands inside Trevor's boxers, pushing them low on his hips while gripping him, stroking and playing with him until a firm blush stained Trevor's cheeks. His hips rolled forward, urging Reed on.

Resting his free hand on the headboard, Reed continued the steady stroke of his other hand, loving the feel of Trevor's satiny, hard as steel cock sliding against his palm. He kept the enticing rhythm steady, going from tip to base to tip again. Reed lowered his head, slowly making eye contact, keeping his strokes firm. If possible, he wanted Trevor's pleasure, and Reed couldn't help but smile as he watched Trevor's perfectly pouty lips quiver just a little before parting slightly. A hiss of breath escaped as Reed's hand twisted wickedly over his swollen tip.

"I'm pleased you're here with me. It's exactly where you should be." Giving in, Reed decided Trevor was up for a quick blow job. What could it hurt? Besides, endorphins were great pain relievers. Leaning forward, Reed closed his eyes, slanting his mouth across Trevor's. Trevor gently rolled his hips forward, again and again, and lay back against the headboard, wrapping his arm around Reed's back. Reed anchored a knee on the bed to slide between Trevor's parted thighs. It took a couple of loud rings for the sound of the doorbell to register in Reed's very aroused brain, ruining all his fun.

CHAPTER 18

"Hello, Reed. How are you, son? I think it's been at least ten years since I last saw you." Dr. McBride stood at the front door, a giant grin spreading across his lean, aged, scholarly looking face. A medical bag in one hand, he extended the other to shake Reed's hand. Reed grinned at the now senior citizen standing in his door. Dr. McBride had been his family doctor for most of his life. He remembered this man to be much different than he looked right now with his white hair and small belly sticking out over his expensive slacks.

"It's been a while, sir. I think it's more like fifteen years. Thank you for coming over." After shaking the doctor's hand, Reed stepped back, opening the door wider with a slight sweep of his arm. "Please come in. The patient's back in my bedroom. I appreciate you coming on such short notice. I wouldn't trust his care to anyone but you."

"I'm happy to stop by. I make house calls for your family regularly. How is our patient? Did the flight go well?" The doctor followed along behind Reed through the house.

"Trevor just got in within the last hour or so. The flight was rough, with lots of turbulence. I'm not sure of the damage it may have caused. Trevor seems in pain but isn't saying anything much about it. I'm finding that is just his way about most things. I do know Trevor's getting frustrated with his arm being bandaged to his chest."

Reed led the doctor through the house to the master bedroom. Just outside the door, Reed stopped, turning back to the physician. He lowered his voice. "Dr. McBride, I'm sure you can see how important Trevor is to me. I need to get him the best care possible. I've taken your advice, but you must know Trevor's a stubborn one. He tries to move around on his own and won't take his meds like he should. If it's possible to remove the bandage keeping his arm secure, I believe he will feel much better about it all. Please keep that in mind while you examine him."

The physician only nodded his reply before Reed reached around to open the bedroom door. Trevor lay propped against the headboard in his boxers exactly as he'd left him. The oversized, stuffed pillow lying beside Trevor quickly came to lie across his lap, hiding the evidence of the beautiful hard-on he'd developed. A deep blush stained his cheeks. Reed couldn't help but chuckle at Trevor's quick movement and uncomfortable look.

"Trevor, this is Dr. McBride. He's agreed to make a house call because we thought you may be more comfortable here as opposed to his office after such a long trip."

Trevor's blush darkened with each word Reed spoke. His soldier gave a nod, but stayed quiet, his eyes flicking between the doctor and Reed. Dr. McBride approached the bed to stand directly beside Trevor.

"Hello, Sgt. West. I understand you were hurt in the line of duty." The doctor extended his hand, and Trevor shook it.

"Yes, sir, that's correct. Call me Trevor."

Dr. McBride nodded, resting his bag on the side of the bed. He unbuckled the clasps and pulled the zipper free. Reed stayed in the doorway, a shoulder propped casually against the frame, watching the exchange between the two.

"Your medical records are being sent to me. I spoke briefly with your physician in Germany. Am I right when I say you took four gunshot wounds and this amputation?"

"Yes, sir," Trevor replied, not saying anything more. He could be as quiet as he was stubborn.

"How are you holding up?" Dr. McBride started a steady stream of questions only requiring simple one-word answers while beginning the exam. The doctor peeled back the layers of bandages and checked each wound. He lifted Trevor's arm, leaning him forward, then back, the whole time asking questions about the events leading to this injury, or certain points during recovery at the German hospital. Reed stayed back, quiet, watching Trevor become absorbed in the exam and finally participating. Dr. McBride was clearly the best at distraction, and Trevor got lost in their interaction.

Reed crossed his arms over his chest and watched the exam. His gaze stayed fixed on Trevor's muscular body while he listened intently to every word the two spoke. Trevor's stunning beauty was never lost on him. It was hard not to stare at the expansive bare chest just a few feet away from him. Trevor's body looked lean and long, but broadly muscular and well defined. It took years of dedicated training and disciplined body building to be that toned and fit from head to toe. He could see Trevor put the time in. Each muscle strained and rippled with the positions the doctor placed Trevor in. From where Reed stood, he couldn't see where Trevor had lost any muscle mass from being down so long.

Reed was again taken back to his thoughts of Trevor looking like a warrior, but his face looked like he could have been sculpted by Michelangelo himself. The deep, full lips answering Dr. McBride's questions gave a natural pout when he sat quietly or slept. Those lips seemed to give Reed fits when he tried to sleep, always invading his dreams, waking him with a raging hard-on. Reed found them incredibly appealing and looked forward to years of kissing just them. Trevor's eyes were arresting, and every time that deep blue gaze landed his way, his heart flew from his chest, landing safely in Trevor's caring hands.

Lord knew, over all the days he'd sat by Trevor's bedside, Reed had more than enough time to study every part of his gorgeous face. Those pouty lips could spread easily into a brilliant smile. Trevor's high cheekbones, sculpted jaw, and strong chin softened when he smiled, yet another reason to put plenty of smiles in Trevor's life from this point forward. And Reed wanted to see many happier, smiling moments in their future. Besides, Trevor's smiles were contagious. They always caused him to stop and stare. Trevor's eyes sparkled when he got excited, much like right now. Zoning back into the conversation, Reed listened to see what had caused this smile from his otherwise somber man.

"Yes, sir. I'll take it easy. You have my word." Trevor nodded as if to affirm his declaration.

"All right then. Let's change these bandages. We won't keep your arm locked to your chest. These wounds look to be healing nicely, but you must continue to take it easy. Your strength will return, but you have to allow your body to heal in its own natural course. No pushing. As hard as this is to say, you've been lucky in your recovery. Let's keep it that way." Dr. McBride turned, looking down to Trevor's leg. "The flight wasn't easy on this leg, was it?"

"No, sir. I jerked around quite a bit."

"Let's take a look." Dr. McBride slowly removed the bandages from the wound just below his knee, making this the first time Reed had actually seen the cut. In Germany, the hospital staff required him to leave the room during any dressing changes.

Reed schooled his features, putting a tight rein on his emotions, showing no sign of the horror Trevor must have endured to cause such an injury. While Dr. McBride worked, Trevor watched Reed closely, not looking at the doctor once. Reed finally lifted his gaze to Trevor's, making sure the sorrow he felt didn't reach his stare. It took quite a bit of effort; the wound looked painful, swollen, and a deep pink.

Reed gave Trevor a quick wink and a little side grin before reaching down to adjust himself from the waning dull ache inside his pants, which hadn't quite settled since he'd opened the front door to the doctor. Hell, that wasn't completely true either. Reed had been hard since he'd watched Trevor enter the grand ballroom at the rehearsal dinner. And anytime he thought about that night, his relentless dick roared back to life again.

The movement successfully distracted Trevor, and he was again rewarded with a touch of red brightening those cheeks. A quick flash of a smile came to Trevor's lips. Reed's heart did a flip in his chest.

Dr. McBride continued the exam, not saying too much more after seeing Trevor's amputation. After every wound was bandaged, the doctor wrote out a couple of prescriptions, explaining each one to both Trevor and Reed, leaving a couple of samples to be taken now. The doctor would also be present at the rehab hospital tomorrow for Trevor's initial appointment.

"There's no reason to live with this pain right now. Take this medication as prescribed. You hear me, son?" Dr. McBride asked, looking down at Trevor.

"Yes, sir."

"Now, is that a 'yes, sir, I hear you' or a 'yes, sir, I'll take my medication'?" The doctor continued his steady stare on Trevor.

"It's a 'yes, sir' to both." Trevor smiled, taking both prescriptions and the samples from the doctor.

"Good." Reaching down, Dr. McBride extended his hand, and Trevor shook it immediately. "It's my honor to meet you. I wish it were under better circumstances."

"Thank you for coming out on such short notice." Trevor clasped his hand.

"Of course. Now take it easy on the arm until we get you assessed tomorrow." Dr. McBride finished packing his bag and snapped the buckle on the leather case. He turned back to Reed while taking the bag in his hand. Emotion played in the physician's eyes the minute he turned away from Trevor.

"I'll walk you out, Dr. McBride. Trevor, I'll be right back," Reed said. The doctor followed Reed through the house, and they stayed quiet. Once they made it past the point where there was any chance Trevor might hear, Reed turned and asked, "How does he look?"

"The wounds are healing remarkably well. It's surprising not one of them became infected. He needs to take it easy, rebuild his body. That leg looks to have had a hard time during the flight. The swelling has increased based on what they said in Germany. I want him to be seen by Dr. Conrad first thing in the morning. He's the best at this sort of injury. Trevor doesn't remember much about that night, does he?"

"No, sir, he doesn't remember much that I know of. It sounded gruesome."

"His body was ravaged. I'm not sure he should've lived through it. I want to get him some counseling, but I have a feeling we need to be inconspicuous with it all. You were right on the phone; he doesn't say too much. He doesn't seem like the kind that would go for a formal counseling session, so I'll work it into his care plan." At the front door, Dr. McBride opened it before looking back at Reed. "I'll be in touch. Keep him down. This is a good thing you're doing." Dr. McBride shook Reed's hand then left through the front door without a backward glance.

With a quick turn of the lock, Reed made his way back to the bedroom, stopping by the refrigerator to grab a cold bottle of water.

"Okay, sexy, per doctor's orders you must take this medication. I'll send out for the prescriptions to be filled. No stalling on this. You promised," Reed said. He came to the side of the bed, sitting down carefully on the mattress. He lifted the small plastic package, peeled back the foil, and let the pill pop out into his hand.

"I feel fine," Trevor began. Reed took advantage and shoved the pill into his open mouth.

"That's not true. Now swallow." After handing Trevor the water, he peeled back another wrapper, popped the tablet out, and handed it over. "If you take your meds, we'll work up to swallowing other things very soon." With a wink, Reed glued his gaze to Trevor, watching him take all his meds with a blush staining his cheeks.

"Now, there's a good boy," Reed teased, bending down to softly kiss those sweet lips, and Trevor puckered up to kiss him back as if it were the most normal thing between them.

"You taste divine," Reed added, staying close to Trevor's face, breathing him in. Holding the moment, Reed looked lovingly into Trevor's eyes. "Now, one of those will make you sleepy, but I think you're already there. Let's lay you down. You need to get some rest. I'll leave the door open. Call me if you need me. Remember, you promised the doctor no undue strain on this left side. I'll get you to the restroom when you need to go. This button on the phone acts as an intercom. Press it, and it'll find me. My home office is just through that door," Reed said, looking over at a side door to his bedroom while positioning Trevor down along the bed. He could already see Trevor was going to overexert his left arm from the way he tried to absorb his body weight and move himself down the bed.

"I have a feeling you're going to be a terrible patient, Trevor West," Reed said, kissing him on the lips again. Reed absently moved the hair from Trevor's forehead before continuing. "I'll check on you. Please sleep for me." Reed could see the fatigue in his eyes. Hopefully a good sleep would chase it away.

"Thank you for all—" Trevor interrupted himself with an unexpected yawn that ripped from his lips. Reed stayed close, staring into Trevor's mesmerizing blue eyes.

"I can see no need for any gratitude. It's nothing more than you would do for me." He reached up again. He couldn't resist gently brushing the auburn strands of hair from Trevor's brow again. "Why must I keep reminding you we're a couple?" Trevor's eyes slid closed. Reed's voice lowered. "You would think you might try to remember such important details." Reed trailed off at the sounds of Trevor's soft snores.

Pulling up the silky duvet, he covered Trevor, tucking him in the way Rylie told him Trevor liked to sleep. Apparently, Trevor liked to be bundled up tight, so Reed tucked the sides of the covers along Trevor's body. He made sure he lay comfortably on the pillows, and his leg was properly elevated.

The realization of how much Reed envied his duvet hit him hard. He desperately wanted his body to be the blanket covering this man right now. The thought struck odd, and he quietly chuckled to himself. Reed was never one for cuddling when he slept. Hell, if truth be told, Reed had never slept with another man before, nothing more than the short post-coital nap he'd had with Trevor after the wedding. But he could feel his need growing at the idea of being wrapped tightly in Trevor's arms. He knew without question his past sleeping patterns were about to change as he watched the handsome man slumbering in his bed. His heart filled with a depth of love he never knew existed before. He bent again for another careful kiss on Trevor's soft, sleeping lips. He couldn't seem to keep his lips or hands off Trevor West.

CHAPTER 19

Stretching out his long body, Trevor turned slightly in the bed, breathing in Reed's cologne. The smell sent goose bumps springing up along his arms. Oh man, he loved this dream. Reed's face took shape in his mind. A grin spread across his lips as Reed stood before him, his toned, muscular body completely naked. His long hard cock jutted out, begging for Trevor's touch.

He licked his lips in anticipation, getting ready to draw Reed's cock into his mouth. Trevor had wanted this for so long. This would be Trevor's first blow job, and he desperately wanted to please Reed. Out of nowhere, the bed jerked out from underneath him, the floor opening up. Trevor gasped as the world shifted, and he fell. Reed grabbed for him, calling out his name as he struggled to keep his own balance even while desperately attempting to grab for Trevor.

Birdseye, better known to the world as Carlos Mendez appeared at Reed's back and Trevor's chest tightened in panic. Evil practically oozed from every pore of the terrorist. Snaking black tendrils encompassed Reed like a thick fog. A sneer tore from Mendez's lips as he lifted a knife toward Reed's neck. Trevor couldn't stop the attack, and Reed didn't notice the man behind him, so focused on saving Trevor.

A gun appeared in Trevor's hand. Perfect! He would kill Carlos for thinking of hurting his Reed, but in a flash, his hands were gone and the weapon fell to his chest. His arms flailed. There were just stumps where his hands had been before. Trevor screamed for Reed to move, but Carlos reached out, grabbed the back of Reed's head, and the knife slashed forward, leaving a trail of blood across Reed's neck.

"Trevor. Trevor, wake up! Trevor West, I need you to wake up."

Jarring awake, fear gripped Trevor. His heart slammed wildly. His mind raced. His eyes remained out of focus, and he blinked, squeezed them shut, blinked again. He woke ready to fight, forcing his body past the pain, gripping the material of Reed's shirt in his right fist. The left side of his body resisted the sudden movement, shooting pain ripped across his chest and shoulder. The searing pain caused him to jerk his body backward, slamming his head against the headboard. Reality slowly sank in. Trevor took in the room, trying to gain his bearings. No terrorists. No evil surrounding the man next to him. He could breathe again. Finally, he wrapped Reed in his arms, pulling him to his chest.

"He had you! Damn it, I couldn't get to you." Trevor's breath shuddered as parts of the dream mixed with parts of the night at the compound. Wave after wave of memory crashed back, all overloading his mind. He pulled Reed tighter to him. His heart raced in his chest, threatening to break straight through his ribcage.

He remembered firing on Carlos. In slow motion, Trevor's mind replayed the moment the bullet hit the dead center of Carlos's forehead, dropping him where he stood. Thoughts of crashing through the compound window with broken glass splintering around him rushed forward. The children's screams of fear pierced his heart. The hard blow and searing burn in his shoulder when he took the first bullet intended for the child crying under his window. The memories pummeled his body as if it were happening in this moment. Trevor was falling, trying to brace himself while the bullets kept driving into his arm and leg.

Another shudder racked his body. Trevor lowered his head to Reed's shoulder, tucking his face into his neck, just breathing him in, anchoring himself in this moment, in reality. Reed stayed quiet, holding him. After a time, Trevor ran his hands up and down Reed's back. Reed gave him more comfort than he remembered having throughout most of his adult life.

After several long moments, Trevor sensed the toll this whole experience had taken on him. Not just the pain of his injuries from the tension still coiling through his body, but fear. He was afraid. And this fear felt more desolate than any he'd ever experienced before. All the memories had flooded back, and he wasn't sure how he'd lived through it all. The onslaught of emotion pouring through him threatened to drag him under. Without question, Trevor knew Reed remained his light in the deep, dark turbulence of this storm he couldn't seem to break free from. And although Trevor was completely unworthy of the man, he said a prayer of thanks for being here with Reed right now. What had he been thinking to send Reed away from him in Germany?

"After I fell, I could see it all coming down on me. I couldn't get my body to cooperate and didn't have time. I hate that they beat me. I can't believe that fucking coward insurgent beat me."

"Babe, he didn't beat you. You got him. He was a coward and died a coward's death. You made sure of that. The reports of what went on in that compound sound horrific. Those men deserved to die for what they did to their women and children alone. Not to mention the horror and pain they caused around the world. They didn't beat you, Trevor. Actually, it's quite the opposite."

Trevor stayed quiet, comforted by Reed's deep, rich, soothing voice and kind words. He kissed Reed's neck and turned his head, laying it again on Reed's shoulder.

"I woke up while they were taking my leg. The pain was so bad, Reed."

"I know, I heard. I can't imagine what you must have gone through," Reed said quietly.

Trevor pulled back, looking at Reed for several long moments. He reached up, touching Reed's cheek, trying to force a small smile, but nothing would come. His heart was just too heavy. Reed seemed to sense his struggle and leaned in to kiss his lips. Reed still kept a tight hold on him; he didn't seem ready to let him go.

"I truly can't imagine and am at a loss as to what to say. I hoped you wouldn't ever remember the pain. Rylie told us you woke when he called. The pain in his voice for what you went through almost did me in. It was more than I could bear for you."

Trevor pulled completely out of Reed's arms, needing to be done with this conversation. It was all too much. Trevor didn't like the pity Reed held in his eyes. His stomach let out a grumble of angry protest, saving him from having to say anything more. He hadn't eaten since before the plane ride. Reed's brows lifted. The look in his eyes changed instantly, holding an amused twinkle.

"Dinner's ready. And just in time, I think. It sounds like you're hungry?"

"I am, but it's hard for me to have you doing all this." While Trevor spoke, he lifted his arm, doing small rotations of his left arm and shoulder. The pain wasn't bad, so he increased the circles in his range of motion, going as far as pain would allow while looking over at the bedside clock. "It's eight thirty at night? Wow, I slept all day. I'm sorry."

"You need rest, sexy. Bodies heal while we're sleeping. It's critical at this stage of the game. Let's get you to the restroom, and I'll bring dinner in. Come on. Let's get you up," Reed said, pulling Trevor from the bed.

The move to the restroom turned out to be a much easier process now that his arm was no longer bound to his side. Being able to use his left hand and arm made all the difference. Trevor's left leg was still sore but not unbearable. The movement and swing of his leg only caused a mild throbbing, something he could easily live with.

The restroom matched the bedroom on the spectacular factor, with a wide sunken bathtub and a massive open shower. Reed helped Trevor to the commode, giving him a minute, then to the sink, handing him a hand towel and showing Trevor a drawer with toothpaste, shaving supplies, and an assortment of colognes and hair gel, all in brand-new bottles.

"This is what I wear," Trevor said, surprise crossing his face. He lifted the bottle of cologne. "How did you know?"

"I love your smell. When I took you home after the bachelor party, I saw it on your dresser. I remembered it. You also wore it the first time we were together. I'll never forget that night. Now, I'm going to step outside the door and give you a few moments alone. Please use whatever you need. Call when you're finished. Then I'll get you back to bed."

Reed spoke casually, saying it all with his hip perched against the granite countertop where he stood. His arms crossed casually over his broad chest, his eyes staring playfully at Trevor. The moment lasted until Trevor tugged his gaze away. Years of practice taught Trevor to hide his spastic nerves, but the blush always gave him away. Hearing those words from Reed made everything right in his heart, but the heat staining his cheeks robbed him of any reply he may have wanted to make. A moment later, Reed stepped outside the bathroom door with that sexy grin in place.

Trevor watched Reed's retreat in the mirror, not looking at himself until the door closed with a decidedly loud click. Then he turned his gaze to the decorative mirror and horror flashed through his eyes as he quickly raked his fingers through his hair. It didn't help. His auburn hair stood in every direction, and his face was in desperate need of a close shave. Trevor's teeth looked as fuzzy as they felt, and he was sure the breath coming from a mouth looking like his couldn't be pleasant at all.

With a critical eye, Trevor looked himself over. Even at his best, he just couldn't see how someone like him could capture the attention of someone like Reed. Trevor loved hearing all those sweet, easily said terms of endearment. All those small hints of love at first sight always stole his heart. He desperately wanted all those romantically sweet fairytales to be true. But Trevor just couldn't see how this man in the mirror was able to capture the attention, let alone the heart, of a man like Reed Kensington.

He forced the wayward thoughts from his mind once again. Even if everything Reed did and said were laced with pity, he would take it for as long as it was offered. Trevor would worry about the future tomorrow. Tonight, he needed to focus on a shave and clean teeth, then food in his stomach. Making fast work of the necessities, Trevor slowly headed to the door. Reed stood ready, grabbing him by the waist, helping him back to his bed.

"I think I could handle dinner at the kitchen table. You don't have to serve me dinner in bed," Trevor said, leaning into Reed as he moved his leg forward step after step.

"Oh, really? I believe that's completely against the advice of your physician, who wants you in bed, resting for tomorrow," Reed said, halting their progress to the mattress, giving Trevor a look that caused him to laugh out loud.

"My mom used to give me that exact same look. For her, it would usually be followed with her signature line, 'Trevor we have to find your brain. It just fell out of your head.'"

Reed's laughter showed in his eyes while he started them forward again. "I've spent the last ten days with you, and I must admit your mother's expression does have merit. Now, handsome, lie down. I'll be back with dinner. No argument, please."

Gingerly, Trevor pulled himself up against the headboard, pulling his leg up, tucking the pillows behind his back. Reed stayed close by, wanting to help, judging by the look in his eyes, but allowed Trevor to do much of it on his own.

After a couple of minutes, Reed seemed satisfied Trevor was settled and handed him the remote before leaving to retrieve their dinner. He flipped on the television and searched the channels while rotating his shoulder, carefully moving his left arm back and forth, gently extending his range of motion. The best Trevor could tell, his left side was stiff but good and working reasonably well, all things considered. Based on the little he knew, he felt like his first goal should be to get to the point of using crutches to get around.

A major news network caught his attention. The anchor recapped his team's military raid and what they now knew from the foreign authorities. Turning the volume up, Trevor listened closely. This was the first report he'd heard since the mission, and apparently the foreign government didn't take breaching their border lightly, which really wasn't all that unexpected. They also released statements to the United Nations that they had no knowledge the drug lord was hiding within their country's borders. All the missing pieces slid together. He'd heard just bits of conversation in the hospital and from Anthony. Apparently, the president of the United States had watched them through the helmet video during the raid. Trevor saw pictures of the situation room while the president and his cabinet sat watching the military work.

He thought it was all pretty cool until it came to the report about the hurt soldier. The reporter had quite a bit of information about him. They knew all his injuries, his amputation, his age, rank, marital status—pretty much everything but his name.

A panel of physicians trained in Trevor's types of injuries split the screen, speculating about what it would take to amputate a leg while in the field. A military adviser spoke of the strain and emotional turmoil not only on Trevor but his entire team as a result of the amputation. The news network reported Trevor left the German hospital early that morning and now stayed in an undisclosed location back in the States, and that his progress was good. They also reported the military public relations department had received thousands of inquiries, cards, and letters on his behalf.

Reed came through the bedroom door, carrying a tray of food. Two plates, napkins, silverware, and drinks were balanced strategically on top. Clicking the volume down, Trevor's stomach gave a solid, loud growl at the smells coming from the plates.

"That smells delicious." Trevor loved those homemade enchiladas from Reed's mom, and his mouth watered with anticipation. "Did she really make enough to feed an army? I seriously think I could eat that much."

Reed brought the tray to him, fitting the legs perfectly over his thighs. Reed took a minute to make sure he was situated before making his way to the other side of the bed.

"She did. And extra spicy. I need to remember my boyfriend likes it hot," Reed said, giving him a wink while kicking off his shoes. Reed pushed himself onto the bed close to Trevor, resting his back against the headboard. They sat side by side now, mostly on his side of the bed.

"You need to eat to keep your energy up. Rehab starts tomorrow." Reed picked up the napkin and placed it across his lap before moving the second plate from the tray onto his own lap. "What're your thoughts on what you just heard?" he asked, pointing with his fork to the television, reaching for the remote with his other hand.

"It's actually all pretty accurate, I think, at least from where I stood," Trevor said, looking over as Reed turned the volume up a little.

"I started listening to part of this earlier. It's a rebroadcast. I know what Rylie told me on the phone, but I was in the hospital with you. I haven't heard all the details yet. You and your team are heroes, and no one will ever know who you are. None of the women or children were killed that night. Some were shot and injured, but so far no one has died. They show images of the men opening fire. I think that video probably came from your helmet. It looks like the angle you were in from what Rylie says."

Trevor stayed quiet, listening to Reed and the television. He remembered using his mirror to see the frightened children in the room and the hate radiating from the insurgents inside. Trevor just didn't understand how things got so out of control to have grown men shooting at children. He lowered his head and bent forward a little, concentrating on his food, but he wasn't eating. His mind couldn't force away the image of the insurgent barreling into the room, opening fire. How did he not kill some of those children?

"I have two thousand channels and rarely watch much TV. Let's see what's on. Do you have any favorite shows? You know, these are probably things I should learn about you," Reed asked casually, effectively pulling Trevor from his spiraling thoughts. Reed's last line was the perfect diversion. Trevor looked over at Reed, finally taking another bite. He paused. He wanted Reed to know how he truly felt about the mission and his job.

"We aren't heroes. None of us see it that way at all. I look at guys like you and think you're the hero. You save peoples' lives every day. You saved mine at the expense of yourself. I just did a job I was trained and paid to do. That's it. No man wants to see children hurt. Mendez kicked a pregnant woman in the stomach. He was gonna have to die because that was my job, but after I saw that... He needed to die sooner rather than later. The guy who opened fire on the room wasn't targeting me or Grigsby in the other window. He came to target those children. He needed to die too. It doesn't make me a hero."

"In my book, it does. In most of the world's books it does, too, but I see what you're saying about how it should be in the world."

Trevor turned back to the food, a frown wrinkling his brow. He was just so uncomfortable with the talk of heroes. He didn't see it that way at all.

"No, handsome, don't pull away from me. And I want you

to keep eating. You need your strength. Besides, I think that's the most you've said to me at one time since the bachelor party. And oh, how I loved the bachelor party. It's the night I knew for sure that you were the one for me," Reed said, shoveling a fork full of food in his mouth. Then he pointed his fork to Trevor's plate, encouraging him to eat.

"That seems like so long ago. I still don't remember the bachelor party. I should have never gotten that drunk. Care to share yet?" Trevor asked with a wince.

"Only after you start eating again," Reed said, then waited, eyeing him with a slight grin until Trevor took a bite. "Let's see, I'll tell you I was greatly disappointed that you didn't call me after meeting you at the rehearsal dinner. I kept telling myself you would call. That you had to feel the pull between us. I bet I checked my phone a hundred times to make sure it still worked. I told my assistant to put every call through, not to screen any of them in hopes it would be you. I ended up talking to an energy company trying to save me money from my current electric provider. As it turned out, they were my current electric provider, who knew? I also spoke to a home security company. Did you know one in four homes is burglarized every twelve minutes? I know, shocking. But none of those calls were you, Mr. West, and my heart and confidence was left in tatters. I couldn't wait to see you that night." Reed looked up from his plate. Trevor's blush was back, but he was also eating again.

"I remember being in the club, winning second place in foosball, and I remember women dancing," Trevor said between bites. "I was afraid the strippers were dancing on me based on the flashbacks I had when I woke. I'm embarrassed as to what I did. I never sleep in the nude, and I woke that way. I'm nervous. I don't drink a lot."

"Yes, I do believe those were the words you said to me, perhaps right before you threw up," Reed said, laughing when Trevor choked on the peach-flavored iced tea his mother had left for them.

"Oh God, I threw up? Did I throw up on you?" Trevor did a sideways wince, looking over at Reed, not quite able to make eye contact.

"Oh no, don't worry. I wasn't in the line of fire. You stumbled away from me, but your pants were around your ankles, making it hard for you to move too quickly." Reed took a bite of food, a wicked grin curling the corners of his lips. Trevor could see Reed struggling to hold his composure over the laughter he wanted to let loose.

"Damn, it's worse than I thought," Trevor groaned, dropping his head back against the headboard.

"No, no, you must eat. No more storytelling until you eat a few more bites, handsome. Besides, it was the day I fell in love with you. It will always be one of the most special days in my life. Now eat, and if you're a good boy and eat everything on your plate, I'll tell you what happened to your bathroom in Rylie's apartment." Reed chuckled, reaching over to cut a bite of Trevor's enchiladas. He lifted the fork to feed him. It took a minute for Trevor to open his mouth, but he finally did. "I love it when you blush, Trevor."

Trevor chewed quickly. "I don't think I can take hearing any more. Did I say I don't drink very much?"

"Yes, you've said that a few times, both now and then as well. Let's get some of our relationship formalities out of the way. What's your favorite ice cream?" Reed asked, his empty plate balanced on his lap. He reached over again, cutting another piece of enchilada. He lifted the fork to Trevor's mouth. "Eat, handsome. Your new antibiotics are strong. You need to take them on a full stomach, babe."

"Ice Cream? Hmm...is vanilla too boring to say? I also like praline pecan. I don't eat it much, but your mom always has it when we visit." Trevor took a bite, chewing. He lifted a finger, pointing at Reed, motioning for him to answer his own question.

"Well, now this is a hard question. There are so many delicious flavors... Chocolate chip cookie dough, chocolate almond, Cherry Garcia..." Reed cut another bite, lifting it to Trevor.

"I've always wanted to try Cherry Garcia. I think it would probably move to the top of my list. I like cherries. Can't see how that would be anything but great," Trevor replied, before opening for the bite.

"It's very good. We'll pick some up tomorrow on the way home. It may just become your favorite. Now, what's your preferred way to eat your eggs?"

"Scrambled, and you?" Trevor answered quickly, then chewed as Reed took the opening, and stuck another bite in his mouth.

"Also scrambled. What's your favorite color?"

"Camo, duh."

They both laughed. Reed handed Trevor his drink before gathering up the dishes onto the tray. Scooting to the end of the bed, Reed got up. "Would you like another plate? There's plenty."

"No, I'm good. I'm full and it's delicious. I need to call your mom." Trevor dusted off the duvet, pulling it up to cover his boxers.

"Here, keep your tea. You have meds to take. Mom and Dad as well as Elise stopped by. They send their love. No one wanted to wake you. They'll come by tomorrow night," Reed called over his shoulder as he left the room with the tray.

"What's your favorite color?" Trevor asked when Reed came back into the room. He stood by the bed with a handful of pills.

"My new favorite color is cerulean blue, which coincidentally is the color of your eyes. Ah...and there's my reward, my second favorite, the color of your blush. Now here you go, beautiful. Let's see here, we have all the colors of the rainbow...a huge red one, a tiny purple one, and this odd-shaped peach one. Which first? Or are you man enough to take them all at once?"

Trevor grinned, raising his eyebrows at the challenge. Reed

dropped them all in Trevor's hand. He swallowed them all in a single go.

"Now, there's a big boy. Trevor West, I do believe you're an expert swallower. Now I'm excited to learn for myself. We'll test the theory again later." Reed winked and kept going, not giving Trevor time to truly absorb the words. "The tiny purple one is a badass antibiotic, the red one is for pain, and the odd-shaped one is an anti-inflammatory for your leg." Taking the tea, Reed placed it on the nightstand before turning to his closet. "It's been a long day and the meds will make you tired. Do you need to use the restroom again?" he asked, making his way to his closet, pulling his shirt free of the waistband of his jeans.

"I can wait, just maybe before bed. You look tired." Trevor's eyes followed Reed while he opened the door to his closet. Reed stepped in but didn't shut the door behind him. Trevor could see him clearly as he pulled off his clothes.

Reed shook out a pair of pajama pants, pulling the new tags free of the fabric. Trevor could see Reed's brow furrowing as he held the pants up, letting the legs fall down while they unfolded. "Why would people wear such a thing to sleep in?" Reed's muttering made him smile.

Laughing, Trevor forced his eyes away, but Reed's comment shed some light on why he'd been put to bed with no clothes on after the bachelor party.

"I'm tired," Reed finally said from the closet. "I wanted everything to be ready for you, so I took a couple of weeks off work. I spent last night transitioning files. It didn't go so well. I wasn't as thorough as I thought. I received several phone calls today. I may be pulled away now and again to answer questions for my staff, but my time should easily be yours."

"It's fine. I hate to be a burden to you."

"You couldn't be a burden, handsome." Reed came from the closet, the pajama pants hanging low on his hips, his lean, muscular chest bare. The small patch of hair leading down into the pajama pants showed just enough to make Trevor want to see more.

"Come on. Let's get you to the restroom," Reed said, helping him up and across the room. The movement became easier each time they did it. Trevor's shoulder and arm were sorer than before but being able to use the arm was critical to his success in getting in and out of bed on his own. After everything was done, Reed settled Trevor back in bed before grabbing a few pillows from the guest room. Turning off the lights, Reed climbed in on the other side of the bed.

"This is another first for me, babe. I've never slept with a man in my bed. It feels comforting to have you here with me." Reed stayed on his side of the bed, adjusting the pillows behind his head. He pulled the duvet up around him.

"It's new for me too," Trevor said. He could feel his eyes already drooping. The meds were making him drowsy. Reed leaned in on one elbow and kissed Trevor lightly on the lips before turning the TV off, plunging them into darkness.

"Good night. Wake me up if you need anything. Promise me."

"I will. Good night. Thank you for everything, Reed. I don't know how I got so lucky to have you in my life..." Trevor's voice trailed off, becoming soft and quiet as he fell asleep.

CHAPTER 20

The red blinking numbers of the clock seared into Reed's brain. It was now three fifty-three in the morning, and he wondered if anyone else knew the clock slightly blinked approximately thirty-three times every single minute, over and over again. Reed knew this with all certainty because he lay in this bed since ten forty-five last night, ready to sleep. Now, five hours and eight minutes later, he was still awake. Awake with a raging hard-on and stupid pajama pants that kept twisting around his ankles.

All Reed wanted to do was sleep. After the first hour and a half, he'd snuck to the bathroom, quietly rubbing one off, hoping the release would make him sleepy. No such luck.

Every time Trevor exhaled, his dick thought it was time to stand up and take notice.

Approximately an hour and a half after that, Reed repeated

the bathroom run, trying to find relief yet again. At one point, he drifted off to sleep, but the terrible pajama pants, which Reed decidedly determined should be outlawed by the federal government as cruel and unusual punishment, tangled around his ankles yet again. Seriously, who really wore these things to sleep in, and why in the hell would anyone invent something as dumb as pajama pants? Clearly no one in their right mind! His normal sleeping habits included no clothing at all, the way normal people should sleep every single night.

Reed ran his palms over his face.

What am I doing? What was I thinking bringing him to my bed?

The feel of Trevor's body next to his, so close yet so far away, had him tied up in knots. Reed didn't know if he was coming or going. Every one of his thoughts centered on some memory of Trevor. Hearing his laughter or seeing his brief smile when their eyes met felt like some sort of great reward to him. A prize he felt completely undeserving of, which made it that much more treasured.

Truly, every one of Reed's life goals had changed the moment he saw Trevor enter the grand hall at the rehearsal dinner party. Now all he wanted in life was to have Trevor stop thanking him so much and commit himself to their relationship and to Reed forever. Hell, if Trevor would just admit there may be an opportunity for a relationship, he may just fall to his knees, thanking the world for the blessing.

Frustrated with his whole line of thinking, Reed kicked the sheets and duvet off his body and pushed himself from the bed. His gaze lowered to Trevor, who continued to sleep like a baby as if it were perfectly normal to be lying in bed with your clothes on next to a man you desperately wanted to touch but didn't want to freak out. God, he wished he was the blanket covering Trevor. That blanket got way more action than he did, and jealousy spiked through his heart.

As Reed stood there, he knew without question, when Trevor was healed, he would do whatever it took to spend every night wrapped in his arms. He would tuck his body close so Trevor would never have need for another blanket again. Or sleepwear. Reed needed to add that to the wish as well.

Pushing the frustratingly binding material down his legs, Reed kicked the pajama pants into the air toward the waste basket. The cool air conditioning hit his lower body, and he paced the room. His eyes stayed on Trevor. He looked beautiful, sleeping so peacefully.

Reed had always considered this room to be his only true private space. No one came inside this room. Most only made it as far as the guest room. The close proximity of the guest room to the front door was the very reason he'd bought this house.

A small prickle of insecurity rippled through his heart. The idea of losing Trevor worried him. It caused him to doubt himself and question all the signals Trevor had given him. Reed absolutely did not want a pity or appreciation style relationship with Trevor. Right now, those seemed to be Trevor's only thoughts. So, he would continue to go against his basic needs, and wait to define them, to secure the words of commitment his heart desperately needed to hear from Trevor. Until then, he would help Trevor as best he could.

A new resolve for his original plan made him strong again. In the meantime, if he slid into bed wearing nothing more than a grin, surely Trevor wouldn't mind. Reed would easily explain it, talk it through with him, and make Trevor understand how the evil in the world certainly must have created the concept of pajama pants. Maybe if he scooted close to Trevor in the middle of the night, lying against his good side while possibly resting his head on Trevor's good shoulder, breathing his scent deep into his body, Trevor would just have to accept his irresistibility. And not be freaked out too badly when Reed licked his way up Trevor's neck on occasion or nipped at the sweet lobe of the man's ear. Truly, it was all Trevor's fault anyway. The man was just too hot for his own good.

   With those crazy thoughts running rampant through Reed's mind, he lifted the covers and carefully crawled into bed with a sigh for his newfound freedom between the sheets. After a moment, Reed inched himself against Trevor's right side. He loved the feel of Trevor's skin against his. He then tugged his pillow over right next to Trevor's pillow. He placed a kiss on his shoulder, checking the urge to lick any part of Trevor's chest. The feel of the man against his body was better than any sleep aid he could have taken. Reed yawned quietly, closed his eyes, and fell asleep with his hand tucked sweetly into Trevor's.

CHAPTER 21

Trevor woke to the sounds and smell of sizzling bacon. He looked up to see the sun filtering through the window shades. It seemed early. The clock on the opposite nightstand was turned away from the bed, making it impossible to read the time.

He looked over at the side Reed had slept on. The linens were barely creased, and the spot vacant. Reed's head print dented the pillow, but the pillow was pushed closer to his. It looked like they both slept on the same side of the bed.

Trevor brought the pillow to his face, breathing in Reed's masculine scent, letting it fill his soul, caressing and comforting like nothing ever had before. Trevor loved the smell of Reed and loved the idea of sleeping all night in bed with this man. He envisioned himself to be a cuddler. He liked the thought of lying wrapped up with someone, and he hoped Reed might someday sleep tucked in his arms.

The pain in his shoulder, fortunately, wasn't unbearable as Trevor pulled himself up to lean against the headboard. He rotated his shoulder to find the movement did hurt this morning, but the discomfort felt more like an overworked, sore muscle, not that of a new injury.

He rose quietly, trying to be as careful as he could. The pain wasn't bad, a little worse than last night, but he managed through it. He found the equilibrium of his balance easier than any time before, and he held onto the bed for leverage, slowly scooting his foot along the carpet. The pain grew, but he forced himself through it, causing a sheen of sweat to cross his brow while he moved along.

He anchored himself across the furniture. Trevor used his arms to pull himself along to the bathroom, doing it all while pushing through the pain. The effort caused all the muscles in his leg and arms to quiver as he finally reached for the door. He looked down at the waste basket and saw the pajama pants Reed had worn to bed last night. Their discarded state caused him to chuckle. Apparently, they must not have been a big hit if they were already in the trash.

Once inside the bathroom, Trevor sat on the side of the tub, catching his breath while trying to work out the strain in his shoulder. The entire left side of his body hurt under the exertion of getting into the bathroom. Every muscle was tight, pulling and straining with each of his movements. Trevor let his gaze fall to his leg. It still took some getting used to, not seeing a foot attached. Self-pity filled him and tears came, but he pushed those away. At this point, it was nothing but counterproductive to focus on what he'd lost.

Trevor rose with the help of the expensive-looking granite countertop. Glancing around the bathroom, he realized again that Reed lived an amazingly opulent life. This bathroom was spacious, very modern with lots of granite tile and polished marble. The color choices were the same patterns as his bedroom.

The house wasn't a sprawling mansion, but it was large, highly decorated, and comfortable. Reed had to make good money to afford something this nice.

Balancing himself, Trevor made his way to the shower, trying to reach the soap and shampoo. He couldn't get his leg wet. The rest of his body was still heavily bandaged, but he needed to clean himself as completely as possible. He made it to the sink, leaning his hip against the counter. He washed his body with a hand towel before ducking his head under the sink, washing his hair under the spray of warm water. Under normal circumstances, he showered a couple of times a day, every day. Cleaning himself now brought a sense of normalcy back into his life. After brushing his teeth, Trevor pulled the shaving gear from the drawer. He did a quick shave before running his towel over the water droplets on the counter.

Trevor stood, looking into the mirror, rotating his left arm. He watched the strain of his tight muscles as he tried to get a larger, fuller range of motion. He left the restroom the same way he'd come in, this time using it more as a workout. The stretching and bending pulled his muscles. The trip to the bathroom had exhausted him, but again, it wasn't terrible. This minor achievement gave him hope as he climbed back into bed, tugging the covers into place, before dropping his head back against the headboard. Reed came through the bedroom door with a tray of food.

"Good morning, handsome. I hope you slept well." Reed came to a dead stop in the middle of the room. He looked at Trevor with an accusing frown. "Did you get out of bed?"

"I did. How did you sleep?" Trevor lifted his head, thinking again how handsome Reed was. Morning looked good on the man. The long silk robe Reed wore looked brand new, much like the pajama pants he had worn last night.

"Trevor, you promised. You're a frustrating patient. You shouldn't have gotten up on your own. In a few days maybe, but not now. It's not a weakness to let your body heal." Reed narrowed his eyes as he walked closer to the bed.

"What's on the tray?" Trevor asked, ignoring Reed's choice of conversation.

"Please let me help you. I don't want you to fall and re-injure yourself," Reed said, waiting for Trevor to nod before he continued. Reed gave a frustrated sigh when he finally did. "I have scrambled eggs, bacon, toast, and the fried potatoes my mother swears you like. I think you must have some spicy southern ancestry running through your veins with all the jalapeños you seem to eat." Reed came closer to the bed, preparing to place the tray in front of him, but Trevor lifted his hand, reaching up to slide under Reed's robe. A grin spread across his lips at finding Reed completely nude and hardening in his hand.

"I suppose those pajamas in the trash can weren't your thing?" he asked, lifting his gaze to Reed as he stroked his thickening cock. Reed's arousal jerked, growing rock hard while Trevor continued to tease him, running his thumb over the broad head now sticking out through the robe. He loved how Reed's cock felt like hardened steel wrapped in warm velvet. His own arousal grew with the knowledge he had such an effect on Reed.

"Mmmm, you're playing with fire. I've wanted your touch too badly not to respond. Babe, I..." Reed's breathing deepened and his hips began a sultry move. The tray was still in his hands, but his eyes were closed, and his head rolled back between his shoulders.

"I've wanted to do this since I was here on our first date. There're lots of things I want to do," Trevor said. He reached both hands under the robe, stroking Reed's cock and gently rolling the tender sac underneath. "Reed, let me taste you before we eat. I've dreamed about blowing you."

Trevor strained his body, reaching forward, trying to pull himself up enough to take Reed into his mouth. Reed still held the tray in his hands. His eyes were closed. Trevor continued to stroke back and forth, but his movements and position were awkward, causing pain to sear through his chest and hip. He gripped Reed a little harder than he'd intended while trying to bear the discomfort to keep Reed from stepping away.

"Mmmm, Trevor, you undo me so effortlessly. Let's make this easier on you." Setting the tray down on a small bedside table, Reed went around to the other side. Untying the sash, Reed flipped open his robe, removing it quickly before tossing it in the general direction of the trash can his pajama pants were in. He climbed on the mattress, placing himself on the right of Trevor at the headboard. Reed stayed on his knees to give him better access. Trevor didn't hesitate. He took hold of Reed, licking his lips while bringing the hard cock straight to his mouth.

The feel and taste of Reed gliding across his lips, along his tongue, and deep into his mouth caused Trevor's own hips to involuntarily jerk forward. His eyes rolled back in his head, closing on their own. Reed tasted like the most erotic dream he could ever remember. He wrapped his tongue around the tender underside of Reed's thick cock and pulled slowly back until only the very tip was left inside his mouth. Trevor took a moment to languidly stroke the broad head, lapping small beads of moisture that gathered on the tip.

Lifting his eyes, Trevor gauged Reed's reaction to make sure he was receiving the same pleasure that Trevor was from doing this. He gripped the base of Reed's erection and stroked slowly back and forth. With his left hand, he reached lower, running his fingertips against Reed's thigh before gently massaging the retracting sac.

It took Trevor a minute, but he created a rhythm between his hand and his mouth, taking Reed deeper, in and out, back and forth, from tip to base, repeatedly. The taste of Reed's pre-come mingled with the feel of the cock moving in and out of his mouth, letting Trevor know he did everything perfectly. With the buck of Reed's hips, Trevor closed his eyes, pushing Reed deeper into his throat, preparing for the release to fill his mouth. He wasn't sure just what to expect but grew excited and hungry at the prospect. Instead, Reed pushed him away, pulling himself from Trevor's mouth.

"What's wrong?" Trevor asked, his eyes darting open.

"If you keep doing that, I won't last much longer," Reed replied, keeping himself just out of Trevor's reach. Reed panted, lowering his upper body until he rested on all fours, about a foot from where Trevor lay.

"I can't see why that's a bad thing." Trevor's statement came out as more of a question than the statement he'd intended. Reed continued to fight him as Trevor reached for him again.

"It is when I want it to last. I don't want to come until you do, but are you sure you're ready for this? I'm prepared to wait as long as I need to." Reed pushed back farther on the bed when Trevor reached out again for him. He'd never done anything like this; all of this was still so new to him. He wanted to experience it all with Reed. He loved the feel of Reed's cock in his mouth, the hard yet velvety feel of it as it slid across his tongue, and the salty taste of his pre-come made his taste buds beg for more.

"I'm ready, really ready. I want you, Reed. I want to make love to you. Please."

Reed's gaze intensified. Trevor knew he was deciding whether this would hurt him in any way. He pushed the duvet down, rising forward to show Reed he meant every word. Reed surged toward Trevor. He quickly captured their lips together in an earth-shattering kiss. Reed worked the duvet to their feet, forcing him down on his back. The kiss turned urgent and demanding. Reed thrust his tongue deep into Trevor's eager mouth. He carefully laid his body all along Trevor's. Trevor wrapped his arms completely around Reed, wanting him even closer. He brushed his fingertips and palms up and down Reed's broad back, down to his perfectly tight ass.

Everything about Reed drew Trevor in. His heart hammered in his chest. His cock pushed hard against his boxers, begging to be released. Reed seemed to innately know. He reached low, sliding his hand straight into Trevor's boxers. A hiss escaped his lips when Reed's fingers gripped his aching cock, stroking him while using his thumb to massage small circles over his tip. Oh damn, Trevor loved that move. He pulled away from the kiss. A loud protesting moan slid from Reed's parted lips.

"Listen to me, Reed. I told you on the balcony I wanted to know what it felt like to be inside you. If my team hadn't been called away, we would have already explored so much more. Life is precious, and I don't want to wait any longer. I need to make love to you. Please, let me." Leaning on his right arm, Trevor pushed Reed over, carefully sliding his left leg forward between Reed's now parted thighs. Every instinct guided Trevor to bury himself deep inside this man. The movement was a little shaky, but Trevor managed to pull himself over and slightly on top of Reed. He thrust his tongue deep into Reed's mouth, binding them together. Reed eagerly returned the kiss while lying slowly down on his back, taking Trevor with him.

They held each other, moving carefully. Trevor lowered his legs while Reed spread his thighs, lifting his knees to cradle Trevor just where he wanted to be. This was the exact position Trevor had dreamed of every day and night since he'd met Reed at the hotel bar.

Trevor tried to rise, using the right side of his body, while Reed reached over to the nightstand and pulled a small bottle and condom from a side drawer. Their lips refused to part from the urgency of the kiss. Lifting himself with his right arm, Trevor reached low to push his boxers farther down. His left leg bumped into Reed's knee. Pain seared, shooting straight up into his body. The unexpected feeling caused Trevor to jerk free of the kiss, hissing against Reed's lips.

The sudden movement made him unstable, and Trevor toppled back down on Reed's chest. Beneath him, Reed held completely still. Trevor took deep breaths, letting the pain end before lifting his gaze, not quite able to meet Reed's. Reed was on him immediately, helping him back over onto his back.

"Reed, God, I just wanted to be inside you. I want to know what that feels like, what you feel like. Damn it, don't stop."

Trevor ran his hand up over his face and into his hair, the pain dissipating under the gentle touch. He kept hold of Reed, not letting him leave their embrace. He used the strength in his good arm to keep Reed anchored along that side of his body when he tried to pull away. Pain be damned, he wasn't letting another day go by where he felt helpless. He was anything but that.

"We have plenty of time. Let's get you healthy before we tackle such an undertaking," Reed murmured, trying again to pull away, but Trevor held fast.

"No, don't leave. Please stay here with me. I'm okay. I can do it." Tears threatened to fall, and, dear lord, wasn't that just the worst thing that could possibly happen at this moment? Reed pulled free of the hold, rising, and pushing back, almost out of his grip. "Please, Reed. Let me just have this moment. I know I'm asking a lot, but I need to know what you feel like."

"Trevor, babe, I don't want to hurt you, and we will if we continue this. It won't be too much longer, I promise. Until then, there are other ways to relieve some of this pressure." Reed came closer but kept a distance between them. Trevor never let go of him.

"You don't understand. I don't care about the pain. My feelings for you are so strong. The entire time I ran through that fucking jungle, I thought of what it was like to make love to you. I thought about the night in the hotel, and it was the thought of being with you again that helped me fight to stay alive. When I was lying in that fucking basement, trying to focus on keeping my weapon ready with rubble falling all around, it was your face that filled my mind. I smiled at you as the blackness crept in from the sides, taking me under. And fuck, Reed, I knew then, like I know now…" Trevor shook his head before continuing, "I don't see you staying with me long term. I'm not dumb. Please, I just want to feel you surrounding me now." Desperation filled Trevor's voice, but he couldn't control it.

Flashes of anger filled Reed's eyes, but Trevor quickly lifted his hand to Reed's lips, silencing him.

"No, listen to me. At some point you'll see me for who I am. It's not the injury. It's me. I'm boring, with very little to offer you. And I just want to have this memory to hang on to. I feel like this is love, Reed. I know without a doubt I'll love you for the rest of my life. No one will ever take your place in my heart. I... I know it hasn't been long, and I get I'm freaking you out, but it doesn't change this inside me. Please let me try again. I can handle the pain. I promise. It wasn't terrible." While Trevor confessed what was in his heart, Reed watched him intently, slowly lowering back down alongside his body.

Every emotion Trevor could name flashed through Reed's emerald eyes until he noticed they finally remained soft and focused only on his face. It took a moment before Reed responded. He ran his fingertips gently over Trevor's lips and jaw.

"I'm somewhat at a loss for words, which is rare for me. You touch my heart like no one ever has before. Only time will show you the truth in my words, but you must know I'm madly in love with you. I have been since I first spoke your name while sitting across from you at the hotel bar. I want nothing more than to be here with you, by your side. Your happiness is my only happiness. I love you completely, Trevor," Reed whispered while rising up to capture his lips.

The kiss was the most passionate of his life. Reed kissed him like their souls were connecting, binding them into one being. Trevor thrust his tongue forward, but Reed consumed him, caressing his tongue with a wet velvety stroke before diving and delving into the far reaches of his mouth. Then Reed abruptly tore free, pulling his body up.

"Trevor, lean against the headboard. Let me lift your leg, babe." Reed worked quickly, pulling him free of his boxers and stuffing pillows behind his back. Trevor couldn't seem to keep his hands off Reed, touching anything within his reach, while he positioned him. "I'm willing to give in to your demands because my need for you is overriding my common sense...but if you hurt, you need to let me know. We'll think of other ways to pleasure one another."

When Reed seemed satisfied with how he sat, he reached across the bed to where he'd left the condoms and lubricant. Reed quickly kissed him. Trevor ran his fingertips over and over Reed's hard abs, and then around to his tight perfect ass, sliding his fingers into carefully massage Reed's tight rim. Reed straddled his hips, being careful of his leg, never putting his full weight on Trevor.

"I don't want to hurt you, Trevor. You must tell me if I do. I'll reposition until we work it out. Promise me you won't stay in pain. There are many ways to make this happen for you." Reed stopped what he was doing until Trevor gave a small nod. The concern and love Trevor saw in Reed's eyes had him pulling Reed to him for another deep kiss. He rolled his hips forward, pushing his cock against Reed's, loving the feel of them mingling together. Reed tore from the kiss and rose. He watched Reed slide a condom on his shaft before applying several drops of cold liquid straight onto his rigid length. The cold sensation startled him, but the lube quickly warmed when Reed reached between their bodies to stroke him.

"I've dreamed about you being inside me," Reed whispered into his lips, stroking him back and forth while running his nose along Trevor's jaw and down across his neck.

"I love hearing you say that."

Trevor's eyes rolled in the back of his head as Reed lifted his body, rubbing Trevor's engorged tip against his opening. Reed slowly worked himself onto Trevor's hard cock. Trevor tried to watch Reed lower himself, but the sensations were too strong. He dropped his head back against the headboard. He gripped and stroked Reed's thick cock, while rolling his hips forward. This was so much better than he'd ever imagined. Their new position allowed him to fully relax into the sensations flowing through him. He groaned as Reed slowly rocked his hips back and forth, taking Trevor inch by delicious inch until he was buried deep in his body.

"Yess...baby...yes," Reed hissed, lifting his hips. "So good. Trevor, I love you."

Trevor slid out to the tip before Reed ground down against him, repeating the move in a steady rhythm. Reed robbed Trevor of all his senses yet gave him the entire world as his orgasm swept through his body, driving him deeper into Reed.

Heaven...yes, this is heaven.

CHAPTER 22

Tapping her well-manicured fingernail on the old newsroom desk, Laurie hung up the phone in a huff of irritation. She, and four other reporters, shared this tiny desk, tucked away in a far back corner of the newsroom. Budget cuts and a decrease in advertising revenue would force upper management to eliminate more jobs. Laurie couldn't afford for that cut to include her.

She had just paid the tuition for an expensive boarding school for the daughter no one knew she had. There was no way she would become a news anchor if anyone found out about her twelve-year-old daughter, especially since she was only twenty-six years old herself. At least that was what she told everyone, even if it wasn't true.

The need to look good on-air seemed the only commonality the five reporters shared. A desktop mirror sat to the right of the phone. Laurie took a moment to stare at her reflection, making sure every hair was in place and she was completely put together. She never knew when a story would pop up, so she had to always be ready, which included the ever-important visual aspect.

She ran a fingertip along her lip, wiping a small smudge away from the perfectly applied all day lip liner. Laurie didn't have a single wrinkle on her smooth, alabaster skin. Her dark brown eyes and brown/black hair was such a contrast to her fair skin type. She worked hard to keep her complexion fair. It absolutely would not do for anyone to know her father was a migrant worker and her mother a housekeeper for a Brownsville, Texas, hotel chain.

Lowering the mirror, she looked around to see if anyone was paying attention to her before she straightened her back, lifting her shapely boobs, compliments of a famous plastic surgeon. The cut of her blouse accentuated their appeal. She resisted the urge to shove her hands into each cup to plump her cleavage a little more. Using her assets to her best advantage came naturally to her. She always left the buttons on her blouse open, ensuring men got lost in the quick flashes of flesh, forgetting to monitor their words.

The quick nipple peeks usually helped her find some of her best stories while out in the field. And if that didn't work, the short, tight skirts she wore on her five-eight frame came in handy when accidentally dropping something on the ground. She would need to retrieve her dropped item, all the while exposing her thong in their direction. Once, the mayor actually reached out and touched her behind. Laurie had loved that moment. In the agreement to keep the indiscretion off the air, she'd gotten several exclusive interviews.

The shrill ring of the '60s era phone put her on alert. Laurie grabbed the receiver before it could ring again.

"Harry, say you have something for me, babe." None of her regular contacts were panning out. It didn't make sense at all. It was never this hard to figure out a name. Especially the name of a soldier who'd received millions of various comments a day from an adoring national fan base. God, who she wouldn't kill for that kind of exposure. The entire country stayed captivated by the images of this unknown soldier protecting all those women and children while being fired upon himself.

Only as a last resort did Laurie ever consider contacting Harry. His payment never required her to dig into her wallet. She'd have to pack a bag and spend the night in a sleazy hotel room. She would wear nothing more than fishnets, lots of eyeliner, and extra hold cheap hair spray. But a girl had to do what she had to do to get ahead in broadcasting.

"What time can I expect you?"

"I'll tell you once I know what you have," Laurie replied, rolling her eyes.

"No, no, no. You know what you have to do." Harry chuckled in his little squeaky voice.

Lowering her voice, Laurie rolled her eyes again, looking around to make sure no one stood within hearing distance. "I'm sitting here naked, thinking of you. My nipples are turning so hard they hurt, and I'm super wet just hearing your sexy voice, sugar," Laurie said, in an exaggerated southern accent she'd spent a ton of money trying to rid herself of before breaking into this business.

"How wet are you?"

"Dripping, just for you." Actually, dried up like the desert thinking of having to be with you, she thought as she spoke. It wouldn't do to share her actual feelings.

"Tell me where you want my dick." Harry's voice lowered, the squeak more pronounced.

"No, Harry. That's all you get until you answer my question."

"Tell me where you want my dick." Had to give it to him. He never wavered from his objective.

"Harry... God! Okay, up my ass. I want it up my ass. Now tell me what you fucking know." Laurie didn't use the southern accent. Her frustration levels were already through the roof with this phone call.

"A flight left Germany with a patient on it yesterday."

"Harry, please don't tell me you just made me go through this—"

"Ask me questions about the flight."

"Goddamn it, Harry." Laurie stared at the phone, contemplating ending the call. Harry worked as a freelance research journalist whose connections were always spot-on when he got the scoop, but this game he played got old.

"Ask me questions," Harry said again. His voice grew husky, and she narrowed her eyes, thinking over her options.

"Damn it. Okay. What kind of flight?"

"No, use the voice," he whined.

"Sugar, what kind of flight was it?" Rolling her eyes, she knew without question he was jacking off to the sound of her voice.

"A, ah...private flight." His voice came out in small, wispy breaths.

"Really? Hmmm. Well, honey, what makes this flight different from any other flight leaving Germany?"

"There was only one military patient aboard." Harry made the small grunts she had grown to hate, but she pushed those sounds aside. His answer had perked her up. Pulling her pen and paper in front of her, she took notes.

"And do we know the passenger's name, sugar?" More eager to play, her mind raced through questions that might help her meet her objective.

"No, it's not listed."

"Well, hottie, what do we know about him?"

"Say it again," Harry said. She could tell by the sound of his voice he had switched her to speaker phone. Such a perv.

"Are you thinking of me while you jerk off?"

"Of your tits bouncing like I like." Harry gave a deep moan and several panted grunts through the phone. Laurie could hear his hand working his cock.

"Well, tell me more, and you'll get to see more than just my tits bouncing."

"Do you promise? Say my name." Desperation filled his voice now when he spoke. The man was close. It never took him long.

"Of course, I do, Harry. Don't I always want to come to you? I mean for you, sugar." Laurie had tried for sultry when saying his name. She doubted she succeeded, but Harry heard what he wanted to anyway.

"Okay, it's...ahh...the plane is...ah...yeah, it's registered to the private company of ahh...crap, I can't think... God, you're such a fascinating little slut to get me here already."

"Say it, sugar, and I'll finish you off."

"It's registered to Carson Kensington here in DC."

"And?"

"The plane was...yeah, it was chartered by the Kensington family. That Kensington mom is one classy bitch," he said between grunts.

"Kensington? The United Nations ambassador?" Laurie knew she was losing him now. Harry had a thing for Olivia Kensington. He always talked about her, and Laurie suspected it was why Harry required her to talk in the southern accent. Laurie should have guessed this was where this conversation originated, and she wondered if Olivia Kensington had any idea Harry watched her so closely. Of course, the stalker would know what that family was up to.

"Finish me, slut." Harry moaned loudly.

"No. That information means nothing to me," Laurie said in her normal voice. She must get it out of Harry before it was too late, once he spilled his seed, his information dried up too.

"Finish me! I'll put it together for you."

Oh, Laurie hated this guy. She hated him and loathed herself for what she was about to do. "Grip your sac, sugar, and pull it just a little. Yeah, just like that. Are you stroking that long, thick sexy dick I love so much? The one I want shoved deep down my throat like you do? Ahh yeah, I can hear it. You're close. God, your voice makes me wet. Dear God, I'm going to come too. You're so sexy, you stud... Ahhh... Ahh...yes...yes!"

"Okay, I'm done," Harry said, his voice already recovered. She wondered how long he let her go on like that.

"Now tell me," she said firmly.

"I've explained all this to you before. Kensington's the father of Rylie Kensington, a Marine Special Ops team lead who recently married. His wedding was cut short. He and his Special Ops team left abruptly during the reception. Kensington is also the father of Reed Kensington. He's a young guy, no more than twenty-nine, and already worth about twenty million dollars all on his own. Recently, Reed moved home and accepted a huge position at Baker & Pruitt, but suddenly took two weeks off work after flying to Germany last week, per his office. And oh, did I mention, Reed Kensington is very gay?"

"No way." Laurie stopped writing at that bit of news. If the implication was true, this information would ensure she didn't lose her job. She might even get an anchor seat or her own broadcast time. The wheels continued to turn.

"Yes, very way. I can just hear your little useless brain ticking." Harry chuckled.

"And we're sure the injured soldier wasn't his brother?"

"Yes, we're very sure it wasn't, but it's someone close to Rylie. He was spotted leaving the German hospital a few days ago."

"So, who do you think was on board..." Back to business, Laurie started writing again.

"That's for you to figure out."

"What? That's it? That's all you have, a bunch of speculation?" she hissed.

"Well, I also have that there's a new VIP at the National Rehabilitation Center. No one knows his name, but it's a leg amputation. Appointment today at one thirty. When am I going to see you?"

"You aren't. A hand job is all this is worth. I still have to dig for this guy, you ass," Laurie said through clenched teeth.

"Look for Reed. My hunch is you'll find your guy. If you do, I want a weekend."

"No, that's just gross." Two nights with Harry... No way. She did have some standards left in her life.

"A weekend away, your treat, with more pictures. I love your big fake tits. I need more pictures. I sold my last set to a guy here in the office and my computer crashed."

"You sold my pictures? No fucking way I'm doing more." Laurie's eyes flew to the phone. Worry crossed her brow, wondering if it would be good or bad for her career if her breasts were made public for the world to see.

"I took your face out of them. And I'm calling CBS if you don't agree," Harry added. She knew he would do it too.

"Damn it, Harry. You fucking suck. I swear to God."

"So, I'll take that as a yes, and I have something you can suck, already growing hard again. Let me know what you find. I'll be watching the news tonight for your story." Harry hung up, not giving her a chance to respond.

She dropped the phone back in the cradle. Laurie felt dirty. She truly hated the things she did just to get ahead. Looking down at her watch, she gathered her notebook, pen, and purse before heading out the door. Fortunately for her, some of their cameramen were on standby in the front of the studio.

"Come on. I need to check something out. We're taking my car so that no one sees us, and bring the smallest camera you have. We need to hide it in my purse." Never stopping, Laurie's high heels clicked along the concrete while walking to her car. Finding out that the current national hero was gay would push her face in front of every major market across the nation, probably across the world. Sure, being gay wouldn't get you tossed out on your ass these days, but the United States was packed full of religious homophobes. This would be too big of a story, sure to blow up the airwaves.

Opening her car door, Laurie slid inside, lost in thought. The cameraman barely opened the door to sit in the passenger seat when she put the car in reverse and began backing out. He better pick up the fucking pace. Nowhere in her job description did it require her to wait for him for any reason.

CHAPTER 23

Reed drove through the underground garage to the secure patient entry far below the first floor. This rehabilitation hospital held many high-profile patients, who for one reason or another, wanted to remain anonymous. It was one of the biggest reasons Reed had pushed for Trevor to enter this facility over other government-owned centers. His continued anonymity was too important to risk. He made a wide turn into an oversized parking space, put the SUV in park, and turned the ignition off before looking over at Trevor, who had won the battle for the front seat.

"You drive like my grandmother used to," Trevor said, looking down at the clock on the dashboard. The twenty-minute drive had taken almost an hour with Reed taking the back roads and never going over thirty-five miles an hour. But he wouldn't apologize for that.

"I wanted you to be safe, my stubborn boyfriend." Reed leaned over to kiss Trevor lightly on the lips, and hopefully wipe the annoyance away. "I can't seem to keep my hands or my lips to myself."

Trevor's eyebrow arched in reply. Reed chuckled, unbuckled his seatbelt, and opened the driver's side door. He hurried to the back of the SUV and pulled out Trevor's wheelchair. By the time Reed made it to the passenger side, Trevor stood waiting, holding on to the passenger door.

"Babe, please let me help you. I don't want you to fall."

This time Trevor made the appeasing move first. He leaned in and placed a soft kiss on Reed's lips, effectively pacifying and silencing him. Reed could never let the cronies in his office know how easily he could be manipulated for fear he may never live it down.

"I'm fine but thank you. It's just me getting out of the car," Trevor said, staying close to Reed's face. He lifted his index finger to run it down Reed's frustration-furrowed brow before turning to sit in the chair. The small touch from Trevor removed all the worry and concern, leaving Reed just staring at the stunning man in front of him.

Trevor no longer held himself back and didn't shy away from his touch. Their ride to the hospital had taken an extraordinarily long time, but Trevor had held Reed's hand the entire way. Their entwined fingers and the small swipes of Trevor's thumb across his palm had caused Reed's heart to flutter, vanquishing some of his newfound insecurities.

"This rehab facility is world-renowned. It was between here and one in San Antonio, but this one has pioneered some new technologies in prostheses, which could aid you better in recovery. Plus, my home is more comfortable for us than trying to stay in a hotel in San Antonio."

Reed continued talking as he pushed Trevor through the sliding doors of the garage and into a private elevator. Trevor didn't respond, which Reed was beginning to understand meant he was getting nervous. He laid a hand on Trevor's shoulder, running a finger along his neck. Trevor's pulse sped up at his touch and he bent down to whisper quietly in Trevor's ear.

"Did I tell you how much I loved hearing you moan while I rode you this morning? I can't wait to get home for a repeat performance. Making love to you is quite an appealing thought."

Trevor lifted his gaze to Reed. A blush spread across his cheeks and a smile lit up his face. He leaned in again, a move becoming all too frequent, and placed a small kiss on those perfectly pouty lips smiling up at him.

"Every part of your rehab will be here in this facility if it suits you. The prosthesis company will come here to measure and fit you. All your doctor's appointments and physical therapy will take place here." Each ring of the bell sounded off as the floors passed by. It cost Reed quite a bit to work it all this way, but in the end, he hoped Trevor's recovery would be more complete.

As he understood it, their first order of business was to clear Trevor to begin rehab. Dr. McBride agreed to be present at the initial exam today and would work with Trevor's new orthopedist, Dr. Carlton, to develop a comprehensive treatment plan for the rest of Trevor's care. Reed had pushed hard at the boundaries of military medical care and had even agreed to cover additional costs to provide Trevor with the best possible outcome. Trevor was never to know.

The elevator opened to a short, perky young woman standing in the standard professional garb of a crisp navy-blue business suit. Her pencil skirt fell just below the knee, blazer to the hip, a modestly cut cream-colored blouse with a set of matching pearl earrings and necklace completed her professional business attire. The woman also came with a giant toothy grin and clipboard in her well-manicured hands.

"Sgt. West, Mr. Kensington, welcome to National Rehab. I'm Natalie, your patient liaison. It's a pleasure to meet you both. I have your exam room ready if you will follow me this way." With a sweep of the arm, the woman led the way through the foyer, small heels clicking on the marble tile floor. She turned back to them every couple of seconds as she spoke. "First, let me start off by telling you how happy we are that you have chosen our facility. I have a folder of information for you with my telephone numbers. I'll be here with you each step of the way. Any question or concern you may have, I'm happy to help you find the best answers. We truly feel privileged you have chosen us to provide your care through this stage of your recovery."

They followed Natalie into a spacious exam room. The room was so large it held a waiting area with a small solid print sofa and flat screen television anchored from the ceiling. Along with a small sink, refrigerator, and a large open area, the room was designed for a wheelchair to easily access everything.

"Here's your room. Dr. Carlton and Dr. McBride will be with you shortly. Until then, please remove your clothing and here's a gown for you to wear. Dr. McBride called and he's running a little behind. We're waiting for his arrival now and expect him at any moment. Again, please make yourself at home. I'll leave this folder with you now."

"Perfect. Thank you for the warm greeting." Reed grinned his sexy grin and gave her a wink, pushing Trevor into the room, helping him from the chair. After a moment, when no answer came from Natalie, both Trevor and Reed looked her way. She stood just staring at them. Her only movement was the blinking of her eyes. All three of them held each other's gaze for a moment before Natalie finally turned on her heels, clearing her throat.

"All right then, I'll leave you two to get ready. Just dial zero if you need anything." Natalie didn't look back as she left the room, pushing the door wide open with the palms of her hands.

***

"Dear Lord, could they be any hotter? Seriously, why do all the good-looking ones have to be gay? I mean, Jesus Christ, did you see those two?" Natalie took her clipboard and fanned herself, muttering while stepping up to the large ornately curved mahogany reception desk in the front lobby of the hospital.

"Did you see them, Nikki? That one in the wheelchair was seriously a brick house, or heck, he looked like he benched brick houses regularly. And, dear God, when the blond smiled at me, I lost all ability to reason," Natalie whispered while bending over the side of the high reception desk. Nikki quietly pointed her finger in the direction of a new tour, standing just a few feet from them in the front foyer of the hospital.

Natalie's assistant, Mandy, was just starting the standard introductory greeting they were all required to give with two potential prospects, and Natalie didn't hesitate. She straightened and ran her hands down the front of her business suit, putting on her game face. Census room counts were down; the hospital needed patients badly. Incentives were handed down earlier this morning. For every new patient admitted, there would be a five-hundred-dollar bonus sent her way. Clearing her throat, Natalie stuck out her hand in greeting to the very pretty young woman talking to her mousy, frumpy assistant, who painstakingly followed protocol to the point of boring the prospective patients away.

"Hi, I'm Natalie Vickery, patient liaison. Welcome to National Rehabilitation Hospital. Thank you, Mandy, I'll take it from here." With that, Natalie effectively dismissed her employee without a backward glance. She turned to the woman, who was standing with a young man. They looked as different as two people could look. They didn't seem to be a couple. The woman was polished and smoothly sophisticated, wearing spiky Jimmy Choo's, large round Prada sunglasses, and carrying a fashionably sensible, large Louis Vuitton shoulder bag. She wore thousands of dollars in just her accessories, while the man beside her looked like he just rolled out of bed—hair askew, face unshaven. Had he even brushed his teeth or put on clean clothes? Natalie forced her eyes away from the man to turn back to the woman.

"I'm sorry, but you look so familiar to me. Have we met before?" Natalie asked, looking the woman over closely, trying to place her.

***

"I'm Michelle Powell and this is my older brother, Josh. We're looking for a place for our father. He was recently in a mountain climbing accident. My father wants to keep things under wraps. His board of directors doesn't know of this accident. There was alcohol involved. So, Father sent us here to start the process. We only want the best for his care. Money isn't an issue, and Daddy usually likes to have a floor to himself in situations like these. Not that there have been a lot of situations like these, but there have been a few. Can you accommodate such a stay?" Laurie spoke quickly, giving a fake New England accent.

On the ride over, she drilled Josh, her cameraman, on possible alibis and accents. This was the only one he could pull off effectively, and they needed to sound similar yet foreign for this to work. Adjusting the straps of her fake Louis Vuitton over her shoulder, the weight of Josh's camera strained her neck and shoulder muscles. She'd have a painful crick in her neck by morning.

"Absolutely, Ms. Powell, I understand the importance of discretion. You will absolutely get it here. It's very responsible of you to do this for your father. The sooner you get him into the facility, the better and faster his outcome will be. We do have the room right now to accommodate a floor request, but you would have to act fast to secure an entire floor dedicated to him. Walk with me. Let's take this conversation to a more private area and I'll show you around. We can end the tour in my office. I can have the contracts drawn up within minutes to get your father started."

"Great, but the stay will be extended. I'm not sure he would be willing to leave until the whole process is complete. Money isn't an issue, I'm sure you know of my father's military background and long-standing wealth. Is there a secure entrance for him?" Laurie could see Natalie sizing her up, connecting her with Warren Buffett, the dollar signs coming to her eyes. Who knew if Warren Buffett had children, but she could tell Natalie fell for her story hook, line, and sinker. Resisting the urge to do the happy dance right there in the foyer, Laurie followed slowly behind. She wished Natalie would just walk and stop looking back over her shoulder.

"Yes, we do, but let me start from the beginning to hopefully answer all of your questions. Your family can rest assured our medical director and his staff of specialty trained physicians will work closely with your father's treating physician to work up a comprehensive treatment plan to accelerate his recovery. Our center is state of the art with the most current technologies and equipment available today. I won't bore you with the specifics, but we are well equipped enough to handle anything thrown our way." Natalie moved them through the front lobby, entering a quick key code into a security pad, without asking for credentials from either of them. Laurie couldn't believe how easy it all turned out to be. Once inside the center, she stood, momentarily shocked at truly being behind the scenes. Most of her competition tried to get into various high-security locations on a regular basis and were always locked out, but she'd done it on the first try.

The first room they entered appeared to be a large workout room. Several patients were receiving their physical therapy, all in different stages of care. Medical personnel stood close by, instructing or supporting the patients in whatever task they were assigned to perform. Laurie quickly scanned the room, looking over the faces of those in treatment, but found no one looking to be active military.

"As you can see, here we have the workout rooms. These are standard traditional rooms, equipped for every stage of the recovery. Your father can have time here to himself, but we have found when other patients are in the room, it helps build a sense of unity. It's very sweet how encouraging all the patients become to one another. Now, if you will follow me, these halls lead to a series of exam rooms and the secure entrance you asked about earlier. These elevator doors to the left come from a private underground parking garage entrance. There's security placed in different checkpoints along the way, blocking anyone from coming down into the garage who isn't pre-authorized. Now, through these doors we have the official exam rooms. Most medical care is done right here in these rooms." Natalie stopped and turned her friendly, fake smile to an older man who looked lost in the hall. "Hi, Dr. McBride, they're in exam room six, sir." Laurie prayed her own fake smile looked as natural as the ugly little Natalie's did.

"Thank you. Have they been here long?" Dr. McBride asked.

"No, sir, just a few minutes."

Dr. McBride gave a nod of dismissal to them all and ducked into the exam room Natalie pointed to. Turning back to Laurie, Natalie continued with what had to be a boring memorized speech. "If your father's physician wants to monitor care, our medical staff will work closely with that person, much like Dr. McBride there, making sure everyone's comfortable with all treatment plans provided."

The tour continued at a swift pace that Laurie desperately needed to slow down. They were moving too quickly, and she needed more time to search. Slowing her stride, Laurie was able to fall behind in order to dig her knuckles into Josh's shoulder. She pushed him forward, whispering with a hiss for him to be useful and ask engaging questions while she searched the hospital. Laurie stayed several feet behind the two, hoping she looked thoughtful. No one in the place looked to be active military or the perfect blond Reed Kensington.

All the pictures of Reed Kensington her research department sent included a tall, extremely good-looking, and always fashionable man. His hair and clothing were never the same style, but they were always in the current trend. In every picture she found online, Reed always appeared to have a different man on his arm, many being reasonably well-known male models. Reed shied away from the camera while his partners always posed, drawing all the attention to them, making it hard to really study his features too closely.

As the tour continued, Laurie's attitude took a nosedive. Natalie couldn't be more boring, and Laurie grew increasingly frustrated. Maybe they were too early or too late, or maybe Harry didn't have any idea what the hell he talked about. Reality crashed in. Perhaps it wasn't her acting skills that got her into the facility; maybe the reason they were able to walk right in was because they had no high-profile patients at the moment. Immediately, Laurie formulated plans on how she could get Harry back for this wasted afternoon trip.

Watching Natalie walk, Laurie thought maybe she could do a story on the ugly clothes marketing people wore. When Natalie glanced down at her clipboard, Laurie's gaze dropped too. The Daily Census Count sheet on the clipboard held a list of every patient in the facility that day. With a gliding step forward, Laurie stayed behind Natalie, getting enough of a glimpse to see she was right. Laurie gradually began asking questions, trying hard to get her to put down the clipboard. It took about ten minutes, but Natalie finally put the clipboard down to help Laurie find the contact lens she pretended to lose. Laurie quickly swiped the top page and folded it, dropping it into her skirt pocket. Feigning more eye problems, Laurie promptly escaped to the restroom with her purse in hand to read over the report.

The center received four new patients that day. Two females, two males, one being twenty-three, the other fifty-seven. Trevor West had to be the twenty-three-year-old. Pulling her phone out, Laurie sent a quick message to her research team back in the office asking for bio information on Trevor West ASAP. Within seconds, photos of Trevor West appeared on her phone.

His bio followed shortly after. Trevor West, a sergeant in the Marines Special Ops. Bingo. Just like that, Laurie had her guy. Excitement built deep within her, and she took a minute to calm herself. She had to think. Her heart began a slow steady pounding as her eyes darted back to the census report, seeing his appointment scheduled for thirty minutes earlier. He was still somewhere in this building.

Relief flooded her as she stuck her head out the door to see Josh talking to Natalie with her back to the door. Taking her Jimmy Choo's off, Laurie dropped them in her bag and ducked out of the restroom as silently as possible. According to the paper, Trevor would be in the exam area they had just left.

She turned the corner, looking over her shoulder to make sure no one followed. Heading back toward the front, she stopped abruptly before silently retreating from the hallway. Two gorgeous, smiling men were exiting a clinic exam room. Their intense focus on one another kept them from even realizing she was there. If her intel was correct, the man in the wheelchair appeared to be Trevor West. The other man must be Reed Kensington, although he looked different from the photos due to his ever-changing trendy haircut.

Laurie pulled the camera from her purse and anchored the purse over her shoulder, tossing the bag against her back. She didn't want to be forcibly removed from the facility and have to leave the purse behind. Regardless of it being a knockoff, it still cost a pretty penny. While her heart slammed in her chest, Laurie flipped the lens open and pushed the record button at the top of the camera. She quietly took the final step around the corner, positioning the camera for the best angle.

For the first time in a long time, Laurie knew what she was about to do was wrong. Just watching these two for the short time she stood there, she could see they were clearly in love. And it looked real and honest, an all-consuming kind of love. Regardless of the circumstance which brought them here, happiness radiated from the couple. Neither of them seemed to be able to stop touching one another, and both smiled at the other the entire time they spoke. Neither man paid any attention to where they were, or to who might be around. They were simply happy. By doing what she planned to do, these two men's lives would change dramatically. For some unknown reason, this felt so wrong after everything the soldier had gone through. She shoved her conscience aside. She needed to focus on propelling her career and this exclusive would do that. Nothing else should matter.

After a couple seconds of taping, Laurie captured Reed squatting down to kiss Trevor lightly on the lips. Her hands shook from the momentary remorse she felt, but Laurie forced herself to become a professional. She must steady herself, look into the lens, and make sure the angle hit the two of them just right.

"Well now, wasn't that encouraging, babe? I had no idea things worked so quickly," Reed said, bending down again to kiss Trevor. Laurie smiled, catching it all on tape. She could feel her old self creeping back in.

"It's surprising. I didn't know I could be on a leg that fast. Thank you for this, Reed. I have to get my arm strength back quickly, though. I need it to help support myself and to help me balance."

Reed lifted a finger to Trevor's moving lips, cutting him off as he spoke. All the while Laurie stayed perfectly still, catching it all on tape.

"Babe, please stop saying thank you. I love you. I want you to have the best care possible." With two kisses and a declaration of appreciation and love, Laurie decided she'd captured enough on tape. Her time was limited. Soon, someone would spot her. She needed to get the questions on tape in her voice. At this point, the most important part for her was to keep this story hers at all cost. Damn, she wished she could get in the shot. Where was fucking Josh when she needed him?

"Mr. Kensington, Sgt. West." Laurie took several steps forward out of the shadows, filming the whole time. "I'm Laurie

Bernard of Truth or Tales. Can you tell us how you are involved with Sgt. West?" Both men turned toward her, startled. Laurie could see they never expected this. They erroneously thought they were secure here, and they hadn't counted on the greedy little Natalie or the super stealth Laurie Bernard on the case.

"Are you supposed to be in here?" Reed asked, rising from his squatting position, turning fully to her. In the movement, Reed pushed Trevor away from the camera, making her only able to capture the back of his head from this angle. Reed's deep green eyes turned icy when they focused on her. She fully understood how he was such an accomplished attorney. His eyes spoke volumes, telling her she needed to hand over the camera and apologize for her lapse in judgment. With extreme effort, Laurie forced herself not to do the bidding his eyes were calling for her to do.

"How's Sgt. West's care since leaving Germany? And how long have you two been together?"

Reed stepped in front of Trevor, now completely blocking him from her view, anger flashing across his extraordinary face. "I believe you have quite enough. You need to leave." Reed stood as an immovable force, blocking her way to any additional footage of Trevor. Her heart pounded, but she kept going, not letting him force her into a defensive position.

"Sgt. West, how long have you been out of the closet? Was it hard being a gay man in the military?"

Reed's icy green eyes became shards of glass, shooting daggers directly into her. He lifted his hand to her camera, aggressively stalking toward her. His body completely blocked her from Trevor. Dr. Carlton came around the corner with two well-built men in scrubs flanking him. All three rushed over. Laurie had no choice but to step back or be run over.

"This is private property, and you're prohibited to film here, but I'm sure you know this. What would it take to relieve you of this camera? I'm willing to pay a substantial amount for this camera right now, but only right now," Reed demanded. He'd successfully herded Laurie backward around the corner and away from Trevor, all while he reached up to turn the camera off.

"Did these injuries really occur by the insurgents or is there more to the story? Does it have anything to do with being a gay man in the military?"

Hospital security barreled down the hall toward her, obviously called by the medical staff. Her time had run out. Rushing her last question before they got to her, Laurie needed to get a reaction from Reed. Otherwise, this could all backfire on her by making Reed and Trevor look victimized by her and her station.

"Mr. Kensington, you can set the record straight. Give me an exclusive interview, and you can stop the rumors before they start."

Reed's lips curled into the smallest sneer. He took a couple of steps back, watching security take hold of the situation to remove her in their normal, none too friendly way. Then Reed turned on his heel, dismissing her without a backward glance. Something Laurie absolutely hated. The guards dragged her through the facility, but her focus remained on Reed Kensington. The highest ratings came from people flipping out on camera, making her look better or even justified for interrupting the privacy of their lives. But not Kensington. He stayed too irritatingly smooth and together. She didn't break him. Not even close. She'd have to flip the narrative, so she didn't look like an ambulance chaser, trying to hurt a beloved military hero.

Laurie stumbled back but stayed on her feet as she was pushed through the front doors of the rehab center. Josh got tossed out right behind her. Straightening her blouse, she tucked it back in before shoving the hair from her face. Laurie blew out a breath, planning her next move. She would dig up all the dirt she could find on Reed Kensington. Between her and Reed, if one of them needed to look bad, it wasn't going to be her.

Reed was too good-looking and too shrewd to not have

a past. She'd find some damning information to help turn this around. Hell, if not, she would just make it up. Her whole angle for this story could be Truth or Tales protecting Trevor West, the US military hero, from the big, bad international playboy.

Oh yes, Laurie was back on track now. She had a plan to execute before the news cycle ended.

"Did you get it?" Josh grunted, rolling to his side as he pushed up off the ground. He hadn't been so lucky to stay on his feet with his abrupt forced departure from the facility.

"Got it. Now come on. We don't have much time." Laurie jogged to the car as Josh limped behind her.

CHAPTER 24

After what felt like a lifetime, Reed came barreling through the thick mahogany door of the exam room, noting the physical therapist standing guard just inside. He wore the crisp clean scrubs of a professional but had an air about him that made one think he'd be more at home in a seedy biker bar. Reed was grateful to have the man on Trevor's side, looking out for him. Reed's heart thumped against his ribcage. His mind raced over how to stop this information leak, his hands curling into fists. A calculating side that he only reserved for the courtroom angled his brow at the physical therapist standing between him and Trevor.

Trevor gave a slight movement with his hand on the wheel, turning the chair toward Reed. The look Trevor gave caused his heart to sink, and the therapist excused himself, quickly leaving the room. Reed watched the man's hurried exit, making sure the door closed solidly behind him.

Being an attorney, Reed appreciated the ability of one to speak so clearly with just his eyes. He turned back to Trevor, who sat there with his face devoid of emotion, his eyes hollow, and his jaw clenched tight. Reed could easily see every bit of the ground he'd made with Trevor was lost at the hands of an overzealous, two-bit reporter. The reality made Reed's unsteady heart slam hard against his chest, hard enough to have him absently push his palm against the thin material of his shirt, rubbing the sudden ache in the center of his chest.

"Did she leave?" Trevor asked, his voice was the same as his face, seemingly uninterested.

"Yes. How are you?" Reed slowly, carefully walked to Trevor. His mind told him not to make any sudden moves, and he bent at the knee in front of the wheelchair, meeting Trevor at eye level.

"How did she find me?" Trevor kept his voice even, his stare distant, and his jaw locked, but he did meet Reed's gaze. Reed reached forward to run a hand up and down Trevor's thigh, willing his touch to bring Trevor emotionally back to him.

"I'm not sure, but I promise I'll find out where this leak originated. They will be dealt with." Reed's hand stopped moving as his words turned pleading. "Trevor. Babe, talk to me. What're you thinking? Please don't close up. We agreed this morning, we're a team. We're in this together. We'll figure it out." Reed leaned in, lifting his hand to trace a finger down Trevor's cheek. His world broke apart when Trevor moved his head out from under the touch.

"It doesn't really matter now. At this point, what do you think will happen?" Trevor pushed his chair back with a small shove on the wheels from both hands. His carefully placed walls were all back up in protection mode to keep him from any more hurt. By design, they also pushed Reed completely away.

"I think the local hero will have his day of fame and then it'll subside," Reed said, watching Trevor closely. He stayed bent at the knee, balancing on his heels while Trevor pushed back another few inches.

"What about the gay thing?"

"I honestly don't know, Trevor. It'll be talked about, I'm sure, but possibly no one will care. We're in a new age now. It's not such a big deal anymore." Reed knew what he said wasn't completely true, probably more just wishful thinking. The people of this country would care. The United States always cared about such things. His gut told him the undying media coverage on the raid would be set to a frenzy, talking about the ins and outs of a gay man in the military. It would never be 'our hero's a gay man' but something far uglier, making it more sinister as the reporter had proved with some of her questions.

Slowly Reed rose to his feet and took several steps away from Trevor, putting more distance between them. His heart broke when Trevor moved away from him, and he didn't want to watch it happen again, so he gave him the space he needed.

"They'll care," Trevor said, finally averting his gaze. He looked down at his lap. The tic in his clenched jaw became more pronounced. Trevor gripped his fist around the wheel, and Reed was surprised the strong man didn't bend the rim or pop the tire.

"Perhaps you're right. Only time will tell. We need to consider your safety. Your name will go international, will anyone come for vengeance? We should get you security." Reed pushed his thoughts forward, trying to think of all the potential effects of the publicity about to bombard the man he loved.

"I don't really know. It makes sense, I guess. Except she didn't care about any of that, or the harm it may cause. All that mattered to her was that I'm gay. Shit, Reed, this is so gonna be awful." Emotion finally showed on Trevor's anguished face. Hurt tore through his heart at the desperation pouring from Trevor's eyes.

"We can't worry about that. I love you. I'm ready to shout it to the world. I'm good with being out. I've never tried to hide. I want you to feel the same way. What others think of you shouldn't matter." Reed spoke while moving back across the small room to Trevor. He ran a hand up Trevor's neck and took his other hand and hooked a finger, lifting Trevor's strongly chiseled chin up to meet his gaze. He needed to look at his handsome Trevor as he said his next words. "Babe, nothing has changed for us, and it won't change. We'll be right here together, dealing as a couple. I love you. I'm not going anywhere. Please let that be enough."

Trevor gripped Reed's hand. It felt very much like the life preserver cast out to a drowning man. They stared at one another. Reed felt like he may have his Trevor back, but Dr. Carlton chose then to come through the exam room door, interrupting his crucial moment. Trevor jerked, looking back at the door, fear covering his features. He shoved his chair back out of Reed's reach, hitting the small sofa sitting against the wall.

"Everything good here?" the doctor asked, looking first at Trevor, then at Reed.

"Yes, sir," Trevor answered immediately, not looking over at Reed who sighed heavily while shoving his hands in his pockets.

"Good. We're calling in public relations now. They'll contact the Marine Corps. The site director is on his way down. I must apologize. I don't know how this happened. We never give out our patient's private information."

"We weren't expecting this. I knew Trevor was still at the top of the news feeds, but I thought it would fade with a little more time. The leak must have come from within this hospital. Very few people, as a matter of fact, only two, know we're here." Reed turned, giving Trevor his space, and took the few steps to face the doctor directly.

"Mr. Kensington, we don't ever have these problems. I assure you every procedure will be reviewed. The somber doctor stood by the door. His seriousness of the situation was focused on Reed.

"I'm ready to get moving. The sooner I'm back on my feet, the better it'll all be," Trevor said, awkwardly wheeling past

Reed. When Reed tried to help, he got a noticeably clear, very decisive, "I got this."

Trevor struggled to push the heavy door open. After a couple of good whacks against the frame and several strong choice words, Trevor made it out to the physical therapy room. From there, Trevor forced one of the therapists standing and discussing the large breach in security to begin rehab on his arm. Trevor didn't take no for an answer or look back at Reed for the entire rest of their time there.

Anytime Trevor was approached regarding the incident with the reporter, he shut down completely and worked his body harder, almost as if he was punishing himself.

Trevor looked exhausted, irritable, and overstressed, both physically and mentally. Several times, the therapist working with Trevor commented on his drive and perseverance. Trevor did not respond to the praise, just kept moving his body, wanting to rebuild what he'd lost. He ignored everything around him, including Reed.

By the end of the day, Trevor talked the center into deeming his upper body strong enough for crutches, making his mobility a much easier thing to accomplish on his own. Neither spoke as they loaded into the SUV. During the long, painfully slow drive home, Reed stayed silent, tired of being ignored when he spoke.

"While I worked out this afternoon, I was thinking I should move into the guest room. Give you your space back until I can get a place. I can't see how it's gonna be anything but a nightmare coming toward us. I think we need to put some space between us until things die down. Especially if anyone decides to come after me. I don't want you to be a factor. I can move to base, I guess, or another rehab center." Trevor said it all while staring out the front window.

Reed knew without question he would rather have the silence than this. He didn't reply right away, just kept his eyes on the road.

"I don't want space between us. We've done nothing wrong. Remember this morning? Remember our confessions to one another? I'll remember everything you said for the rest of my life, and I meant what I said to you. I don't want you to leave me. From where I'm standing, the worst-case scenario from this media situation isn't as bad as you deciding to leave me." Reed spoke from his heart but kept his eyes forward for fear the tears he felt might actually fall if he looked over at his handsome Trevor and saw anything resembling disdain or resolve.

Trevor didn't acknowledge he'd heard Reed. An uncomfortable silence filled the SUV for the rest of the drive home. He pulled into the driveway, quickly parked the truck and jumped out, but Trevor wouldn't allow his help to move from the front seat or walk up to the porch. Trevor did all the work with the help of his crutches. Reed knew Trevor's arms must be sore and aching, ready to fall off from the exertion of the day, but Trevor didn't complain or stop.

The doorbell rang just after they closed the front door. Reed turned to answer it while Trevor continued farther into the house. He was encouraged that Trevor was working his way in the direction of his bedroom while he answered the door. He expected to see a neighborhood child, but instead a local news crew shoved a camera in his face and pummeled him with questions.

At the same time, the home phone and his cell phone began to ring. Another news van came to a screeching halt behind the other parked on the street. Reed slammed the door in their faces. The pounding on the door and the ringing of his doorbell did not stop, nor did the phone stop ringing.

By the time Reed was able to get the doorbell dismantled, all the windows locked, and curtains drawn, the police were involved, controlling the multiple news agencies in his front yard. They roped off his porch and assisted him in moving the SUV back to the garage to give them secure transportation in and out of the house.

Reed's father sent several private armed security guards,

who stood at the front and back doors of the home, keeping trespassers away. His father also sent a burner cell phone to keep communication with his family open.

He had a moment of panic when he finally made his way back to his bedroom to check on Trevor to see no one in the room. The new items Reed had bought for Trevor were folded neatly on the end of the bed. The extended moment of panic gripped his heart for fear Trevor may have left his house, but he stopped that line of thinking. Even if Trevor wanted to leave, there was no way he would make it an inch out the door without being attacked by the bloodthirsty group of reporters.

He forced himself to calm as he took long quick strides through the house to the front guest room. A few steps from the door, he heard the television and deep relief flooded through him.

Slowly, Reed came to a stop in the open doorway, looking at his heart's desire sitting on the guest bed with his eyes focused on the television. Reed never crossed the imaginary line of the threshold. There was no possible way Trevor could miss Reed standing there, but he refused to acknowledge him from where he sat on top of the bedspread in the sweatpants he had arrived in. For the briefest moment, Reed wondered what Trevor would have chosen to wear had he known Reed purchased those sweats for him before leaving Germany.

"This is where you would prefer to sleep tonight, Trevor?" Tension laced Reed's words regardless of how casual he tried to be. Trevor did little more than nod, keeping his gaze on the television. "All right, whatever makes you the most comfortable. I'd planned on dinner being brought in, but that may be a little impossible at this point. I'll reheat the enchiladas my mom made for you."

"I'm fine. I'm not hungry. I'm learning you're a wealthy man. I assumed you made some money, but I had no idea how much. They're reporting you're worth somewhere around sixteen million dollars. Is that true?" Trevor asked, finally lifting his eyes from the television, turning an accusing glare his way.

"My financial worth means very little to me at this moment. I'm more concerned about your welfare, and you being in this bedroom. Didn't our morning set anything right between us?"

"So, it's true then. I hoped it was a lie like so many of the things they're spreading about me. You've been with a lot of men over the last ten years. The one just interviewed believed he was the love of your life. They interviewed him in France. His English wasn't so good, but they captured enough to know you two spent years in love. Others have also been interviewed. It's all over social media. I guess I understand the reason for all the condoms in this nightstand. They're also really pretty men. Lots of pictures. They fit you very well. None look anything like me." Every word came out in a strong, unmistakable tone of accusation. Trevor didn't wait for an answer, just moved his gaze back to the TV.

"Trevor, I've only ever said 'I love you' to you. I told you I never went out with anyone more than once. Those are lies, and you know they're lies. The reporters are lying about you, what makes you think they wouldn't lie about me too? We need to focus on what's important. We need to get you your meds, let you eat, and get off to sleep. You had a big day. All this will die down. Until then, we have to focus on the important thing, and that's your health."

Reed stood there several long minutes, just staring at Trevor, who purposely ignored him. A sense of deep hurt radiated from Trevor. Reed didn't know how to stop it.

Frustrated, he took a step inside the door, crossing that imaginary line, determined to get Trevor to listen to him. His new burner phone rang, and Rylie's number came across the screen. He pivoted on his heels, abruptly leaving the room to take the call.

"Little brother, tell me this hasn't reached you. Where are you?" Reed tried to hide the strain of the last few hours from his voice and concentrate on making sure his brother was safe.

"I'm just getting back in town. Elise picked me up from the airport. She's filled me in. Dad gave me the new number. You okay?"

Reed came to a stop in his living room. He leaned back against the wall, dropping his head with a small thump. His eyes closed. "Not so good. I haven't heard any of the reports, but Trevor's pretty torn up about it," Reed said openly and honestly to his brother, his heart breaking in half as he spoke.

"Shit, it doesn't sound like something he should be watching. They're digging up dirt on both of you," Rylie said. "Elise said there are lots of lies, and one of the French guys is really from our area. He's an actor. She also said the reporter who broke the story is getting interviewed on all the national news, telling bigger lies with each interview. Did they really barge into the rehab?"

"Yeah, I don't know how long they were behind us filming. Trevor's completely withdrawn from me and I'm worried. He says he's going to find another place to stay. This morning things were so good between us. Really, just perfect. Now it's like none of that happened. I don't want him to leave, Rylie, but I don't know how to keep him with me."

"I'm on my way over. Let whoever know I'm coming, so they let me in when I arrive."

CHAPTER 25

Trevor sat quietly on the bed in Reed's guest room. He ignored all the extra preparations Reed had made to ready this room for his arrival and kept his eyes steadily focused on the forty-eight-inch flat screen television. Trevor watched with interest as the latest clip of headline news reported from Reed's front yard. The showcasing of the house was excellent. The shots and backdrops of the on-air reports were of the rich colorful blooms contrasting against the greenery of the assorted shrubs, and the wood, brick, and rock all along the front of the large custom-built home. The only eyesore Trevor could see might be the long wooden ramp snaking up to the wraparound porch.

Trevor had ridden up to this house several times, but always stayed too focused and taken with Reed to pay close attention to his surroundings. Now, Trevor saw the home in its true glory. He was dumb not to have figured out Reed made so much money, but even with this impressive house, multi-millionaires could afford so much more.

Maybe Reed kept a home in one of the other countries he lived in. Perhaps he still paid for some of those men's homes across the world. Paying them off or paying them to remain there, ready for Reed when he went back into those parts of the world. Honestly though, none of it made any sense to Trevor. Reed didn't have to keep men on call. He was too charming and too smooth not to have access to regular hookups.

The bigger problem for Trevor right now wasn't one he really wanted to concentrate on. He was stuck. He tried to call his commander to explain and to see where this might leave him, but Reed's home phone line was dead. Trevor supposed Reed had the device disconnected with all the calls coming in.

For the first time since the accident, Trevor realized he was completely stuck without anything. His cell phone and all his belongings were spread between Rylie's apartment and the foreign country where his life had gone to shit. Trevor didn't have his wallet or even a dollar bill to his name until Rylie brought his things to him. The best he could do at this point would be to wait and call as soon as he got to the rehab hospital tomorrow.

Sitting back against the headboard, Trevor continued to watch the complete coverage of his story. Much as he'd suspected, he watched everything about his all-important mission become sidelined to the video of Reed bending down beside his chair, reaching to kiss him while running his hand over Trevor's hair. The footage ran over and over, across every channel on the satellite dish. The coverage ran in Spanish, French, and Italian. All showing the same images of him looking back at Reed with the most love-struck gaze. It turned his stomach. He seriously couldn't look more pathetic. Especially in contrast to the others in Reed's past. In that one shot, it showed Trevor giving his heart and soul to a man who left a string of broken hearts and tattered souls behind all over the world.

As the night wore on, a few of Trevor's team members were identified, found, and interviewed. All of them were completely surprised to learn Trevor was gay. At least on-air, his team stood up for him. They said either it couldn't be true or gave a "who cares" shrug with no further comment. One of his buddies just kept asking the reporter questions on how well Trevor was doing in recovery, not responding to anything said or asked of him. Trevor prayed those casual responses were true and not what they were trained to do.

Reed brought Trevor a plate of food, but he didn't stay to eat this time. Nor did he say much of anything after that first discussion they'd shared when Reed stood in the doorway. It didn't matter that he needed to eat and take his meds. Instead, he stayed obstinate, refusing to give in to the aroma of those delicious enchiladas or take the pills lying right beside the plate. He was just done with this whole mess.

By eight thirty that evening, Reed's tax returns had been aired. Trevor didn't take it well at all. It was much worse than initially reported. He had family money—Trevor wasn't oblivious of the Kensington name—but Reed had made millions on his own.

Randomly, throughout the evening, Reed would come to stand in the doorway and quietly stare at Trevor. Trevor never acknowledged him and kept his eyes glued to the television. After a few minutes, Reed would leave, solemn-faced, his hands in his pockets.

Trevor couldn't understand why Reed might be so dejected. He led a fascinating life. A video surfaced on TMZ of a camera hungry threesome. Two men talked openly to the cameras following them, but Reed stayed in the background, waiting for the guys to finish their session with the photographers. The whole video lasted about ten minutes as they readily discussed their evening. Trevor felt sick to his stomach. How had he believed for a moment he could have someone like Reed Kensington?

"Hey, man. You look a hundred percent better than the last time I saw you." Rylie came through the bedroom door, a big grin across his face. Elise was close behind. She stepped forward, moving around Rylie to give Trevor a big hug.

"How are you?" Elise asked, wrapping her arms around him, kissing his cheek before she pulled away.

"I'm better. I heard you came by last night. I'm sorry I was sleeping," Trevor said. He finally looked over at the door, wondering if Reed might be there listening, but there was no sign of him.

Trevor hated bringing all this down on the people who helped him the most in life. He couldn't see how he could continue being a part of the Kensington family after bringing all this drama down on their heads. Those thoughts caused a strong ache through his heart, settling in his gut. Rylie's family was all he had in the world. He didn't want to lose any of them.

"No, silly, you needed rest. I'm going to let you and Rylie talk. I just wanted to say hi." Elise hugged Trevor again, then gave Rylie a quick kiss before leaving, shutting the door behind her.

"How are you really feeling?" Rylie asked. He pulled Trevor's backpack off his shoulder, setting it on the floor by the nightstand. Rylie grabbed the nearest chair from the corner of the room, pulling it close to the bed before he sat down.

"I'm better, getting the use of my arm back," Trevor said, flexing the arm in question before turning his eyes back to the TV.

"Brody asked to be relocated. He doesn't want to move here," Rylie casually said.

"Since all this came out today?" Trevor whipped his head around, staring hard at Rylie.

"Nah, yesterday, way before all this." Rylie looked up, making eye contact with Trevor. They sat there contemplating each other for a moment before Trevor turned away.

"Why?" he finally asked. He hadn't talked to Brody since the mission, not even in the hospital in Germany. Before that, things had gotten a little weird between them, but he still thought of

Brody as a partner, a teammate…family.

"My guess is he knows what he lost, but he just said he needed to move on. He'll call you soon. He told me to tell you not to be stubborn and to do all your rehab."

Trevor just stayed quiet to that remark. Truth be told, he hadn't really thought much about Brody since he'd met Reed. It was odd to him; Trevor had spent his entire adult life wanting Brody to pick him, and not even understanding what that meant until he found Reed. He'd have to let that relationship run its own course. He couldn't force Brody to remain friends, even if now he realized he never wanted anything more from him than just that.

"What're you hearing on the inside? I can't imagine they'll let me stay with the team."

"Yeah, I can't really see it either." Rylie ran a hand through his short hair. "They're worried about your security. We'll all have to lie low for a while. That reporter did a lot of damage to our team for just a simple story that doesn't really matter anyway."

"I'm sorry. I should have thought this through better." Trevor lowered his gaze to his lap, remorse edging his words.

"Don't be. They were going to figure out names, eventually. You're not the one to blame here. You did nothing wrong. And for the record, I'm glad you're finally happy. I've talked to Reed several times a day since all this happened. He's seriously happy, concerned as hell, but really very happy. That's what's important. The rest of this doesn't matter." Silence ensued for several long moments. Trevor could feel Rylie's eyes on him, but he didn't turn to look at him.

"Why didn't you tell me Reed was a multi-millionaire?" Trevor's voice came out small, almost a whisper.

Rylie laughed. "So what? I might pull in forty-five grand this year. Do you think less of me?" Rylie shot back.

"It looks like I'll be pulling in much less than that now that I'm unemployed."

"You aren't unemployed and this is not of your own doing.

You were seriously injured in the line of duty. You're lucky to be alive. That's what should be considered, nothing else. My whole family considers you part of us. If it weren't Reed here with you, it would be my mom. You aren't going at this alone."

"They aren't going to keep me in, Rylie, and I don't have a skill. I planned on being career military. What am I going to do without that?"

"They'll do something with you. This publicity's too big, but it'll die down."

"Reed told me he loved me," Trevor finally said, his voice small. Why was it so hard to say out loud?

"Yeah, I can tell. He's different now."

"Apparently he's loved many before me." The hurt from that one thought had to show on his face.

Rylie scoffed. "You know that's not true, and if you don't know, you just need to trust me on it." His direct stare never faltered.

Trevor tried a different approach. "Look at this shit-storm tonight. They attacked him over me. I can't let that happen. Reed did nothing to have his personal life spread all over the place like this. It's all because of me. Rylie, I have nothing to offer him and I'm ruining his life."

"How can you say that? I've never seen Reed so happy."

"It was only three days."

Rylie reached out, resting his hand on Trevor's thigh. "Trevor, look at me. You need to be looking at me when I say this."

Trevor turned his eyes toward Rylie.

"Buddy, you know all the stories. It's just how the men in my family work. I knew the first time I saw Elise that she would be my wife. It didn't matter that I was eleven years old, and it was the first day of fifth grade. I told her that day I loved her, and I have loved her ever since. Same with my dad. He met my mom and proposed by the end of the evening. He was nineteen and in Dallas for a Cowboys-Redskins game, and she was on the JumboTron. He searched her out and proposed to her that same night. Same with my granddad. Surely, Reed's the same. It just took longer for him to find you. That's how we know it's real."

Trevor stayed quiet, his gaze drawn back to his lap. His brow furrowed and his lips pursed. He didn't respond. His heart was too heavy, thumping wildly in his chest. The magnitude of this situation caused Trevor to resist what was being said to him. All evening, the new coverage speculated that Reed was one of the best-looking men on the planet, and in that, Trevor wholeheartedly agreed. It was in seeing him and Reed together that he realized how completely mismatched they were. At his best, he was just an average-looking man. Reed dated gorgeous people with interesting lives and jobs. At some point soon, Reed would tire of him and leave. It would just be better for everyone involved if it ended now before the pain of separation got too unbearable to handle.

"Look, I can see you're thinking, and it doesn't look good. I've been worried for Reed for a while now. He's been all alone for so long. Then you came into his life and all my concerns have disappeared. You're the perfect guy for him, Trevor. You complement him on every level. You fill in the holes of his life. You'll be Reed's anchor throughout the years, and I know you'll be his best friend as well as his lover. If Reed was what they portrayed him to be on television tonight, I promise I wouldn't have let you spend any time alone with him. Instead during my own wedding reception, I watched the two of you slip away onto the balcony and my heart was relieved that my big brother was gonna be okay."

Rylie continued, "Buddy, you're a good man with traditional values. Do you have any idea how rare that is in today's world? You have honor and integrity. You'll always put my brother before yourself. And Reed will do that for you because he's those same things. I promise. My family's your family. We love you. And if I know you like I think I do, what's going through your head right now is not that Reed lied to you, but that you aren't worthy of him." Rylie leaned forward, placing his elbows on his knees to look Trevor directly in the eyes. "But I'm telling you right now, you are worthy, and you need to embrace this and trust me on that."

"I don't want things to change between you and me. When Reed's had enough of me wrecking his life, I could lose you all," Trevor said.

"You aren't going to lose anything and only time will show you that we Kensington men stick around permanently. It's how we're built."

Trevor stayed quiet, just staring at Rylie, thinking through everything. Rylie sat back, pushing forward on the seat to rise. "Just think about what I've said. I know it's been a lot to deal with and you're used to dealing with your shit all by yourself. Reed told me he loves you. He said it at the hospital in Germany. He's never said those words to me about anyone before. If you return the feeling, wipe the pain from his eyes now. He's hurting for you, and he's a little desperate. Put him out of his misery." Rylie walked to the bedroom door. "I'll be back tomorrow. Elise just picked me up from the airport. I'm going to go have my wedding night. I just wanted to check on you first."

Trevor nodded. "I'm sorry you came to me before spending time with Elise."

"I wouldn't have it any other way. Take it easy tonight. I'll see you tomorrow. Damn, I forgot. I'm turning into such a baby, thinking about relationships more than war and battle. Dad told me that they passed the Medal of Honor for you. You'll be hearing from them soon, I'm sure."

Trevor nodded again; his heart eased quite a bit talking to Rylie. And the Medal of Honor was a huge deal. Almost unimaginable to think he could be associated with such an honor.

"Hey, quick question. I may need you to pick something up for me at the store in the next few days, is that possible?" Trevor asked as an afterthought, pulling Rylie back in the doorway he'd just stepped through.

"Sure, just let me know when and I'm on it. I'll talk to you later. Call me if you need me."

"Thanks for the talk. I needed it badly."

Rylie tapped the door jamb with the palm of his hand, giving him a wink before disappearing down the hall.

CHAPTER 26

The cameras in the front of the house began flashing through the blinds. Trevor supposed that meant Rylie and Elise were leaving, making their way through the masses of news crews. His mind stayed on his conversation with Rylie as he flipped off the television to stare at the darkened screen. If he were going to try to make amends with Reed, he needed to get his head right in this relationship. Self-doubt and insecurity were his lifelong traits, but he had to find a way to put them aside. His focus must stay on how to become the best possible man he could be in order to stand beside Reed comfortably, as his heart desperately wanted him to do.

Trevor's body hurt from the workout he'd put himself through this afternoon. He reached for the crutches resting against the nightstand and hissed from the pain. His left arm jerked in a cramp, sending the crutches flying. They scraped against the wall, banging as they crashed onto the hardwood flooring. It was late, Trevor was tired, and now the crutches lay out of his reach. He used the nightstand and his right leg to move from the bed, awkwardly bending to the floor. His body resisted, but he forced through it until he managed to reach a crutch with his fingertips.

"Trevor, what happened? What're you doing?" Reed broke through the imaginary line he'd stayed behind all night, rushing to his side.

"I dropped my crutches. Reed, I'm sorry," Trevor said, bending over, trying to reach the other crutch. At his awkward angle, Trevor watched Reed rush to him from under his own arm.

"Did you fall? Are you hurt?" Reed gathered the crutches while sliding an arm around Trevor's waist, absorbing his body weight to help hold him up. He pushed Trevor back to bed. His concerned gaze scanning Trevor's body.

"I'm sorry. Please stop fussing over me for a minute. I'm fine. I just dropped my crutches." His hands went to Reed's cheeks, drawing his face up. "I'm sorry for all of this tonight. I'm just overwhelmed." Trevor kept his hands and his eyes on Reed. He knew the blush was forming; he was shit at finding the right words for anything. "You've overwhelmed me, and I didn't feel worthy of you."

The concerned tension eased off Reed's face. "You don't need to apologize. You've overwhelmed me from the first minute our eyes met across the grand ballroom. The only thing I'm certain of is I love you completely," Reed said, sitting on the side of the bed.

"I love you too. I do. It's complete for me too. I've robbed us of a normal beginning. Of dating, getting to know each other, learning how we fit. I'm sorry about that, but if you'll have me back, I want to stay here with you."

"I never wanted you gone. I've always wanted you right here with me," Reed said, taking his hand, wrapping their fingers together in a tight grasp.

"It's gonna be hard. If at any point you can't handle all this attention, I can go. Promise me you'll tell me. And if your feelings change, just say it. Promise me, Reed. If you promise me, I'll try hard to stop second-guessing everything and just go with it." Trevor gripped Reed's hand tighter, bringing their joined hands to his lips for a kiss, waiting for Reed to answer.

"I'll promise you that will never happen, but I can see by that angry brow you want my oath. Very well, I do promise to tell you if anything changes in my feelings for you." Reed brought his lips to Trevor's for a soft, sweet kiss of his own, sealing his answer. "Now, let's get you back to our bedroom. No more of this guest bedroom business ever again. Promise me. Otherwise, I may have to make this room into a large closet or something of the sort. I don't like you being in here away from me." Reed reached down, slinging his backpack over his shoulder while handing Trevor his crutches.

"I promise. I like the idea of our room."

"Me too, very much."

CHAPTER 27

Three Months later

"Do I look okay? I think the uniform's too big now. I lost some weight. Baby... Reed...seriously, you have to get up." Leaning over the bed, Trevor kissed a sleeping Reed on his soft lips. Reed kissed him back, but Trevor had to dodge his arms or be pulled back into bed. Reed groaned loudly when their alarm sounded again after hitting the snooze button for the third or fourth time. Trevor was already up, freshly showered and completely dressed in his dress blues, too excited to sleep.

The last three months were a constant whirlwind for the both of them. Trevor's prosthesis came in and it was bad ass, totally state of the art, just as promised. Trevor wore it proudly. His leg still required periods of rest, as the swelling wasn't completely under control, but he tried hard to stay positive and encouraged about the future. He still felt like he looked a little awkward while walking. It didn't bother him. He was fully focused on his recovery, knowing it would work itself out soon.

"Mmmm...good morning to you. You smell delicious. Are you wearing my favorite cologne? You know what it does to me," Reed growled, his deep voice even huskier from sleep. "It can't be time to wake. Just give me five more minutes. And it would be better if you lay here with me that same five more minutes..." Reed tried to turn over, tucking the pillow under his head.

"No. Come on. Dress quickly and meet me in the kitchen. I'll have breakfast ready. But you have to open your eyes and get out of bed to do all those things, Reed Kensington. Shake a leg! I have something I need to tell you before we go." Trevor popped Reed on his partially exposed naked butt. He grabbed the bed covers, moving quickly around the mattress, getting as far away from Reed's reaching hands as he could while Reed darted up in an attempt to grab him.

"Damn, you're too quick on that leg already. I think we should revisit the rule in which you don't wear the leg in the house so I can catch you better. Come back here. We have plenty of time. I need my morning lovin' from my sexy boyfriend." Reed sprawled across the bed now. His head on his elbow, his nude body fully exposed, showing a nice enticing view of the curve of his tight ass.

"Get dressed. Meet me in the kitchen." Trevor wadded up the bed covers, tossing them on a side chair and not looking back. He made his way to the kitchen. Reed was too handsome and convincing. If he stayed in the room any longer, he would be back in that bed, making love to Reed, forgetting about the importance of what they were about to do.

Pulling bagels and fresh fruit from the refrigerator, Trevor opted for an easy breakfast. He didn't want to mess up his uniform before the big event. Reed always ate breakfast in the morning, and usually it was something sweet. Trevor had removed most of the bad foods from the house over the last few months, loading the cupboards with healthier brands and items. Reed still snuck a few bad things in, but Trevor always pretended not to notice.

He smiled when his man wrapped his arms around him from behind. Trevor leaned his head back, reaching his left arm up to wrap it around Reed's head. He pulled Reed to him for a small but thorough kiss.

"Sexy, you could tell me your little secret back in bed. Do you feel how badly I want you?" Reed whispered into his ear, while brushing his rock-hard cock against Trevor's ass.

"It's time to get moving. It's not everyday someone gets the Medal of Honor and meets the president of the United States. Chop, chop, baby, get to movin'." Trevor tried to pull from Reed's arms, but he wouldn't let go. Instead, Reed placed small kisses along his neck, ignoring Trevor completely. "You know, you need to look your best. My beautiful boyfriend will be all over the tabloids as he stands beside me today."

Reed gave a little groan; he could almost see him stomping his feet. All he could do in return was laugh. It wasn't often Reed didn't get what he wanted, but this morning held too much importance to give in and they were running out of time. Reaching across the table, Trevor grabbed a little box he placed there earlier that morning, close to Reed's normal place setting. He saw that a sit-down breakfast wouldn't be happening for them at that point.

"Okay, wait. I have something for you. I've had it for months. Rylie picked this up for me right after he got back into town. I just waited for the right time. And then I chickened out. But I want you to have it before we go today. I want you to wear it if you want to." Turning on his heel, Trevor forced Reed back a step, not letting him go in for the kiss he intended. "Stop making this harder than it has to be and listen to me."

Carefully, Trevor dropped to one knee. He wasn't completely comfortable on the prosthesis yet, so he lowered as he had practiced, trying to keep balanced properly, praying it all worked.

This seemed to finally capture Reed's attention, making Trevor all the more nervous. Heat rushed to his cheeks as he opened the little box before turning it up for Reed to see. Trevor forced himself to man up and ignored his pounding heart. After a second, Trevor raised his gaze to Reed's deep green eyes and watched his perfectly arched brows lift in surprise.

"We've only known each other for a short while, but it's been the best time of my life. I've fallen deeply and completely in love with you. You make every one of my days better and nights special. You're my best friend, my lover, and my life." He took a deep breath, and exhaled on a huff, nervous as hell, but forging on with his prepared proposal. "Reed Kensington, you would make me the happiest man in the world if you would promise to someday marry me. One day. In the future...I'm not saying right now, just someday, but sooner rather than later. If you agree." Trevor's heart pounded so hard in his chest he couldn't hear his own words, and he knew he was rambling. Just like he had to force himself to speak, he now forced himself to shut up, waiting for Reed's reaction.

Reed took Trevor's hand and lowered to his knees. His eyes twinkled as his smile widened. "Yes! Yes, of course I'll marry you." Reed lifted his hand, placing his palm tenderly on the side of Trevor's face. "Baby, you're the reason my heart beats. You know you're my love, my life, my everything."

"Thank you for saying yes," Trevor said, releasing the anxious breath he held. Relief flooded his heart. He gathered Reed in his arms. His smile wouldn't leave his lips, but the alert on his phone sounded. Knowing what that meant, Trevor quickly kissed Reed on the lips before pulling him up and spinning him around, pushing him toward his bathroom. "You have thirty minutes before the car picks us up. Correction, twenty-nine minutes. You have to hurry. No primping today."

The time passed quickly with Trevor pacing through the house, his anxiousness getting the best of him. At the end of the driveway, the driver pulled through the gate Reed installed after the dreaded night the reporter broke their story. The horde of reporters were camping out in the front yard. Trevor had no idea why they continued to come day after day. On occasion, Reed would send cold water bottles or iced drinks when the late summer weather got too hot.

"The car's here," Trevor called, watching the time. Even with the extra time built into their schedule, they were officially late.

"You look dashing, and we're barely late. Only by five minutes. Let's go," Reed said as he walked toward Trevor who pulled open the door off the kitchen, leading to the garage, lifting a single brow. Five minutes his ass. A driver jumped out, opening the door to a Jaguar XJ, effectively stopping everything.

"I don't even know what to say. It's a Jaguar, Reed. Did you arrange this?" Trevor stood stock-still, looking over the car, wanting to see everything about it.

"No, babe, it's customary. Come on. We're late."

Trevor didn't respond, but bent in the driver's side door, looking inside, trying to see everything he could. Hell, if he could have figured out a way to drive the Jaguar today, he would have jumped in the front seat. Reed only chuckled at Trevor's enthusiasm, ushering him inside the back seat.

The trip to the White House was a short one but took well over an hour with traffic and all the protestors. They passed several picketing groups along the way; their causes were wide ranging and diverse, but most of them were centered on the pros and cons of homosexuality. Inside the car, Reed kept Trevor busy by kissing him behind the slightly tinted glass of the car windows and showing off the wedding ring he wore on his left hand as Trevor had requested of him.

He stayed so distracted with the kisses and the ring that he didn't notice when Reed pulled a small black box from his pocket, placing it in his hands. Trevor pulled away, surprised.

"I planned for a proper proposal too. Something grand and memorable, but I find I want this on your finger today as well.

I do want the world to know they didn't beat us and that you're truly mine. I want a proper wedding. I would like for it to be soon, but my mother will never let us get away with a small affair. She's too excited and proud to let this slide by without a large, eventful wedding. She made that clear when we went to pick this out together, shortly after you flew home from Germany."

"Reed...I...babe, you're such a blessing to me. I can't believe how lucky I am to have found you." Tears filled Trevor's eyes, causing his vision to blur. He pulled the stunning diamond band from the little black box.

He looked at it closely, reading the words engraved on the inside of the band. I love you, forever. A grin spread across his lips. His eyes darted up to Reed's, excitement filling his heart.

"I know, baby. We engraved the same words, and I do love you forever, my Trevor love."

EPILOGUE

Security at the White House took extreme to a whole new level, but the process remained efficient and reasonably easy to navigate. The horde of reporters became frustrated when they were left at the gate without so much as even a peek at either Reed or Trevor.

Reed stayed close by Trevor's side as requested. They were escorted into the White House through a secure entrance and welcomed the way visiting dignitaries were greeted. Reed knew his way around, having spent time there as a child with his father. Occasionally, Reed would comment on some change, or point out something, giving Trevor a quick history of the object or area. They stayed together, holding hands the entire time. After three months of dating Reed, PDAs just became second nature to Trevor.

"Babe, come this way," Reed said. "We have a briefing to do. They'll go over protocol with us before we meet the president. The Rose Garden is beautiful. It's spectacular this time of year, and I'm surprised they've allowed this award to be given there today. They must know the world will be watching you closely."

Reed continued to make random small-talk while Trevor became increasingly nervous, shutting down and not saying much at all. This also had become their way of communicating. Reed could always sense when Trevor might be nervous or unsure. Reed would begin talking, trying to distract and draw Trevor's attention away from the uncertainty racing through his mind. When that didn't work, Reed would whisper words about the sex they shared, or were going to share, into Trevor's ear, promising Trevor his favorite position that night, or teasing him about finding a bathroom for a quick blow job. Every time, without fail, those comments would effectively take Trevor's mind off his worries to center them straight into the hope of their future. Today though, Reed didn't take Trevor there. Probably because he didn't want Trevor to have a raging hard-on while the world watched him and took his picture.

"Sgt. West, hello, I'm Griffin, the third aide to the president of the United States. I'm here to go over a few things with you regarding the ceremony. The event will go exactly like this. We will exit through these doors. You will walk the runner, and then be escorted to the garden area.

"You will stand at the front of the podium to the left of the president. The vice president is going to be in attendance today, along with the majority leader and Speaker of the House. Also Lt. Honn, a Marine officer, will be standing by your side. The president will say a few words, then read from the doctrine in the award. You will be handed the award and then you are to—"

"Excuse me," Trevor stopped the clerk mid-sentence. Griffin looked up from his portfolio where he read from his notes. He looked irritated at the disruption. The aide craned his neck to look at both Reed and Trevor, not sure who interrupted him. "Where in this will Reed be standing?"

"Mr. Kensington will be escorted to sit by his family in the audience in just a couple of minutes. They have front row seating. Now, as I was saying before I was interrupted, Sgt. West will be handed—"

"I'm sorry, but I would like Reed to stand beside me." Trevor casually shoved his free hand in his pocket, looking the aide in the eye waiting for his response.

"Well, Sgt. West, I'm sorry, but that will not be possible. Only spouses and fiancés can stand up at the front with—"

"We're engaged," Trevor replied, not removing his gaze from the aide. His stance remained casual, very easygoing.

"Sir, I'm sorry…"

It was then that everything about Trevor changed. Reed began to speak, but Trevor lifted a finger silencing him and looked down at the aide again.

"I'm sorry, I'm not making myself clear. Reed will be beside me when I get this award. I wouldn't be here if it weren't for him. He needs to be beside me." Trevor's voice hardened with each word, his face grew fierce, and Trevor waited to give the aide time to say nothing more than "yes, sir."

"Sir—"

Trevor stopped Griffin by lifting his hand. Reed gave a little chuckle when the aide stomped his foot, anger flashing in his eyes.

"No. I can see by the look in your eyes you're going to try to tell me no again. Let me be absolutely clear. I don't want the award unless Reed's standing beside me when I receive it. If any part of what I just said is unclear, please ask questions." Trevor released Reed's hand, crossing his big brawny arms over his chest. His jaw clenched tightly.

"If you will excuse me for a minute, please," the aide said, spitting the words out. Completely exasperated, he turned quickly and aggressively, walking several feet away, before hitting his earpiece and talking. Griffin's tones were hushed, but you could easily make out his anger with his hands going ninety to nothing, as he looked like he was talking to the air.

"Handsome, you know I appreciate this, but I want you to receive your award," Reed said, leaning in to whisper into Trevor's ear.

"No. I'm not giving in. We can just go home where I would be so much more comfortable than here. Don't try to distract me." Trevor kept his eyes on the aide, arms crossed over his chest and his feet firmly planted in his decision, refusing to look at Reed when he spoke.

"Babe…" Reed tried again.

"I'm not getting it without you there. You agreed to marry me. You're my future and you helped me build this future I'm living now. This is our award. Not just mine. And I ask you to please not say anything more until a decision is made."

Reed chuckled at him, lifting his eyebrows. Trevor never took that tone with him, and he wisely kept his mouth shut, only leaning in once to ask in a whisper if they could play hard-core soldier man tonight in bed. He bumped Reed's shoulder, letting him know he'd heard him, but didn't take his attention from the situation happening in front of him.

"Sir, I've been asked to ask you again to reconsider your stance. It would not do to have this canceled with so much publicity tied to this event, but it's an election year which must be considered." The aide spoke to him in small little words, in an overly calm manner.

"Politics have nothing to do with my life. Do we need to call a cab? Reed, are your parents here to take us home?" Trevor asked, while looking at the aide. The look of disgust radiating from the man caused Reed to finally laugh out loud. The aide hit his earpiece again, not even turning away from them now.

"He won't budge. No, he's completely unreasonable. Yes, yes, okay." Taking a minute to gather himself, the aide finally spoke. "All right, since your apparent cause is the most important thing to you, you can promote it at the expense of others. Mr. Kensington, you will stand in the back and to the side with your entire family. We'll have—"

"No, I'm not doing this. Let's go, Reed." Trevor swung a finger toward the door as if his directive weren't completely obvious and wrapped an arm around Reed, turning to leave in the direction they came.

"Okay," the man shrieked. Trevor didn't smile even though he knew he'd won. "Okay. He can stand beside you. It's all about you! What you want… Fine." The little man stormed off in a huff.

"He's a little high-strung, but he really is harmless." The president stepped out of his office, shrugging on his suit jacket, adjusting his tie. The grin on his face let Trevor know he'd overheard the entire exchange between the two of them.

"Mr. President, sir, it's nice to see you again." Reed held out his hand, stepping forward to take the president's hand.

"Hello, Reed, it's good to see you again, son. I understand your family's here today." The president continued to chuckle as he spoke.

"Yes, sir, they are. Trevor has been special to them for many years. They wouldn't miss this. Please let me introduce Trevor West to you, sir." Reed wrapped an arm around Trevor, smiling at him with such pride it caused Trevor to release the anger he'd felt toward the aide go and concentrate on the bigger moment. Trevor was meeting the president of the United States.

"It's a pleasure to meet you, Sergeant."

"It's an honor to meet you, sir." Trevor saluted the president before taking his hand. They both gave a little laugh because the tough sergeant who had given the aide hell became flustered, not really sure what to do in greeting his commander in chief.

The president's eyes became serious as he said, "I watched you that night. Your bravery and dedication were admirable. I was thoroughly impressed by you and your team. You made me proud to be an American."

"Thank you, sir. I'm a fan of yours. I voted for you." The heat of a blush blasted Trevor's cheeks. He was doing that crazy ramble thing he did when he got nervous, so he forced himself to shut up.

"Thank you. I'm glad to hear it. I'll need that vote again in the next election, but for now, I think they're ready for us. Let's do this."

The grin was still on the president's face as they walked out the back doors of the White House and into the back garden area. Several gasps were heard from the reporting area when Reed came out with Trevor, hand in hand. Cameras flashed like crazy, but Trevor held his head high. He clasped Reed's hand the entire way. The president gave a nod to his vice president but went straight to the podium. Trevor tried hard to remember which side he was to stand on, and of course, he got it wrong. Reed gently guided him over before respectfully taking a step back, letting Trevor stand close to the president as he spoke.

Trevor weighed his options, deciding not to embarrass Reed or the president by throwing a fit on national television. But he would be talking to Reed about that little step back later. The president spoke on acts of heroism and the history of the medal. Trevor listened, but also looked out into the crowd, seeing Reed's family all on the front row. They were his family now. Many members of his team, including Brody were on the second and third rows. Brody winked at him and lifted a fist in an all-air knuckle touch. They'd become friendly again. Returning easily to what were always destined to be…friends and brothers-in-arms

In fact, Trevor had heard from many of his team members since the accident. Not that there had been much time for him to do anything more than fully recover and figure out the new direction of his life. He watched them closely; they seemed proud to be there. Whenever he made eye contact with one of them, he got a thumbs up and a grin. It surprised him how relieved he felt that they'd come to support him.

After a minute, Reed nudged him in the back. Trevor looked up again at the grinning president, who held his hand out to shake Trevor's. Trevor quickly shook the president's hand before leaning forward, allowing the award to be placed around his neck. A cheer erupted from his team and the audience. Both leaders of Congress came forward to congratulate him and shake his hand. Lt. Honn stood a step back, clapping until it was his time to congratulate Trevor with a salute and handshake.

After accepting their handshakes, Trevor turned to Reed, who stood back a couple of steps clapping, smiling, and watching it all. Trevor didn't want Reed to be reserved. Everything the two of them had gone through, all the hardships only brought them closer. His heart was truly happy. As he lifted his hand toward Reed, Reed came immediately to Trevor's side, that sexy grin in place. Trevor didn't hesitate, but bent in, matching the grin, kissing Reed for the world to see. Again, there was a collective gasp, followed by a few cheers from various sections of the audience. The clicking of the camera flashes became a roar in the background.

Turning back to the president, Trevor never lost his smile. Reed's hand stayed in his. In that moment, he realized he would do everything over again just to be standing there with Reed right then.

Trevor turned back to his grinning fiancé, saying loudly, "I do love you forever," and kissed Reed's smiling lips again.

The End

Ducky's story is coming late spring 2022!

NOTE FROM
THE AUTHOR

Send a quick email to kindle@kindlealexander.com and let us know what you think of It's Complicated. For more information on future works click here to sign-up for our new release newsletter or come friend us on all the major social networking sites.

✦ Facebook ➔ https://www.facebook.com/
AuthorKindleAlexander/
✦ Twitter ➔ https://twitter.com/KindleAlexander
✦ Instagram ➔ https://www.instagram.com/
kindlealexander2.0/?hl=en
✦ Book+Main Bites ➔ https://bookandmainbites.com/
KindleAlexander
✦ Goodreads ➔ https://www.goodreads.com/author/
show/6421828.Kindle_Alexander
✦ Amazon ➔ https://amzn.to/2JXnKRF
✦ BookBub ➔ https://www.bookbub.com/profile/kindle-
alexander
✦ Newsletter ➔ https://www.kindlealexander.com/
contact-us/

HAVOC & ORDER

(Tattoos And Ties, Book 1)

Keyes Dixon's life is challenging enough as a full patch member of the Disciples of Havoc Motorcycle Club but being a gay biker leaves him traveling down one tough road. With an abusive past and his vow to the club cementing his future, he doesn't believe in love and steers clear of commitment. But a midnight ride leads to a chance meeting with a sexy distraction that has him going down quicker than a Harley on ice.

Cocky Assistant District Attorney Alec Pierce lives in the shadow of his politically connected family. A life of privilege doesn't equal a life of love, a fact made obvious at every family gathering. Driven yet lonely, Alec yields to his family's demands for his career path, hoping for the acceptance he craves. Until he meets a gorgeous biker who tips the scales in the favor of truth and he can no longer live a lie.

Can two men from completely different worlds…and sides of the law…find common ground, or will all their desires only wreak Havoc?

BOOKS BY
KINDLE ALEXANDER

If you enjoyed *Up In Arms* then you won't want to miss
Kindle Alexander's bestselling novels:

Breakaway
Reservations
It's Complicated
Painted On My Heart
The Current Between Us (with Bonus Material)
Closet Confession
Secret
Texas Pride

Reservations
Reservations
It's Complicated

Always & Forever Duet
Always
Forever

Nice Guys Novels
Double Full
Full Disclosure
Full Domain

Tattoos and Ties
Havoc
Order

Better If Read Together
The Current Between Us
Secret
Painted On My Heart
Reservations
It's Complicated

Made in the USA
Middletown, DE
16 March 2022

62768061R00144